The SECRET DETECTIVE AGENCY

BOOKS BY HELENA DIXON

The SECRET DETECTIVE AGENCY

HELENA DIXON

Bookouture

Published by Bookouture in 2025

An imprint of Storyfire Ltd.
Carmelite House
50 Victoria Embankment
London EC4Y 0DZ

www.bookouture.com

The authorised representative in the EEA is Hachette Ireland
8 Castlecourt Centre
Dublin 15 D15 XTP3
Ireland
(email: info@hbgi.ie)

ISBN: 978-1-83618-105-7
eBook ISBN: 978-1-83618-104-0

In memory of my dad, who was so excited for this book.

There is a tide in the affairs of men.
Which, taken at the flood, leads on to fortune;
Omitted, all the voyage of their life
Is bound in shallows and in miseries.
On such a full sea are we now afloat,
And we must take the current when it serves,
Or lose our ventures.

Julius Caesar, William Shakespeare

CHAPTER ONE

JANUARY 1941

Miss Jane Treen's office deep in the heart of an anonymous-looking government building in Whitehall was cold. The meagre electric fire in the hearth of the shabby black fireplace threw off barely any heat. Her desk, as usual, was as neat and tidy as Jane herself. Her coffee, half drunk, was also almost cold.

Jane did not take much notice of the chill. She was more annoyed by the offending tiny scrap of crimson crêpe paper that remained attached to the ceiling right in her line of sight. She had given explicit instructions that she wished for no Christmas decorations in her office and had been overruled. Now it would remain there until she could persuade someone to obtain a set of steps to remove it. That would probably be in July the way her day was currently progressing. Morale boosting poppycock.

The other thing bothering her was the manila file she held in her hand. Another one of her agents was missing. To lose one was bad enough but for a second one to disappear smacked of carelessness. Especially when this particular agent had been placed in a safe house. It did not bode well, and she could only hope the girl would turn up unharmed.

In the distance through the closed door of her office she

heard the faint bellowing of Brigadier Remmington-Blythe. No doubt he was making one of his notorious phone calls. He still believed it necessary to shout in order for the person on the other end to hear him. If it had not been for the war he would have retired by now and been sat happily by the sea somewhere, or tending a vegetable patch in rural Suffolk. Jane had no choice. Once he had finished his call she would have to go and beard him in his den. She lit one of the cigarettes she had stashed in the top drawer of her desk. She really needed to try and make her dwindling supply last a little longer. They were becoming increasingly difficult to obtain, despite them not being rationed. However, a moment like this called for some kind of Dutch courage.

When the noise from the brigadier's office had died down, she stubbed her cigarette out in the glass ashtray on her desk and rose reluctantly from her seat. She swallowed the last mouthful of coffee, smoothed down the fitted tweed skirt she always wore to the office and checked her brown hair was tidily pinned at the nape of her neck. Appearances mattered when you were a woman in a male dominated world. Then she gathered up both her courage and the file before setting off along the corridor to see her superior.

The brigadier's secretary, Stephen, was seated as usual at his desk in the outer office. His lips lifted in a smirk as Jane entered. She knew he was considered a catch by the girls in the typing pool, however there was little love between the two of them ever since Jane had made it quite clear she was uninterested in his advances.

She had been forced to make this clear with the sharp point of her elbow and the heel of her shoe on his foot before he had received the message. She strongly suspected he had been the instigator of the unwanted decorations which had blighted her office.

'The brigadier is busy. Not to be disturbed he said.' Stephen's pencil-thin moustache lifted in a fake smile.

Jane returned his smile with one that was equally insincere. 'I'll bear that in mind, Stephen.'

She promptly ignored him and rapped on the brigadier's door before he could leap up from his chair and prevent her.

'Come.'

Jane's smile widened and she squared her shoulders and entered the lion's den, leaving Stephen to stew quietly behind his desk. It took her a moment to spot the brigadier through the blue haze of cigar smoke.

'I'm sorry to disturb you, sir, but we have a problem.' She closed the door behind her.

The brigadier was a formidable figure with a neatly trimmed silver toothbrush moustache and erect bearing. Jane had no idea of his actual age, but she knew he had seen active service in the last war. Hence her suspicion that he would have retired had the current conflict not arisen.

She saw his shaggy eyebrows lift at her words. 'Hmm, take a seat, Jane.'

He held his hand out for the file she carried as she seated herself on the bentwood chair in front of his desk. He flipped it open and read her report. She stayed silent while he studied the contents of the folder.

'Another agent missing.' He closed the file.

'Yes, sir, I'm afraid so.' The heavy feeling in the pit of her stomach that had started when she had received the news, intensified.

'Any word from Maura Roberts?' he asked.

Jane shook her head. 'No news at all.'

CHAPTER TWO

The room Arthur Cilento had occupied at Half Moon Manor as a boy was unchanged. His notebooks, full of diagrams and mathematical puzzles, still on the dresser. He had not known back then how valuable his codebreaking and puzzle-solving skills would become. Benson had been in to remove the dust covers and throw open the curtains, the dark-red brocade now sun-faded at the edges.

Even his telescope still stood on its stand, its nose pointing out skywards towards the pool beyond the leafless trees at the far end of the garden. The window was cracked slightly open, allowing a stream of icy air into the room that had been long closed.

Arthur had been away from the house for months, working on various projects for the War Office around the country. He was looking forward to settling back in his old home. Something he had been unable to do since the death of his uncle had coincided with a rush of important government work.

Arthur crossed the faded Turkish rug to pull the sash down. Outside, the sky was late January gunmetal grey, pregnant with rain or sleet. The long length of lawn muddy and tattered, the borders bare beyond a few bold white snowdrops poking nervous heads above the red earth. The Anderson shelter an ugly addition near the chicken coop.

He had spent so many happy summer holidays from school there while his parents had been working abroad. He smiled to himself and gazed at the familiar view. Then he realised that past the trees, in the backwater of the river that reflected the colour of the sky, was something that should not be there. Something blue and bright, a jarring note in a mute palette. He frowned and applied his eye to his boyhood telescope, adjusting the sight to focus on the object.

Bile rose in his throat, even as he frowned in disbelief. He took one final look and ran from the room, calling for his manservant as he did so. Benson emerged from one of the rooms off the hallway, his long narrow face, normally without expression, betrayed his astonishment at the sight of Arthur running towards the back door of the house.

'Come quickly, bring a rake or something, there is someone in the water.'

Arthur didn't wait for Benson to follow him. His focus was on reaching the pool as swiftly as possible, all the time hoping that he had been mistaken in what he had seen from the window. He barely had time to register the cold air hitting his face as he ran the length of the lawn, the leather soles of his shoes slipping on the grass.

Once in the wood, he was forced to slow his pace and pick his way between the trees to avoid tripping over the exposed roots. The pool was an inlet from the river, it rose and fell slightly with the tide as the village of Pennycombe was not far from the coast. His breath came in rasping gasps from the unaccustomed exercise, hanging in small clouds in front of his face. Arthur was not supposed to run.

He emerged onto the claggy bank to see his worst fears materialised. The body of a woman lay face down in the water, a little way out from the shore. The bright-blue wool cloth of her coat rising and falling gently with the ripples of the water. Her arms spread loosely at her sides, partly submerged, fingers pale in the fading light. There was no sign of life.

Behind him, in the wood, he heard Benson crashing his way through the thicket. 'Over here, there is a woman.' His heart hammered in his chest, and he forced himself to suck in lung-fuls of the icy air.

Arthur glanced behind him to see his manservant approaching bearing a broom that looked as if it had seen better days. The man stopped short when he spied the woman. Arthur peered closely at the river pool and realised she wasn't breathing.

'I fear she is beyond help.' Arthur placed a cautionary hand on Benson's arm when the man went to step forward. 'Wait, we must be careful. There may be evidence here on the bank that the police will wish to see.' He was relieved to hear his voice had returned to its normal tone.

Arthur had noticed footprints in the mud near the edge of the water. Small indented heel marks that looked as if they would match the brown leather button boots the woman was wearing. However, there were other prints as if the woman had not been there alone. A man's footprints perhaps, it was hard to tell. A shiver ran along his spine.

'Shall I telephone the police, sir?' Benson asked, his gaze still fixed on the woman in the water.

'Yes, return to the house and call them. Hurry.'

The manservant turned, and, as if not thinking clearly, passed the broom to Arthur before he hurried away, crashing his way back through the shrubby undergrowth. Once he was gone from sight, the wood fell silent again. Even the birds were absent, the only sound the gentle slap of the river water against the bank.

The cold air had penetrated the tweed of his jacket, and he

shivered once more. He should, he supposed, return to the house. There was nothing more that he could do here. Certainly, there was nothing he could do for the poor soul in the water. Yet, it seemed disrespectful to leave her just floating there, like so much debris.

What had brought her here? It wasn't easy to get to. As a child it had been a favourite spot when he had been allowed outside. It was out of sight of the house, away from the servants. She must have entered the garden via the gate at the side of the house and made her way to the river. And who had accompanied her, and why? Who was she?

He looked around the bank side noticing where the winter greenery appeared slightly crushed, as if trodden upon. The rotting wooden platform where his uncle had spent his time fishing was losing its fight with the river, sagging into the water and of no use to retrieve the woman floating nearby. The leaf mould in one spot appeared disturbed as if someone or something had been digging, an animal perhaps.

She could not have been in the water too long he judged, or surely the heavy wool of her coat would have pulled her lower beneath the surface and her appearance been more disarranged by the ebb and flow of the tides.

A few pellets of icy water fell from the sky, splashing into the river and marking the pale tweedy fawn fabric of his coat with dark marks. It was foolish to continue to stay there. He could do nothing for the woman in the river.

The sound of footsteps returning through the wood made him turn. Benson was approaching carrying his winter overcoat and bearing a large, open, black umbrella.

'The police are on their way, sir. I took the liberty of bringing these.'

Arthur shrugged his way into his overcoat and pulled on the leather gloves he habitually kept in the pockets. The after-effects of his recent exertions were making themselves felt and he was glad of the additional layer. Benson held the umbrella above them both as the sleet began to pummel down.

'I wish we had some way of retrieving the poor woman.' The deluge seemed to be adding further insult to the still figure in the blue coat.

'The police requested we do nothing, sir. They should be here shortly. I have asked Mrs Mullins to direct them here when they arrive.'

'Thank you.' He was about to instruct Benson to return to the house when the sound of footsteps rapidly approaching alerted them to the arrival of the police in the form of a uniformed and somewhat breathless young constable.

The constable's ruddy complexion paled when he looked towards the river. 'The chief inspector is on his way, sir. I came ahead on my bicycle.' Sleet dripped from the edges of his helmet and from the hem of his heavy, navy serge cloak.

A harsh cough wracked Arthur's slight frame as the cold and shock of the discovery enveloped him. He pressed his white linen handkerchief to his lips in an effort to suppress the spasms and allow him to recover his breath.

'Sir, if I might suggest we leave the constable here and await the chief inspector at the house?' Benson's tone, as always, was respectful, but Arthur recognised the underlying note of concern in his servant's voice.

When he could speak once more, Arthur nodded consent, accepting the inevitable. 'Very well.'

He permitted Benson to steer him through the trees. Together, they picked their way across the muddy lawn back to the house, the sleet bouncing off the taut material of the black umbrella Benson held so solicitously above his head. The constable's bicycle was propped against the rear wall, near the kitchen door.

For a few years in his youth, Arthur's physical frailties had been a cause of distress and rebellion. Now in his early thirties, he had come to accept his limitations and to live within them. The discovery of the dead woman at the end of his garden had been the first unplanned event to touch his life and disturb the even tenor of his days for years. Arthur Cilento was very much a planner.

He was careful to wipe his feet on the coconut matting at the back door, mindful of his housekeeper Mrs Mullins's clean quarry tiles.

'The fire is lit in the drawing room, sir. Mrs Mullins has prepared a tray of tea.' Benson placed the sodden umbrella in a bucket in the boot room. He assisted Arthur with the removal of his overcoat, ignoring Mrs Mullins's pursed lips at the drips of rain landing on her floor.

'You will show the chief inspector through when he arrives?' Arthur asked. His limbs ached and his breathing was still raspy from the change in air.

'Of course, sir,' Benson assured him.

Arthur made his way from the kitchen along the hall to the welcoming warmth of the drawing room. There was another, larger room that the household used in the summer months, but he preferred the cosy comfort of this part of the house in winter. A fire burned brightly in the grate and a lamp was lit next to the comfortable chenille-covered armchair next to the fireplace.

He took a seat in the chair. The promised tea tray was ready on the side table and his inhaler was also prepared. Arthur checked the apparatus and pumped the rubber bulb to receive the medication. After a moment his chest began to loosen, and his breathing became less laboured.

Out in the hall, the front doorbell chimed, and he heard Benson's heavy tread on the parquet as he went to answer it. There was a rumble of masculine voices before Benson showed in a tall, sharp-featured man of a similar age to himself, wearing a heavy overcoat and dark hat.

'Chief Inspector Thorne, for you, sir.'

'Mr Cilento, please don't get up.' The man approached with an outstretched hand.

Arthur shook his hand. 'You will no doubt wish to get straight to work, Chief Inspector. My man will direct you to where the constable is waiting.'

'Very good, sir. Will you be available to answer a few questions later?'

'Of course.' Arthur watched Benson show the man out, leading him away in the direction of the kitchen. He poured himself a cup of tea, grateful the tremor in his hand had ceased.

He hoped they had retrieved the woman from the water. It didn't seem right for her body to be left out there overnight. It was rapidly growing dark outside now and soon they would not be able to see what they were doing. They would be unable to use lanterns, as the blackout would be in effect.

The tea was reviving, and he was content to sit in the growing darkness listening to the steady tick of the clock on the mantelpiece and the crackle of the logs in the fireplace.

Benson came through to draw the heavy, old-fashioned curtains, shutting out the incipient darkness. 'They have recovered the lady, sir. The chief inspector will be joining you shortly.'

'I am glad to hear it. Perhaps Mrs Mullins would be good enough to provide more tea. I'm sure the chief inspector may be in need of a hot drink.'

Benson assented and removed the tray. Arthur tidied his inhaler out of sight and prepared to receive Chief Inspector Thorne.

The chief inspector was shown through a few minutes later. He gladly accepted a seat on the vacant armchair opposite Arthur. Benson carried in a fresh tray of tea and withdrew.

'Thank you, Mr Cilento, this is most kind of you. Your manservant said you have only returned to the house today to take possession?' He nodded a reply to Arthur's unspoken query with the teapot.

'Yes, that is correct. My late uncle passed away some eight months ago. I have been away on war work, so my uncle's solicitor was instructed to let the house on a short-term lease. The tenant quit the house on New Year's Day, and I returned only a few hours ago.' He poured the chief inspector some tea and passed over the delicate china cup and saucer.

Chief Inspector Thorne accepted the tea and took an appreciative sip. 'Your manservant said you did not know the lady in the river?'

'I didn't see her face, obviously, but I haven't lived in this part of the world for a few years now. I only visited here to see my uncle for a few days at a time. I was last here about a year ago to stay and then just for a few hours for the funeral. My work for the government is confidential and very demanding. Apart from the house staff and a few of my uncle's friends, I don't know very many people in the area. I am not a social person.'

'You did not meet the tenant for the house yourself?' The chief inspector's gaze was sharp.

Arthur sipped his own tea before replying. 'No, never. Mr Hooper, the solicitor, knew of Miss Trevellian's family I believe, and he dealt with it all. I was away in Scotland, on war work, and was then taken ill. I have asthma and was advised not to travel for a time. Is there some connection between Miss Trevellian and the poor lady down at the river?'

He suspected the policeman had a good reason for his question.

The chief inspector surveyed Arthur with a shrewd gaze. 'Your cook, Mrs Mullins, was also employed by Miss Trevellian, I believe?'

'Yes, all the house staff were. Mrs Mullins, her son, Bendigo, who is the gardener and chauffeur, and the lady that comes daily from the village to assist with the housework. It kept all the staff in employment in my absence. I understood from Mr Hooper that Miss Trevellian only intended to bring her companion with her, a Miss Perez.'

He wondered at the chief inspector's interest in his tenant. She had left the house a few days ago. He had considered other, darker reasons for the woman's presence when he had found the body, but had discounted them. He held no information at present that others would find of interest.

'The woman found in the water wore a very distinctive coat.'

Arthur rested his cup down on its saucer. 'Yes, it was the bright-blue colour that attracted my attention when I looked out of the window.'

Chief Inspector Thorne's expression was grave. 'Mrs Mullins has informed my constable that Miss Trevellian possessed just such a coat.'

'I see, Chief Inspector. That is most disturbing. Mr Hooper is due to call on me tomorrow. He is arriving by train at ten fifteen and coming straight here. If you would like to call in and talk to him yourself about Miss Trevellian's tenancy, I'm sure he would be able to assist you.' Arthur wondered afresh what had brought Miss Trevellian back to the house, if indeed the body was hers. It was most peculiar.

'That would be most helpful. You know of no reason yourself, sir, why Miss Trevellian would have returned to the house or grounds? Nothing she had forgotten or left behind to collect at a later date? No post or parcels?' the chief inspector asked.

Mr Cilento shook his head. 'I'm afraid I only arrived here a few hours ago. My servants would be better placed to answer your questions in that regard.' He paused for a moment. 'Whilst I was at the riverbank, I couldn't help noticing there was another set of footprints. Also, and this may well be nothing, it appeared as if something or someone had been digging at a spot under the trees near the fallen log.'

Chief Inspector Thorne gave him a keen glance. 'Yes, sir, I had noticed.'

Arthur smiled apologetically. 'Forgive me, I am not presuming to tell you your job, Chief Inspector. It's simply that as a mathematician I like things to be orderly and have rational explanations. I tend to notice anomalies.'

'Not at all, Mr Cilento. Someone with a sharp pair of eyes can be very useful in cases such as this.' The chief inspector drained the last of his tea.

'May I ask, do you know how she died?' Arthur asked.

'The doctor will take a better look back at the morgue, but at present it appears as if she was hit over the head and either fell or was pushed into the river.' Chief Inspector Thorne placed his empty cup on the table and prepared to take his leave. 'It's a bad business.'

Arthur nodded thoughtfully. 'Indeed. I shall expect you in the morning then, sir, and we can discover from Mr Hooper if the lady is Miss Trevellian, and what he may know of her and her family.'

CHAPTER THREE

Miss Treen took the telephone call at her desk. As usual she was one of the first people into the office, passing the cleaning woman on her way up the stairs.

'I see. A woman's body in the river at Half Moon Manor.' She repeated the message back to her informant, her heart sinking. 'Thank you for letting me know.' She replaced the receiver and went to her filing cabinet.

She sorted through the manila folders until she found the one she wanted. A black-and-white photograph of an attractive young woman with fair hair and wide eyes looked back at her. Jane muttered a curse under her breath and tossed the file onto her desk. The same file she had shown the brigadier the day before.

Another one of her agents dead.

She walked along the corridor to the brigadier's office. He too preferred to get to his desk early, and often stayed late. Stephen had not yet arrived, so she knocked on the door and waited to be called through.

'Jane, my dear, I take it you have news?' he asked, once she was seated.

She told him of the phone call from Devon.

'Then you will need to go to Pennycombe and take care of this personally. As soon as possible. I think that given what we know already, you and Arthur Cilento will need to work together on this matter.'

Jane's heart sank a little at this. Not about taking charge, she preferred running a show to being commanded. It was working with Arthur. She didn't dislike him as a person, it was just that he was so different from her. Annoyingly different.

'I need to take care of a few things first, and I shall have to take Marmaduke with me,' she said, rising from her seat ready to return to her service flat in Pimlico.

A brief smile flashed across the brigadier's face. 'Of course, my dear. Although I am not certain how Arthur will receive your cat. Still, I understand that Half Moon Manor is a generously proportioned house so I dare say he will cope. Take a car from the pool.'

* * *

Mr Hooper arrived at Half Moon Manor promptly by taxi the following morning. A sprightly man in his early sixties now, he had been his uncle's solicitor for as long as Arthur could remember.

Benson showed him through to the study.

A discreet, thorough gentleman of the old school. As always, he was dressed immaculately in a dark-grey pinstripe suit with a fresh red carnation in his lapel.

'Mr Cilento, I was most perturbed to hear of your experience yesterday. My secretary informed me of it this morning when I called in at the office to collect the documents for our meeting. She said that a Chief Inspector Thorne had telephoned for information on the letting arrangements for this house.' Mr Hooper's brow was furrowed with concern as he greeted Arthur and shook his hand, before taking a seat opposite the ornate walnut desk.

'Chief Inspector Thorne will be joining us shortly,' Arthur said.

As he spoke there was a knock at the door and Benson showed the chief inspector in. Arthur made the introductions.

'Thank you for seeing me, Mr Hooper. I'm sure Mr Cilento has told you that we are trying to identify the lady found murdered in the backwater yesterday. The clothing she was wearing was quite distinctive and she has tentatively been identified as Miss Kate Trevellian.' Chief Inspector Thorne had settled on the other carved wooden chair opposite the desk.

'It was definitely murder then, Chief Inspector?' Arthur asked.

'Yes, sir. The police surgeon found a large contusion on the back of her head and there was water in her lungs confirming she was alive when she entered the water,' the chief inspector said.

Mr Hooper looked quite distressed. 'How terrible, the poor woman.'

'How did Miss Trevellian come to take the tenancy?' the chief inspector asked.

Mr Hooper cleared his throat. 'Mr Cilento had been working away and has been unwell. He needed to recuperate elsewhere, which would have meant Half Moon Manor standing empty. He asked me to find a short-term tenant to avoid the house being empty over the coldest months. This is an old house, so needs to be occupied or problems tend to arise: damp, mould and, well, infestations. I duly advertised the house as requested and Miss Trevellian came forward. She said she wished to rent somewhere quiet short term for herself and her companion. Her own property was undergoing repairs and she needed somewhere suitable to stay for a few weeks.'

Arthur considered Mr Hooper's reply. Half Moon Manor

was the last house in the village, situated by itself with no nearby neighbours to overlook the property on any side. It was a large, handsome Tudor house and the staff had been on board wages. It would have been an attractive proposition for a woman in Miss Trevellian's circumstances.

'Did you know Miss Trevellian before she applied for the tenancy?' Arthur asked. He vaguely remembered some mention from Mr Hooper that he knew the family.

Mr Hooper nodded. 'I knew Miss Trevellian's late father many years ago. I had not met his daughter since she had been a small child. She furnished the required references, which were dutifully followed up by my secretary.'

He produced a worn, dark-brown leather attaché case and plucked some documents from its innards. He popped a small pair of wire-framed spectacles on the end of his nose and peered at them.

'Yes, a letter here from Lady Godmaston. She used to be very involved with a project caring for Basque children displaced by the civil war in Spain. She vouched for Miss Trevellian. I understand that it was through Lady Godmaston that Miss Perez came to be in Miss Trevellian's employ.' He shuffled the papers. 'And the other reference was from the Bishop of Truro. An old friend of Miss Trevellian's family.' Mr Hooper passed the papers over to Chief Inspector Thorne.

He read them carefully and passed them to Arthur. Both references were on headed notepaper and confirmed Mr Hooper's assertion that the references were good.

'Did you meet Miss Trevellian when she applied for the tenancy?' Chief Inspector Thorne asked.

Mr Hooper took the letters back from Arthur and restored them to his case. 'Yes, she came to the offices to sign the tenancy agreement and to make the financial arrangements. She paid everything in full up front in cash. She was a pleasant woman in her early thirties. Her companion did not attend on that occasion.'

'And when the keys were returned at the end of the tenancy, did she return to your office herself?' Chief Inspector Thorne asked.

'No, her companion, Miss Perez, called and returned the keys and made the arrangements to complete the handover. A charming young lady in her mid-twenties. Attractive, spoke English very well with a slight accent on certain words. She said Miss Trevellian had been delighted with the house and that the works were now completed on her own house, so she had travelled on ahead to supervise the staff, leaving Miss Perez to finish the business of the tenancy on the manor.' Mr Hooper frowned at the chief inspector. 'Everything appeared perfectly above board, I assure you.'

Arthur could tell from Chief Inspector Thorne's manner that things were not so straightforward.

'You have concerns, Chief Inspector?' he asked.

Thorne drummed his fingers absent-mindedly on the arm of his chair. 'We are anxious to identify the lady found in the water. To this end I have made enquiries at Miss Trevellian's home in Cornwall. The house is empty, and the staff have not seen their mistress since the autumn. They know nothing of a Miss Perez and stated that no works had been carried out on the house that would have necessitated Miss Trevellian having to take a tenancy on another house.'

Mr Hooper started in his seat. 'But that's impossible.'

'Did Miss Trevellian give a forwarding address for any post or messages that might come to Half Moon Manor after her departure?' the chief inspector asked.

The elderly solicitor was clearly perplexed. 'The address I have is for Trelisk in Cornwall, Miss Trevellian's family home.'

Chief Inspector Thorne turned his attention to Arthur.

'You have never met Miss Trevellian, or had any contact from her during her tenancy?'

Arthur shook his head. 'No, Chief Inspector. Mr Hooper handles all my business affairs and I had never heard of this lady until she rented my house.' He had a strange feeling, however, that his employers in Whitehall might well know something about his mysterious tenant.

'Hmm.' The chief inspector's brow furrowed. 'I wonder, Mr Cilento, you did not see the lady's face yesterday?'

'No, Chief Inspector, she was face down in the water when we discovered her and, as you know, I had retired to the house while the recovery was made.' He didn't like to think of it. The body floating on the dark water, the bright blue of her coat bobbing and swaying, had haunted his dreams.

'Mr Hooper, would you be able to confirm her identity if you saw her?' the chief inspector asked.

Arthur could see the solicitor was reluctant to undertake such a task but sensed its inevitability.

'I expect so,' he said.

Chief Inspector Thorne gave a small, grim smile. 'Mr Cilento, I would very much appreciate it if you too would accompany us. I'd like to be certain that you did not recognise Miss Trevellian.'

Arthur was a little surprised by the request. 'If you feel it would be helpful, Chief Inspector. However, I have spent much of the last year in London and then working and recuperating in a rest home in Scotland, so am unlikely to have encountered this lady.'

'Thank you, gentlemen. I am most obliged to both of you. I have also requested photographs of Miss Trevellian to be sent from her home in Cornwall for the purposes of identification. The lady has no close family.' Chief Inspector Thorne rose from his seat.

Benson appeared bearing their outer garments. The rain of

the previous evening had petered out overnight leaving behind a dull, grey day. Arthur accompanied Mr Hooper and the chief inspector to the latter gentleman's waiting police car.

Arthur was not looking forward to the task ahead. Until yesterday he had not seen a dead body for quite some years. His work did not usually bring him into physical danger. It really was dreadfully inconvenient. Mr Hooper appeared to be equally reluctant. The older man looked pale and was quiet as he took his place alongside Arthur in the back of the car. The chief inspector took the front passenger seat. A uniformed constable performed the office of chauffeur.

Arthur settled the plaid travel rug across his knees. His breath hung in a mist before his face and his chest invariably tightened with the change in temperature. Half Moon Manor was at the end of the road leading from the town, and it was some minutes before they were passing through the busier streets that led to the small cottage hospital and the morgue which was situated within its grounds.

The car passed along a narrower street of terraced workers' cottages and then through the wrought-iron gate leading to the rear of the hospital. The morgue was a single-storey red-brick building with a tiled roof standing apart from the other buildings. The constable stopped the car and their party alighted.

Arthur adjusted his thick woollen scarf and followed Mr Hooper and the chief inspector in through the dark-green painted door. The doctor and his attendant met them in the small anteroom in which they found themselves. The chief inspector performed the introductions.

'Thank you for coming, gentlemen. Please come through.' The doctor opened a set of double doors. Arthur's pulse sped up as they progressed into a brightly lit room. A row of grey, steel cabinets were banked against the far wall. In the centre were two metal tables. The floor was of stone and the walls tiled in white. It felt colder inside the morgue than outside the building, and smelled of disinfectant.

One table was occupied. A white sheet covered the person lying beneath it. They approached the table, and the doctor drew back the sheet, exposing the woman's face.

Fair haired with a snub nose and ordinary features. Her time in the river had undoubtedly caused some puffiness and distortion, but Arthur was relieved to see that her appearance was not as alarming as he had feared.

'Yes, this is the lady who came to my office and presented herself as Miss Kate Trevellian,' Mr Hooper said. He raised his handkerchief to his lips.

'Thank you, sir. Mr Cilento, have you ever seen this lady before?'

Arthur was conscious of the chief inspector's sharp gaze resting on him as he studied the dead woman's face. He had acceded to the chief inspector's request to view the woman's face with no expectation of recognising her. Why would he?

And yet, there was something about the woman that tugged at the fringes of his memory. Something vaguely and disconcertingly familiar. Something which he was now certain was connected with his work. The unsettled feeling in the pit of his stomach grew stronger.

'I cannot say, Chief Inspector. There is something familiar about her features, but I cannot think where I could have met her before.' Troubled, he turned to Chief Inspector Thorne. He disliked being unable to recall where he had met the woman. Normally he had a very good recall for faces, and he could only assume that it was seeing the woman dead that was affecting him.

The policeman merely nodded, his expression impassive. 'Thank you, sir. If you do recollect later where you may have encountered her, please let me know.'

The doctor replaced the sheet back over the woman's face and Mr Hooper released a tremulous sigh of relief.

'Thank you, gentlemen.' Chief Inspector Thorne led their small party out of the morgue and back to the anteroom where they had entered. Arthur's mind was preoccupied with trying to recall where he had seen or met the woman before.

They bade farewell to the doctor and his team and took their places back in the police car. Arthur noticed that Mr Hooper's hand trembled as he arranged the travel rug back in place over his knees. The elderly solicitor closed his eyes as the car pulled away.

'Are you feeling all right, Mr Hooper?' Mr Cilento could see that the experience in the morgue had greatly affected the man.

The man opened his eyes and blinked a couple of times. 'I must confess I found the experience most distressing. Such a young woman, murdered in cold blood it seems.'

Arthur understood his companion's distress. 'I wish I could recall where I knew that young woman from, for I have seen her before, I'm certain.'

The solicitor frowned. 'Would your uncle perhaps have known Miss Trevellian's family?'

Arthur considered the possibility. But he was suddenly certain that it had not been with his uncle when he had encountered the young woman. He was equally sure the encounter had not been at Half Moon Manor.

'No, I don't think so, and you yourself hadn't seen her since she was a child?'

'Indeed no. I knew her father as he conducted some business with our firm, but Miss Trevellian would have been perhaps four or five years old when I saw her previously.' The solicitor fell silent. Arthur could tell from his demeanour that he was as troubled about the case as Arthur himself.

* * *

'I made the telephone call the brigadier requested and have spoken personally to Miss Kate Trevellian.' Stephen lounged nonchalantly against the door frame of Miss Treen's office as he passed on the message.

'The real Kate Trevellian, I assume? Thank you.' Jane continued to sort through the files she wished to take to Half Moon Manor. Several of the ones she had searched for had not been in the cabinet.

'Swanning off to Devon then, eh?' Stephen said. 'It's all right for some.'

'It is work, Stephen, something that I'm certain you have plenty of.' She waited for him to take the hint and leave her in peace. There was a lot to do before she could leave for Penny-combe in the morning.

'Another agent dead? Tsk, tsk, Jane, darling, that's not going to look good for when the old man retires and you go sniffing around after his job,' Stephen said.

Jane paused in her sorting to glare at him. 'I'm glad you have time to stand around gossiping like an old woman, but I am busy. There is a war on, in case you'd forgotten.' She knew that Stephen simply liked to wind her up. On top of her rejection of his advances over Christmas, she knew he was jealous of her position in the office.

'By the way, I ran into your mother the other night at a dinner party. She sends her regards.' Stephen straightened up from the door frame as Jane spun around on her heels to face him.

'How very nice for the both of you. Now get out of my office and let me get on with my work.' Her tone was icy and even Stephen seemed to sense he had gone too far with the mention of her mother.

'Keep your hair on, Jane, darling. Just passing on a message.' Stephen beat a hasty retreat when Jane took a step towards him.

With her tormentor gone, Jane attempted to focus her mind back on her work. Mentioning her mother was a low blow. She knew that Stephen was fully aware of how things stood between the two of them.

* * *

Upon their arrival back at Half Moon Manor, the chief inspector excused himself to go and revisit the scene of the murder. Mr Hooper joined Arthur in his study. Over a welcome cup of tea and a small home-made biscuit, they concluded the probate paperwork for the estate, which had been the original purpose of Mr Hooper's visit.

Arthur proposed a removal to the drawing room and offered Mr Hooper lunch before he set off back to the station.

'I understand there is a fine meat and kidney pudding to be had; Mrs Mullins struck gold at the butcher's,' Arthur offered. He had already asked his staff to ensure there would be enough for both Mr Hooper and the chief inspector should he choose to join them. He was slightly troubled by the vagueness of meat, rather than assigning a particular cut such as steak or lamb. However, one had to take what one could get and be thankful, he supposed.

'That would be most kind.' Mr Hooper took a seat opposite his host. 'I take it your plans are to stay here for a time? No more travelling for work in the offing now you are recovered?'

'Not for a while. I find travelling quite exhausting. Despite the cold at present, the air seems to suit me quite well here and I have a contract to publish some more academic texts.' He would remain at Half Moon Manor unless he was sent for again. He had a horrid feeling in the pit of his stomach that the mysterious woman might necessitate a visit from one of his Whitehall contacts.

Benson opened the door to show Chief Inspector Thorne into the room. 'Luncheon will be ready shortly, sir.'

'Thank you, Benson. Chief Inspector, you are joining us I hope?' Arthur asked.

'That's very kind of you, sir.' The chief inspector came to stand nearer to the fire. 'The scene is finished with now, Mr Cilento, so you and your staff are free to enter that part of the garden again.'

'Unlikely, I fear, in this cold weather, Chief Inspector, but thank you.'

The lounge door opened once more, and Benson reappeared. Arthur expected him to announce that they could proceed to the dining room. Instead, however, he handed over a manila envelope to the chief inspector.

'A constable has just left these for you, sir.' Benson departed once more.

Chief Inspector Thorne opened the envelope and took out what appeared to be photographs. Arthur assumed they must be the ones he had requested of Miss Trevellian, from her home in Cornwall.

He watched a range of emotions play across the chief inspector's sharp features as he looked at the pictures in his hand. Shock, disbelief, he wasn't sure which emotion was uppermost.

'Well, gentlemen, it seems we have a puzzle on our hands. If these pictures are correct, the lady residing in the morgue is not Miss Kate Trevellian.'

CHAPTER FOUR

'Preposterous!' Mr Hooper leapt from his seat, his face a ghastly white in the cold winter light coming in through the large bay window. 'There must be some mistake.'

Chief Inspector Thorne passed the photographs across to the solicitor. Instead of his spectacles, the elderly man extracted a small gold-framed pince-nez from his pocket and examined the pictures closely. His hand trembled as he verified for himself the truth of the chief inspector's statement.

Silently, he offered the pictures to Arthur and sank back down onto the armchair, clearly greatly perturbed by the sight of the photographs. Arthur studied the pictures. One was of a family group taken at the front of what he assumed must be Trelisk, the Trevellian family home. It showed a youthful woman with her parents and the family dog. The second picture was a posed studio portrait taken at a photographer's shop in Newlyn, judging from the stamp on the back. A plain, rather awkward young woman with fair hair, a patrician nose and a small pursed-lipped mouth. Definitely not the woman lying on the mortuary table.

He gave the pictures back to Chief Inspector Thorne. 'I

concur, Chief Inspector. It would seem we have been deceived.'
He had a growing suspicion as to the purpose.

Arthur had taken the precaution late the previous evening,
once the household was quiet, of placing a telephone call to a
certain number in Whitehall. The subsequent conversation had
been brief and succinct. His call had been noted and further
instructions would follow if necessary. He had been uncertain
at first if he should have done so, but the events of this morning
appeared to be proving that his instincts had been correct.

Benson cleared his throat discreetly in the doorway. 'Luncheon is served, sir.'

Arthur showed his guests into the dining room, and they
took their places at the elegant mahogany dining table set with
sparkling crystal glassware and polished silver cutlery.

Mrs Mullins had produced a delicious luncheon of a meat
pudding with winter vegetables, followed by a steamed pudding
with custard. The meat had a beef-like taste and texture, much
to Arthur's relief. Offal was all very well but sometimes he
longed for a decent roast. Conversation was steered away from
the mystery of the dead woman until they returned to the sitting
room for coffee.

'When do you expect the inquest to be held, Chief Inspector?' Arthur asked.

The officer accepted his cup of coffee from the attentive
Benson. 'I expect the county coroner will open it and adjourn it
tomorrow morning. That will hopefully give us a little time to
try and establish the woman's identity. I have arranged for the
newspapers to carry a photograph and description.'

Mr Hooper nodded his approval of Chief Inspector
Thorne's instructions. 'I am a little troubled though, sir, by the
whereabouts of the real Kate Trevellian. Did no one at her
house know where their mistress may have gone?'

Arthur had also been thinking about this conundrum.

'Miss Trevellian's staff were under the impression that the

lady was in Wales. They were not expecting her return for quite some weeks.' The chief inspector sipped his drink.

'They had heard from her then?' Arthur asked in a mild tone.

'Yes, shortly before Christmas. She had met with some old friends and did not intend to return until the end of February.'

'How very convenient for the imposter,' Arthur observed, his tone causing Mr Hooper to look curiously at him.

The chief inspector offered to take Mr Hooper back to the station as he was returning to town. An offer which was gratefully accepted by the elderly solicitor as his business with Arthur was concluded.

With the gentlemen gone, Arthur settled himself before the fire with a book. The events of the previous twenty-four hours had unsettled him, and he needed to clear his thoughts. He suspected that he would be hearing from London very soon.

He had not been there above an hour when the doorbell sounded, and he heard Benson ushering visitors into the hallway. But it was not who he had expected.

'The Reverend Andrew Fenwick and his sister, Miss Diana Fenwick, sir.' Benson proffered him a card.

Arthur put aside his book. 'Please show them in and offer them some refreshments.' He knew them both vaguely, having met them briefly when his late uncle had still been alive. They had been in the parish for about four years now, having previously come from London. It seemed he had a small reprieve from a visitation from Whitehall.

Benson withdrew back to the hall and returned moments later to usher in the guests. He stood politely to receive them. Andrew Fenwick was a medium-sized man with a slight potbelly and a pleasant demeanour. He appeared several years older than Arthur and was dressed in his clerical attire.

Miss Diana Fenwick was clearly much younger than her brother. Not classically pretty but with a certain something about her which drew attention. Her dark-blonde hair was fashionably short and waved and she wore a tweed suit with an ivory blouse.

Benson vanished to collect tea for the visitors and Arthur settled the Fenwicks on the lounge furniture. Miss Fenwick opposite him on the armchair, and her brother on the sofa.

'I do hope we are not intruding, Mr Cilento? We had heard from Mrs Mullins that you were returning from your travels and had intended to call later this week. However, when we heard about the terrible tragedy befalling that poor woman, my sister felt we should call somewhat earlier. These kinds of events can be most distressing.' The reverend petered to a halt. His earnest, good-natured face showing what appeared to be genuine concern.

Benson returned with a tray of tea for the guests and began to serve.

'I have less genuine motives than my brother.' Diana Fenwick flashed a brilliant smile and her eyes gleamed with mild amusement. 'I must confess I am alive with curiosity. Nothing exciting ever happens here.' She spread her hands in a disarming gesture.

Arthur noted the quick appraising glance his manservant bestowed on Miss Fenwick. He appeared to approve of her as he gave one of his rare smiles as he offered her a cup of tea. Arthur knew his man to be a good judge of character. They had encountered a good many interesting characters during their travels together and Arthur relied on his judgement, knowing he was not especially skilled in that area.

'I am delighted to see you both. Yes, it has been a most unusual homecoming.' He told the Fenwicks of the discovery that the lady who had been occupying Half Moon Manor for the last eight weeks was not the person they had imagined.

Normally, he would have kept that information to himself, but he was curious to see what their reaction to this news would be.

'Oh dear.' Reverend Fenwick looked most distressed.

His sister on the other hand was more forthright in her opinion. 'I told you there was something odd about Miss Trevellian and her companion, Andrew.' She cast a triumphant glance at her brother.

'I take it you met the lady and, a Miss Perez, was it?' Arthur asked.

'Oh yes,' Diana cut in eagerly, before her brother had the opportunity to reply. 'Andrew called on them shortly after they took up the tenancy. We had quite a few events on at the church during December you see, and we thought Miss Trevellian might wish for some company.'

'Did Miss Trevellian – I suppose we must call her that until we know her real identity – appear keen to attend any events?' Arthur asked.

Mr Hooper had said the lady wished for a quiet life. He was keen to know how she would have received the Fenwicks' well-intentioned invitations.

'Diana and I called shortly after the lady arrived. She greeted us with her companion. They were pleasant enough, but somewhat distant.' Reverend Fenwick's brow puckered as he recalled the visit. 'Miss Trevellian said she had poor health and was recuperating from illness, so was unable to participate in many social outings. Her companion was a young Spanish lady. She spoke excellent English with a slight accent, she was of the Catholic persuasion.'

'I rather think she attended Mass a few times at the church there. I bumped into her the one Sunday as she was coming out,' Diana said.

'What was your impression of them?' He was interested to

know what Diana Fenwick thought. She appeared to be a sensible young woman and, he suspected, she was no fool.

'I only met Miss Trevellian twice to talk to, I think. Our first visit here, and then she attended the Christmas Day service. She had a young man with her who she introduced as her cousin. He was a good-looking sort of chap but, I don't know, Andrew will say this is unchristian of me, he seemed rather smarmy. Do you recall his name, Andrew?'

Her brother frowned as he set down his empty teacup. 'Richard Trent. Yes, that was it, Richard Trent. It stuck in my mind as I was at school with a chap called Trent. He seemed very full of the Christmas-tide joys.'

Arthur stored the information away in his memory. No doubt Chief Inspector Thorne would find the information useful. It might even provide a clue to the dead woman's true identity.

Diana Fenwick appeared to be deep in thought. 'Richard Trent was dressed very well but his clothes weren't the best quality, if you know what I mean.' When Arthur raised an enquiring eyebrow, Diana coloured. 'He wore cheap shoes. A gentleman may have threadbare clothes, or his footwear may have holes, but it will never be cheap.'

Arthur nodded. Diana, it seemed, was a good observer of people.

'I asked Miss Trevellian if she was feeling better, and she said she was much improved. She introduced us to Richard Trent, her cousin, who had come to stay for a few days before they returned to Cornwall. He was on leave, I think,' Andrew Fenwick added to Diana's tale.

'Oh, I say. You don't think this Richard Trent might be her murderer, do you?' Alarm spread across Diana's face, and she looked anxiously at her brother.

Arthur gave a little cough. 'I think Chief Inspector Thorne will be interested in the information, Miss Fenwick. I take it

Miss Perez was not at church with Miss Trevellian and her cousin?'

Diana smiled. 'No, Miss Trevellian said she had gone to her own church and was meeting them back here later.'

'Thinking about it now, Miss Trevellian appeared uncomfortable in her cousin's company somehow. He was quite jovial and chatty, like Diana said, he was full of bonhomie, but Miss Trevellian kept looking about her, as if eager to return to the house. At the time I put it down to her feeling a little unwell after the service. You know, not having been out much.' Reverend Fenwick was clearly uncomfortable at the idea that he might have somehow missed something important.

'What about this companion, Miss Perez? You said you met her a few times, Miss Fenwick?' Arthur asked. Diana hadn't exactly said that, but she had implied it in her earlier comment.

'Yes, I met her, as I said, coming from her church. I was wheeling my bicycle back to the vicarage. I had a puncture. I'd been out to visit an elderly parishioner who was sick, and I happened to see her. She walked with me for part of the way.'

He waited for Diana to tell him more of the story.

'I was chatting to her, as you do, you know, asking her where in Spain she was from and that kind of thing. With the civil war over there and everything, I couldn't help feeling rather sorry for her. She was clearly a well-educated young woman and it seemed she had suffered a great deal,' Diana said. She looked at Arthur. 'She said she was from the Basque region, and she had come to England in the first instance to find her younger brothers. They were eight and ten when they were sent here to escape the conflict in Spain. She had originally hoped to go and collect them from where they had been staying with friends in the Cotswolds. She had wanted to make a home for them here until the troubles at home were over, and they could return to Spain. She is apparently their guardian. Of course, now with the war and everything, well...'

'I presumed that was why she was working for Miss Trevellian for a spell. To get some money together,' Reverend Fenwick said.

'Very possibly,' Arthur agreed.

One of the references that Mr Hooper had produced was from Lady Godmaston. She had been one of the leading figures in finding places for Spanish refugee children. Perhaps another clue for Chief Inspector Thorne to follow.

It was all terribly interesting.

The telephone call from London came through just before supper. Arthur was to expect assistance from Whitehall imminently.

CHAPTER FIVE

Arthur woke with a start. His bedroom was still dark, and he couldn't say what exactly had disturbed him from the bizarre dream he had been having. Something about the river and nursery rhymes.

He sat up in bed and listened. The house was silent. The cool air of his bedroom wrapped itself around his pyjama-clad shoulders in a cold embrace. Arthur snapped on his bedside light. *Nursery rhymes.*

'Little Polly Flinders.' Arthur leaned back against his pillows and scrubbed at his face with his hands. He now knew exactly who the woman in the water was, and that knowledge troubled him deeply.

There was a light tap at his bedroom door and Benson looked in dressed in his night attire.

'Begging your pardon, sir. I thought I heard a noise.'

His manservant was accustomed to sleeping lightly in the event of one of Arthur's asthmatic attacks. 'It's all right, Benson. I had a bad dream, nothing more. I fear there is a problem, however.'

Benson entered the room and closed the door quietly

behind him. 'Sir?'

'The woman in the water. I know now who she is.'

Benson, as usual, betrayed little emotion.

'Polly Flinders. Two years ago, in Berlin.' An icy shiver ran up his spine.

'Operation Firebird, I believe, sir. Just before the commencement of hostilities.'

'Indeed.' Polly Flinders had been his contact. He'd met her twice, briefly. Once when she had delivered the codes, and again when his work had been completed.

'I shall inform Mrs Mullins to expect more guests.' Benson waited for a moment. 'With your permission, sir, I think it might be as well to check the guns.'

'Yes, thank you, I think you may be right, and goodnight. I'm sorry you were disturbed.' He waited until Benson had seen himself out before switching off his light and sliding back into the welcome warmth of his blankets.

As Benson had predicted, Arthur had scarcely finished his breakfast before the first arrival appeared. He was in his study at the front of the house when he heard the purr of a motor car crunching its way along the gravel drive. A glance out of the window at the murky morning revealed a black car with mud splashes marring what must have been immaculate, shining paintwork when the car had started its journey.

Arthur sighed and put away his paperwork as Benson went to answer the bell. Hopefully, his Whitehall visitor's stay would be brief. It was most inconvenient having house guests. He noted that the manservant had indeed made good on his word about firearms. He locked the drawer, ignoring the revolver that had been placed there. Arthur did not care for guns or violence. There were voices in the hall, then Benson entered the study.

'A Miss Treen is here to see you, sir. I have put her in the lounge. The chauffeur and her, er, cat are in the kitchen with Mrs Mullins.'

'Thank you, Benson. I expect she will require coffee and an ashtray. Did you say cat?' He had hoped that Whitehall would not send Miss Treen. She was the least favourite of his contacts there. A small, brisk woman in her mid-to-late thirties, she seemed to survive on coffee, black with two sugars preferably, and cigarettes.

The coffee he didn't mind. Even with the shortages, sugar was rationed, but the cigarettes always troubled his chest somewhat. He had worked with her several times in the past, although usually their meetings had been brief. But why on earth had she brought a cat?

'Yes, sir, a large, fluffy orange animal with one eye,' Benson said.

'Oh dear.' It wasn't that Arthur disliked animals, but cats and his asthma did not go well together, and it sounded as if Miss Treen intended her visit to last longer than one day. No doubt this was why the caller from Whitehall had sounded slightly amused when he had said assistance was forthcoming.

Miss Treen was ensconced in his favourite armchair beside the fire, large ginger cat at her feet, when he opened the lounge door. Benson had clearly been mistaken about it remaining in the kitchen. She turned her head in a swift, bird-like movement as he entered the room, surveying him with sharp, beady, bright-blue eyes that, he was certain, missed nothing.

'Miss Treen, it's good of you to call.' He offered her his hand. She gave it a brisk, firm shake and waved him to the other seat as if Half Moon Manor were her office and he were the guest. Arthur sighed inwardly.

'This is a pickle, Arthur, isn't it?' she said, her tone implying subtly that it must be his fault in some way that Polly Flinders was dead. Not that he supposed Polly Flinders had been her real name, of course. He wondered if Miss Treen was really Miss Treen. She could be a Mrs Smith for all he knew, hurrying home each day at five thirty to an unsuspecting Mr Smith and a family of little Smiths.

He studied her more closely. No, she was definitely a Miss Treen. The neat heather-coloured tweed suit, steely gaze and immaculate patent shoes all spoke of ruthless single efficiency. It took one to know one he supposed. And, of course, there was the cat. He became aware that she was expecting some sort of response from him.

'Polly Flinders.' He watched for her reaction. Not that he expected to see much, Miss Treen was too well trained.

'You recognised her, then?' She raised a delicately shaped eyebrow.

'Yes.' He didn't tell her that the recollection had not been immediate, nor that he had not yet shared this information with Chief Inspector Thorne. Something he felt certain that Miss Treen would issue advice about.

She nodded. His answer clearly not surprising her. 'I take it that you placed her here?' He was unsurprised but rather annoyed that Miss Treen had appropriated his home as some kind of safe house. Something that had dawned on him in the small hours of the morning.

'A regrettable necessity. These are difficult times, as I am sure you appreciate, and I have reason to believe that security in our department has been compromised. I needed a safe house but couldn't use one of our regular places. Half Moon Manor appeared at just the right time.' She gave Marmaduke a scratch under his chin, and he nuzzled her hand appreciatively.

'I take it the reason for her placement here was classified?' he asked mildly.

Miss Treen gave him a sharp look. 'It's rather complicated.'

His chuckle turned into a cough and Miss Treen tutted.

'Isn't it always? And her companion? Miss Perez?' he asked.

'Placed with her for her security.' Miss Treen lifted the fluffy cat onto her lap.

Arthur nodded. 'I assume you know of her whereabouts? Miss Perez, that is?'

Benson reappeared and placed a tray with a large pot of coffee with all the accoutrements on the table before them.

'Will there be anything else, sir?'

'Nothing for now, thank you, Benson.'

His man gave a slight bow and retreated from the room. Miss Treen helped herself to coffee and poured an additional cup for Arthur.

'Miss Perez's whereabouts are known to the department.' She took a sip of her drink.

Arthur added more steamed milk to his coffee, eyeing with some distaste the evil-looking inky black concoction in Miss Treen's cup. 'I don't suppose she will be in a position to assist with any enquiries into Polly Flinders's murder?' He had his own suspicions about where the mysterious Miss Perez might be. He suspected that she was probably no longer on British soil.

Miss Treen gave a barely imperceptible shrug. Her shrewd gaze appeared to be assessing him as if she were undecided about whether she should confide in him. It had the effect of making him feel very uncomfortable, as if he had been summoned for some undefined, unknown crime.

'I mentioned that the department has a problem.' She surveyed him over the rim of her cup.

'A traitor in your midst,' Arthur said. It seemed to be an obvious deduction to him.

'Yes, and worse, a murderer. Intent on removing certain agents. I have no idea why Polly returned here.'

Miss Treen had his full attention with her statement. 'How

do you know this?' There had to be something that made Jane Treen believe particular agents were being targeted.

She hesitated for a second, before carefully setting her cup and saucer aside. She delved into her handbag and handed him a small, slim brown file. 'This. Polly is not the first victim. Take a look. The others that were killed had messages left with them.'

Arthur opened the folder, while Miss Treen took another sip of coffee. His eyebrows rose as he considered the contents.

'There was no note left with Polly, at least not one that Chief Inspector Thorne has mentioned. Difficult I suppose, given that she was found in the water.' Arthur studied the file. 'The other agents that have been killed were all engaged on the same operation when it went wrong? Operation Exodus?'

'There were six agents involved in Operation Exodus at first. One was lost during the operation, five survived. And since then, it seems as if someone is out for vengeance. Two of those five survivors have already been killed and now there's Polly. That leaves two more at risk.' Jane blew out another narrow plume of blue-grey smoke.

'Where are they now, the remaining two?' Arthur lifted his gaze and looked at Jane.

'One is abroad at present, in deep cover. I can only assume he is safe from whoever murdered Polly and the others, at least for now.' Jane frowned as she spoke.

'And the other agent?' Arthur asked. 'Where are they?'

Jane sighed and shifted almost imperceptibly in her seat. 'We don't know. He's vanished.'

Arthur's eyebrows rose at this. 'I see. You said there were letters or rather notes left at the scene with the first two deaths? That's how you linked the deaths together?' He preferred the term deaths to murders. Murder sounded, well, too harsh, even though he knew that was what had happened.

Miss Treen nodded. 'Yes. The actual notes are there in the back of the file.'

Arthur turned to the rear of the folder and found a brown envelope. He opened it with care and peered inside before sliding out two sheets of cheap, lined writing paper. A cursory glance revealed that words had been clipped from what appeared to be a newspaper and pasted onto the sheets of paper.

'No fingerprints?' he asked.

Jane shook her head. 'Nothing. The words appear to have been clipped from a daily newspaper so nothing there. The paper and envelope are readily available from any stationer's.

Exodus 21:23-25 But if any harm follows, then you shall give life for life, eye for eye, tooth for tooth, hand for hand...

'Miss Treen, I learned yesterday that there was another visitor here over Christmas.' Arthur told her what he had learned from Diana and Andrew Fenwick. 'Who was he? This Richard Trent, was he a department member?' Arthur asked as he read the messages once more. The pasted words clearly indicated the deaths were linked to Operation Exodus.

'I don't know anyone of that name.' Miss Treen looked worried. 'Polly was due to send a report after she had left your house. To date, nothing has been received in the department. They had been instructed not to contact the office while they were in the safe house unless there was an emergency. Therefore, I can only assume that this man must have been known to them. After leaving your house, Polly promptly disappeared until she was found dead at the bottom of *your* garden. She didn't report to her handler, at least we don't know that she did. Anna Perez received her new orders and left before we could ask her any questions.' Miss Treen's brow knitted into a fearsome frown.

Arthur resented the inference in Miss Treen's tone when

she said Polly had been found in *his* garden. He was the person who had been ill-used. No one had asked him how he felt about his home being used as a temporary safe house. Or seemed even slightly apologetic about having embroiled him in the middle of a murder enquiry.

Miss Treen had finished her coffee and seemed at a loss for something to do with her hands, with Marmaduke now fast asleep. 'Obviously, I conducted enquiries at my end yesterday to check if any fresh reports had been received about Polly's stay here and nothing was said about any visitor at Christmas.' She drummed her fingers on the arm of the chair.

'Nothing?' Arthur was surprised. Anna and Polly had clearly accepted this Richard Trent and had told people he was Polly's cousin. They were experienced agents, so he had to have either been known to them or had given them convincing evidence about his identity and the purpose of his visit.

'I have no idea who he might be or how he discovered their whereabouts. I cannot communicate with Anna at present and it's unlikely that I shall be able to reach her for some considerable time.' Miss Treen produced another cigarette. 'I'll telephone the office in a minute and make enquiries, but the name is not one that I'm familiar with at all.'

'And where was Polly supposed to go after she left here, and Anna returned to London?' Arthur asked. 'I assume Anna was not part of Operation Exodus?'

'No, she wasn't. They travelled together into Exeter. Anna returned to London after delivering the keys as planned to your solicitor. Polly was to report to her handler and to return to her own home for a day, before leaving on another mission.'

'What happened?' Arthur asked. 'Did she fail to report in?'

'Anna fulfilled her part. The handler Polly was supposed to report to hasn't left a note in the file to say if she heard from her. We have no way of knowing what went wrong. And we are now unable to reach Polly's contact.' Miss Treen looked distressed. 'The bombing raids in London have been particularly bad. The smooth running of the department has been impacted.'

Arthur sighed as she lit up and inhaled deeply. 'Then I think if I am to assist you, you will need to tell me more about Operation Exodus and what went wrong.'

CHAPTER SIX

'It is the brigadier's wish that we work together to solve this problem, so I will fill you in. However, it goes without saying that everything I am about to tell you about Operation Exodus is top secret.' She fixed Arthur with a steely gaze.

She knew that Arthur was well aware of the need for secrecy already, but it never did any harm to remind people.

'Of course.' His tone was slightly scornful, and he had that expression on his face which never failed to slightly annoy her.

'Operation Exodus took place in spring last year. Their mission was to ensure that certain people were given safe passage back to England. A small number of our field agents had been working under deep cover behind the lines. The people needing passage were key agents and escaped prisoners of war who had vital information. But intelligence began to gradually trickle through to London that something was amiss with the plan.' Jane paused, taking a moment to recall exactly what had happened.

'Were the field agents based together?' Arthur asked.

Jane shook her head. It would have been highly dangerous and unusual if that had been the case. 'No, they were in the same area of the country, but deployed in different occupations. Each agent only knew of one contact.'

'So, if caught, they could only ever betray one person if they succumbed to pressure under interrogation.' Arthur had clearly grasped the concept.

'Exactly, although each agent was working to the same end. It was a highly complex and unusually sensitive operation. Those involved in assisting the escapees were all hand-picked. I oversee several other similar operations, but the people we were getting out through Operation Exodus had been at the heart of the German government, so the stakes were very high. And it was very successful to begin with. It had been one of the brigadier's ideas and approved at the highest levels here. The risks were enormous, something all the agents had been aware of when they had undertaken the task.'

'Who were the agents involved?' Arthur asked. 'You said that two were still alive and you indicated that both of them might now be at risk? Or do you think one may be at risk and the other the assassin?'

Miss Treen's lips compressed into a line, and her frown deepened as she considered his questions.

'Polly Flinders, you knew already. The operatives were all given code names. You'll see that in the files. She was murdered here. Peter Piper was the agent killed during the operation. He was the main contact back to London, operating the radio, we believe he was shot. Jack Horner was the first of the murders here, followed by Lucy Locket. Tommy Tucker is still under deep cover abroad and Georgie Porgie is the agent that is missing. I don't know if both are at risk or if, as you suggest, one may be the murderer. There is no motive that I know of for the latter suggestion to be true.'

Jane rose from her seat and paced up and down in front of the fireplace. Arthur's questions were increasing her agitation.

Arthur was silent for a moment as he continued to leaf

through the file. She knew that he could speed-read and she had no doubt that he was committing every letter, full stop and comma from the documents to his incredible memory.

'I presume you have other information with you?' Arthur asked as he closed the folder.

Jane nodded. She had anticipated the question and had brought other files from the archives with her. At least, she had brought what was still available.

'Polly, Peter, Jack and Lucy,' Arthur read the names from the front of each slim brown dossier. 'Where are the other two files?'

Jane paused in her pacing. 'Missing. I looked, the brigadier's secretary Stephen looked, even the brigadier himself went and searched. Just a gap in the cabinet where they should have been. All I could find were these.' She handed over two smaller documents containing a photograph of each agent and a few sparse details.

Arthur raised an enquiring eyebrow. 'I see. What else should I know, Miss Treen?'

Jane was unsurprised by his perspicacity. It was partly why she was there, presenting him with the problem. 'There is one more person unaccounted for, who is also missing and whose file has also mysteriously vanished.'

'The handler?' Arthur asked.

'Each agent knew one operative in the field and the handler who was based back in London. They coordinated the operation.' Jane blew out a breath and went to retrieve her cigarettes.

Arthur waited until she had struck a match and lit up before speaking. 'And that person was?'

'Maura Roberts, code name Little Miss Muffet. She usually reported directly to the brigadier but in Operation Exodus, I was her senior officer.' Jane expelled a thin stream of smoke from her mouth.

Arthur settled back in his seat, his gaze fixed on her as she too dropped back down onto the armchair opposite his.

'If you want me to help you then you need to be completely frank with me.'

Jane fought the urge to roll her eyes. Arthur might be useful to the department, but he was still annoying. 'If you want to know more about Maura, there isn't much to tell. I've only met her on a few occasions to discuss the operations or when we passed briefly in the corridor. Her role was to direct the operations on the ground as she is fluent in several languages. I simply oversaw and intervened if there was a problem. As I said, I have charge of several similar operations all working in a similar way. This is the only one where there has been this issue, but it was the most important. Maura was, or appeared to be, as distressed and confused about the murders of Jack Horner and Lucy Locket as the rest of us.'

'But you say she too has now vanished?' Arthur asked.

'The street where she lived was hit during an air raid. You may know that there was heavy bombing on the twenty-ninth of December. She made brief contact to say she had got out all right, but she was obviously deeply distressed. That was the last contact we had with her.'

'You have no idea where she's gone?' Arthur asked. 'And her file is also missing?'

Jane nodded and stubbed out her cigarette in the ashtray. 'No idea at all. I looked for her file so we could try her next of kin. I thought she may have had a sister or aunt or someone locally that she could have gone to. I tried the police and the hospitals. The damage from the bomb was extensive. Most of Maura's street is blocked off still while they fetch a wall down.'

Arthur flicked through the files in his hands. 'I see. Any connections between any of the agents or with Miss Roberts other than through the department? Any personal connections you are aware of?'

'I'm not in the habit of probing into any of my agents' personal lives unless I have operational cause to do so. They were all vetted, of course, when they joined the department.' Jane was aware that her tone sounded stiff and starchy. However, it was true, she had little interest in people's private lives unless it impinged upon their efficiency. Perhaps that was a weakness. Since she herself did not have much of a life outside work, she did not attach much importance to other people's.

She refilled her coffee cup. It was clear that her answer had not been useful.

'Who else could have had access to these files?' Arthur asked.

'Anyone within the department. Myself, Stephen, the brigadier, a couple of secretaries, and Maura herself. The room where the cabinets are stored is kept locked, but I suppose if one were determined it wouldn't be difficult to gain entry.' She had not given a great deal of thought to how the files had gone missing. There had been no visible signs of damage to the door of the room. Or to the cabinets, for that matter, and no one had reported discovering the door unlocked.

Arthur shuffled the files together and handed them back to her. 'What do you want me to do, Miss Treen? Two people are missing and the third is deep undercover overseas.'

She didn't care for the dismissive note in his voice. 'A woman, a fellow agent, was murdered here at *your* home. It's clear that someone with close links to the department or, even worse, in the heart of Whitehall, is a traitor. This may just be the tip of the iceberg. Other lives may be at risk. Even our country's security. For all I know, you and I may be targets.'

Irritated further by the impassive response her speech received, she drew out another cigarette. Ignoring the expression of distaste on Arthur's face she lit up and inhaled. The nicotine rush helped, calming nerves that she hadn't realised were feeling fraught.

'Then how do you suggest we proceed?' Arthur coughed and flapped his hand about in front of his face as the smoke drifted towards him.

She redirected the cigarette away from him. 'We need to find Maura.' Jane had been thinking about this on the journey to Devon. 'In her message to the office she said that she was unhurt but needed to relocate. I understand that she lost family members in the raid. Now, it may be that she will resurface in the next few days. If anyone has any insight into the agents involved in Operation Exodus, then surely it will be her.'

'You said she knew of the first two deaths?' Arthur asked.

'Yes, the brigadier insisted she be told even though the operation had shut down. He was concerned that she too might be at risk. We had also hoped she might have an idea of who might be responsible and why.'

There was a rap at the door of the room and Benson entered with an apologetic air.

'I'm sorry to disturb you, sir, but Mrs Mullins wishes to know how many there will be for lunch.'

'I shall, of course, be staying for the foreseeable future. Please ask my driver to unload my bags from the car, then he may return to London.' She didn't give Arthur time to object.

'Very good, miss. The, em, animal too is remaining, miss?'

'Yes, I have supplies for Marmaduke. I'll be along in a moment to attend to him,' Jane confirmed.

Benson inclined his head and retreated from the room.

'You are intending to stay here? And the cat?' Arthur had sat upright in his chair. She thought she detected a look of alarm in his expression.

'Well of course, we need to put our heads together to work out how we are going to sort this problem out. Clearly, I shall need to speak personally to whoever is handling the investigation into Polly's death. Then we need to determine our course of action.' Her eyebrows rose. Surely, even Arthur, with his vague, wishy-washy otherworldliness could see that she had no choice.

Left to herself, Jane had very little desire to remain in the old-fashioned Tudor manor house in the middle of nowhere with Arthur Cilento for company. Heavens above, she had far better things to do back in London. She was the brigadier's right-hand woman and, as she had just told Arthur, had a lot of important work to do.

* * *

Arthur was not a happy man. Jane Treen had installed herself in what had been his uncle's bedroom, and was currently occupying his study barking orders into the telephone. Her wretched cat was in his kitchen. He had not enjoyed his lunch since what was usually a quiet, peaceful repast had been spoiled by Miss Treen's constant questions. To make matters worse he hadn't really had the answers to many of them.

'Excuse me, sir. Chief Inspector Thorne is here. I believe Miss Treen has requested him to call.' Benson stood aside to permit the policeman to enter the sitting room.

'Thank you, please let Miss Treen know he has arrived, would you? Chief Inspector, please take a seat.' Arthur waved his hand in the direction of the sofa. At least Arthur had managed to claim his favourite chair.

'A Miss Treen telephoned the police station and said she had some information regarding the young woman we found dead in your garden.' The chief inspector took a seat. His sharp-eyed gaze locked with Arthur's.

'Yes, Miss Treen will be joining us shortly.' Arthur noticed that Benson had emptied Jane's ashtray whilst they had been eating lunch. The room had also been aired, leaving it still feeling a little chilly.

Jane entered the room with her hand outstretched to greet

the chief inspector. 'Thank you so much for coming, I do hope this is not too inconvenient a time for you? My name is Jane Treen and I work for His Majesty's Government in the War Office.' She took the chair opposite Arthur, tucking her feet in their sensible patent brogues neatly together.

The chief inspector resumed his place on the sofa. 'Not at all, Miss Treen. You told my officer on the telephone that you had information regarding the young woman Mr Cilento found in his garden?'

Jane nodded. 'I must check before we go any further with this conversation that you understand that the information I give you is classified and is subject to the Official Secrets Act?'

If Miss Treen had whipped out a fountain pen and a copy of the act for the chief inspector to sign right there and then, Arthur would not have been surprised. Really, the woman was impossible.

The chief inspector's expression remained impassive. 'Of course, Miss Treen. Please, do continue.'

Jane straightened her tweed skirt and provided Chief Inspector Thorne with a succinct précis of who the young woman had been and why her identity had been concealed.

'Would you mind if I take down a few notes? Purely so that I can brief the coroner. I shall, of course, redact anything that may compromise your agency.' The policeman took out his notebook.

Miss Treen raised her eyebrows and looked the inspector directly in the eyes. 'This information is on a need-to-know basis. Nothing must get into the public arena that risks compromising either my department or any of my other agents.'

Arthur looked at each of his colleagues in turn. He hoped Jane would refrain from producing her infernal cigarettes. 'I'm sure Chief Inspector Thorne will act discreetly.'

Miss Treen glared at him and ignored his comment. 'It may

be better if some parts of the case do not make the newspapers. Obviously, the coroner will need to know her real name.'

'There are others who know that the dead woman was not the real Miss Trevellian,' Arthur said.

Jane shifted in her seat to face him. 'Who?'

'Mr Hooper, the solicitor.' Chief Inspector Thorne sounded apologetic.

'We can telephone him.' Miss Treen dismissed the issue of Mr Hooper.

Arthur had the uncomfortable feeling that he was included in Miss Treen's use of the word *we*.

'Then there is the vicar and his sister. If you recall, I told you they called at the house yesterday. They met Polly and Anna whilst they were here. They also met this Mr Trent.' Arthur could see that this information was not being well received by Miss Treen.

'Mr Trent?' Chief Inspector Thorne asked.

Arthur passed on the information he had gleaned from the Fenwicks. 'The staff also have no idea who he was beyond the story they were told during his stay.'

'Thank you, sir. I shall speak to the reverend and his sister. Miss Treen, you don't know who this man might be?' The policeman looked at Jane.

'I'm afraid not. I have been in touch with my office, and they are trying to find out,' she confirmed.

'If you do discover his identity, please let me know,' the chief inspector said.

'Of course, Chief Inspector. In the meantime, I can see there is quite a lot of containment to be done. It's fortunate that I'm here.' Miss Treen looked at Arthur as if daring him to contradict her.

Chief Inspector Thorne tucked his notebook away. 'I shall speak to the coroner and prepare a statement for the newspapers. Thank you for the information, Miss Treen. I shall, of course, keep you updated with any progress we make in our investigation.'

'Thank you. Arthur and I shall do the same. Perhaps before you leave could you show me where Polly's body was discovered?'

'Of course. It is rather muddy; you may wish to change your shoes.' The chief inspector glanced at Miss Treen's feet.

'I have galoshes with me.' She rose.

Arthur slumped down further in his chair, resigned to being saddled with his unwanted house guest. At least she had not asked him to traipse back down the garden to the backwater.

The chief inspector took his leave and Miss Treen, thankfully, went with him. Left to himself once more he picked up the folders she had provided and began to study them again more closely.

CHAPTER SEVEN

By the time Miss Treen rejoined him for afternoon tea Arthur had recovered some of his equilibrium. He had also drafted a list of questions ready for her.

Benson delivered the tea tray with his customary discretion and withdrew.

'I've telephoned Mr Hooper and sorted things out with him. I also checked in with the office again, and still nothing on this Trent character.' She shivered. 'Brr, it's quite cold outside. The chief inspector has left for the police station to try his contacts there.'

Miss Treen took a seat on the armchair opposite Arthur and picked up the lid of the teapot. She glanced at the contents and gave them a stir before replacing the lid.

Arthur knew Miss Treen was not over fond of tea, preferring coffee instead. 'Was Mr Hooper all right about it all? He was very distressed by the viewing at the morgue.'

She poured them both a cup of tea and added milk without bothering to ask Arthur for his preference. 'He was annoyed that I couldn't give him all the details, but he understands that there is a war on.' She stirred the contents of her cup, clanging the spoon against the rim.

Arthur winced at the noise and picked up his cup and saucer. He would have liked sugar but was learning to do without. 'I've been going over the files again.' He paused to take a sip of tea.

'Find anything useful?' she asked as she settled back in her chair, her sharp gaze fixed on his face.

'I've compiled a list of questions.' He tried to ignore the smoke already wafting in his direction. 'This Maura Roberts, have there been any other issues with any of the other operations she was involved with?'

Miss Treen paused to consider. 'Not that I'm aware of. I obviously went through all the other cases she had been responsible for before coming here. I'm certain the brigadier would have said if he had been aware of anything. Maura is an experienced agent despite her youth.'

'And you said you didn't know of any connections between Miss Roberts and any of the agents in Operation Exodus. No personal connections or family ties?' Arthur had set down his tea and picked up his notepad and pencil.

Miss Treen gave a slight shrug. 'I don't really know Maura terribly well, but she was from London according to people I spoke to in the department, so I presume her family are from there. She lived with her mother and a younger sibling, a boy of about fourteen, I think. Polly Flinders is from the West Country as was Georgie Porgie, not sure if it was Devon or Cornwall. It's in the files. Jack Horner was from Essex and Lucy Locket from Yorkshire. They were both murdered in London when they were on leave between assignments after we had retrieved them from France. Tommy Tucker is Scottish and Peter Piper was from Cornwall.' She waved her hand towards the files and Arthur tried not to groan aloud when a sprinkle of ash detached itself from the end of her cigarette.

'Is Miss Roberts close to anyone else within the department at Whitehall?' Arthur asked as he scribbled a note in his book.

'In the offices, you mean?' She took a pull on her cigarette, narrowing her eyes as she thought about his question.

Arthur nodded and waited for her reply.

'There is a girl in the typing pool. Similar age to Maura, they used to go to tea sometimes together I believe. I only know because I followed them out of the building once at the end of the day and Maura had come to call for her. What's her name?' The frown on Jane's brow deepened. 'Rose, yes, that's it, Rose Hall.'

'Hmm, then she may know where Maura has gone,' Arthur said. It struck him that this Rose may also have some connection to the dead and missing agents. A typing pool would have sight of a good deal of confidential material.

It was clear that Miss Treen had been struck by the same idea. 'I'll telephone the office again shortly. Although I'll probably get Stephen, the brigadier's secretary and, well...' She stubbed out the last bit of her cigarette with some force in the ashtray.

Arthur gathered that Miss Treen and the mysterious Stephen were not on the best of terms.

'The first agent, the one killed in the field during Operation Exodus...' He paused and looked at Miss Treen.

'Peter Piper?' She took a sip of her tea and grimaced.

'His file is very slim. Do you know much about him? Anything that is not included in here?' Arthur asked as he looked at the black-and-white photograph attached to the contents of the folder.

Miss Treen abandoned her tea. 'He was twenty-eight, Cornish. I believe he lived not far from Miss Trevellian's home funnily enough.'

'Polly Flinders's borrowed identity?' Arthur was intrigued

at this seemingly random connection. 'Polly too was from' – he flipped open her file – 'Saltash, so Cornish too.'

'Do you think that is significant?' Miss Treen asked.

Arthur shrugged. 'I'm not certain at this point. However, it's worth noting.'

Miss Treen stood. 'I'll go and telephone the office before everyone finishes for the day, and see what I can learn about Rose Hall and her connection with Maura Roberts.'

She left Arthur to finish his tea while she made her call from his study. He had finished his drink and returned his cup to the tray when Benson entered to clear away the tea things.

'Thank you, Benson. I wondered if you might ask Mrs Mullins to step in for a moment if she has time,' Arthur said as the manservant collected the tray.

'Sir?' Benson's gaze met his.

'I'm curious about the male visitor who stayed at the house at Christmas. I know we have spoken to her already, but I should like to check some things,' Arthur answered Benson's unspoken query.

'Of course, very good, sir.' Benson nodded and headed out of the room, passing Miss Treen in the doorway.

'Rose Hall is also missing, believed dead. Her house was one of those hit when Maura Roberts's house was bombed. She hasn't been in to work, and no one has seen or heard from her. The site hasn't been cleared as a further unexploded bomb is sitting in a crater nearby.' She retook her seat opposite Arthur.

He could see that the news had affected even Miss Treen's usual impermeable shell.

'Oh dear, it seems nothing further can be discovered there then. At least not until there is confirmation of her death.' Arthur suppressed a shiver at the news that yet another young woman had seemingly perished in such a horrible fashion. 'I have asked Mrs Mullins, my housekeeper, to join us. She may know more about this Richard Trent who stayed here at Christmas now she has had time to think about the matter.'

Before Miss Treen could reply there was a tap at the door.

'Mr Benson said as you wished to see me, sir?' Mrs Mullins peered into the room.

'Yes, Mrs Mullins, please come in. This is Miss Treen, a colleague from London. She will be staying for a day or so, as you know.' Arthur waved a hand in Miss Treen's direction.

'Pleased to meet you, miss.' Mrs Mullins had clearly come straight from the kitchen. Her dark floral-printed dress was swathed in a white wrap-around apron that covered most of her clothes, protecting them from grease and dirt as she cooked. Her grey curls were tidily arranged, and her rosy-cheeked face bore a wary expression.

'Mrs Mullins, I realise that it has been most upsetting lately with the death of Miss Trevellian. I know Benson and I asked before, but I wondered if you could recall anything else about the man who visited the house over Christmas. I believe he had said he was a cousin of Miss Trevellian's?' Arthur asked.

'That's right, sir. A Mr Richard Trent he said his name was and he were on a few days' leave. Miss Anna didn't seem too happy to see him when he arrived. Miss Kate, though, she were different.' Mrs Mullins screwed up her face in concentration as she tried to recollect the events of a few weeks ago.

'His arrival was unexpected?' Miss Treen asked.

'I don't know, miss. By Miss Anna, I should say, as she had no inkling. Miss Kate, though, I don't know if she were quite as surprised as she made out to be.' Mrs Mullins's tone was thoughtful.

'What makes you think that?' Arthur asked.

'I don't know. Miss Anna, she were a bit put out by him coming and I think as she and Miss Kate had a few words over it. I heard them late on Christmas afternoon. Miss Anna said something like, "Why is he here and how did he find you?" and

Miss Kate says, "It doesn't matter, he'll be gone soon."' Mrs Mullins looked at Arthur. 'Miss Anna were cross about it though, I heard her muttering to herself in foreign.'

'That is a good question, whoever this Mr Trent is, how did he find them?' Miss Treen looked at Arthur. He could see the concern in her sharp eyes.

'Could you describe Mr Trent for us, Mrs Mullins? I appreciate that the chief inspector will no doubt have asked you to do this already, but it would help Miss Treen and myself enormously to picture this man,' Arthur asked.

'Well, he were tall, about six foot, light-brown hair and a bit of a charming way to him. You know, made little jokes and would try and flatter the young ladies. His clothes were good, and he dressed nice. Brylcreemed his hair like they do in the films.' Mrs Mullins frowned as she tried to recall all the details of the Christmas visitor.

'Diana Fenwick thought he had cheap shoes,' Arthur remarked mildly.

'Oh, he weren't a gentleman, I'm certain of that, but he weren't badly off neither,' Mrs Mullins explained.

'Miss Fenwick thought Miss Trevellian was uncomfortable in his company when she saw them in church at Christmas,' Arthur continued.

'Miss Anna had tried to persuade Miss Kate as they should stay here and not attend the service, but Mr Trent were keen to go. Miss Anna went to the other church, her being a Catholic and all.' Mrs Mullins looked slightly disapproving of this.

'And after Mr Trent had departed, before Miss Trevellian and Miss Perez left the house, how were things between them then?' Arthur asked.

Mrs Mullins paused for thought at this unexpected question. 'Miss Anna were, well, worried. She kept asking Miss Kate if she knew what she was about. They obviously didn't want me to hear anything. Kept dropping their voices if I were in the room. Miss Anna mentioned telephoning London, but Miss Kate told her no. She said it weren't safe.'

Miss Treen availed herself of another cigarette. Arthur could see that the information Mrs Mullins had provided had deeply troubled his colleague.

'There is something else, sir.' Worry lines creased Mrs Mullins's brow and she was twisting the hem of her apron between her fingers.

'Yes?' Arthur asked mildly. He knew Mrs Mullins well. Since the discovery of Polly's body at the end of the garden, the older woman would have fretted over every interaction she had had with the manor's tenants.

'Mr Trent, well, he always seemed quite cheery and a bit, well, cocky when anyone was about, but, well, I think he were scared of something.' Mrs Mullins looked relieved to have told Arthur what was on her mind.

'What makes you think he was afraid?' Miss Treen leaned forward in her chair, her cigarette dangling unheeded between her fingers. Arthur could only hope the ash didn't fall and damage the Turkish rug.

Mrs Mullins licked her lips as if her mouth was dry. 'It were how he kept looking about him. Jumpy as a cat he was. A door would bang, or a bird would shoot out of the hedge unexpected like and he was like as if he was about to be shot at. I was surprised as he wanted to go to church at Christmas, but he persuaded Miss Kate as they should go.'

Much to Arthur's relief, Miss Treen recollected her cigarette and stubbed it out in the ashtray in the nick of time.

'Thank you, Mrs Mullins, that has been quite insightful.' Arthur's mind raced over the information his cook had provided.

Mrs Mullins's plump cheeks creased in a smile. 'Will that

be all, sir, only I don't want my pastry to burn.' She looked towards the door as if eager to return to her kitchen.

'One last thing.' Arthur was suddenly struck with a flash of inspiration. He didn't care to call it a hunch, preferring his ideas to have a basis in practicality. A mathematical process of eliminating random factors or the proving of a theory.

He collected up the folders Miss Treen had provided and took out the photographs of each of the male agents. 'Do you recognise any of these men?'

Miss Treen stared at him as if he had lost his mind.

Mrs Mullins leafed through the top two before her hand stilled. 'That's him, sir, that's Mr Trent.' She passed the photograph back to Arthur.

'You are quite certain, Mrs Mullins?' he asked.

'Oh yes, sir. That's him.' Her tone was definite.

'Thank you.' Arthur dismissed the cook.

'Begging your pardon, sir, miss, but the cat, is he all right to be let out in the garden? Only he's yowling his head off. I can butter his paws to stop him straying.' Mrs Mullins paused on her way out and looked at Miss Treen.

'Yes, that's fine, Mrs Mullins. Marmaduke is quite a character. Just place a dish outside with some of his pilchards and he won't go far.' She smiled and waited for the cook to close the door behind her.

'Very good, miss.' Mrs Mullins departed.

Jane burst impatiently out of her chair to circle round behind Arthur. She peered over his shoulder to see which picture Mrs Mullins had selected as the mysterious Mr Trent.

'Georgie Porgie.' She retook her seat, frowning as she did so. 'So, Polly knew Georgie. He must have been her link man during Operation Exodus. You remember that each agent was connected to one other agent in the field.'

'Perhaps, or maybe they had a more personal connection.'

Arthur concentrated on the photograph, committing the image to memory. 'So where is this Georgie.' He paused to look at the agent's real name in the slim file. 'George, also known as Richard Trent, now?'

CHAPTER EIGHT

Jane drummed her fingers restlessly on the arms of her chair. 'The last information I had was that he was en route to the Low Countries. Beyond that I don't know. The mission he was moved to has a higher security clearance. I was lucky to be able to get hold of his file, and I'm sure you can see the contents have been redacted. As indeed have some of the others.'

She was most unhappy about this unexpected turn of events. How had George managed to find Polly and why had he come to visit her? The cook had said he had seemed afraid of something. If Whitehall had discovered he was at Half Moon Manor he would have had cause to be afraid. He was supposedly hundreds of miles away, behind enemy lines. Had he come before he went abroad?

Was he Polly's murderer? Or had he come to warn her of something or someone?

'Can we find out? At the very least we need to know why he was here,' Arthur said.

Jane blew out an exasperated sigh. 'I can try, but you know yourself that it may not be so easy, and we may be waiting quite a while for any information.' Arthur had no idea how difficult it could be at times to extract information from the different departments. Especially when she was trusting tasks to Stephen.

She left the room and placed yet another telephone call to Whitehall before returning to her seat.

It had sounded from what Mrs Mullins had overheard that Anna had not been party to whatever arrangements Polly and George had made. Not that she could ask Anna anyway since the girl was also now behind enemy lines and unreachable. But why had Anna not said anything before leaving? Or had she spoken to Maura? It was terribly unsatisfactory.

She glanced at Arthur who appeared to have drifted off into some kind of trance. Sometimes she wondered how anyone as intelligent as Arthur could appear to be so useless.

'I've asked for more information, so where should we go from here?' Jane asked, startling Arthur from his reverie.

'Well, I expect you'll need to return to the office in London.' There was a hopeful note in his voice which wasn't lost on her.

'Possibly, but I doubt it, not yet at least. I shall telephone the brigadier again early tomorrow and see if he managed to find out where George might be and what kind of operation he is attached to.' Jane knew the brigadier was always at his desk early so she could speak to him before the offices became busy. Stephen had sounded quite sulky when she had informed him that she had another task for him.

If Polly had been concerned about Anna contacting White-hall, she could have thought that someone there was the traitor. For a moment Jane considered Stephen, before dismissing the idea. He might be irritating but she had no reason to question his loyalty. At least not yet.

'I think too, that tomorrow we should call on those people you mentioned, who were they? The vicar and his sister, the Fenwicks? You can introduce me.' She looked at Arthur.

'If you think they may have more information to give?'

Arthur's mild response sat uneasily with the slightly sour expression on his face. It was obvious that he would rather she returned to London and looked at things from that end.

Jane, herself, would have infinitely preferred that too. However, she was nothing if not thorough and it was important that she gathered all the intelligence she could while trespassing on Arthur's begrudging hospitality. Plus, the brigadier had been emphatic about them working together, using both their skills to resolve this case. Arthur would simply have to put up with it.

After gathering the files together, she left Arthur to his thoughts while she went upstairs to dress for dinner. It was fortunate that she had prudently packed a selection of clothes in the small case she had brought with her. She also checked on Marmaduke who appeared to have claimed a nice, cosy spot in the kitchen.

After a brief lie down on a rather lumpy bed and a splash of cold water to revive her, Jane changed and was back downstairs a couple of hours later. She made her way to the sitting room where Arthur was sitting in much the same place as she had left him. Except that he had now donned an evening jacket and had apparently combed his hair.

It was a relief that at least some standards were being maintained despite the war, she thought as she accepted a glass of sherry. The wind outside the house seemed to have picked up and she could hear it roaring about the twisted red-brick chimneys. With the blackout firmly in place and the curtains shut up tight, the atmosphere inside the house was oddly intimate.

'What exactly do you hope to discover from the Fenwicks tomorrow?' Arthur asked her.

'I'm not sure. I'd like to know if they detected anything between George, Anna and Polly. As you know, the smallest things can reveal the most sometimes. I may also go and speak to the priest at the other church. If Anna attended regularly, she may have confided in him,' Jane said.

Arthur gave her a smug look. 'I wouldn't hold out much hope of getting anything from the priest. You know they are bound to an oath of confidentiality?'

'Obviously, the confessional falls into that category, but I was thinking more of her general demeanour and anything she may have said to him in passing. If she spoke about Trent arriving, for instance.' Jane took a sip from her glass and grimaced. So much for standards. Really, Arthur could do with acquiring a better-quality drink. This one reminded her of one her late father had brewed many years ago using pea pods.

'Dinner is served, sir, madam.' Benson had arrived silently in the room while they had been talking.

She followed Arthur into the cooler air of the hall and into the dining room. Two places had been set at one end of the large oval table. Benson pulled out a chair for her and Jane took her place opposite Arthur.

A dish of parsnip soup was set before her, and she sniffed it appreciatively. At least it seemed that she would receive acceptable food while staying at Half Moon Manor. Jane led the conversation over dinner, keeping firmly off the subject of their case.

Instead, she focused on the changes made in London due to the war with the theatres and restaurants. She talked of music and films and radio plays in an effort to make dining together a more pleasurable experience. However, Arthur was not the most scintillating of companions and offered her little in return. It seemed he only cared for classical music and crosswords.

Dinner over, she was glad to return to the sitting room for coffee and a much-needed cigarette. Arthur did his usual business of looking disapproving, whilst pointedly placing the chrome ashtray next to her.

Jane lit her cigarette and sighed contentedly once the first burst of nicotine reached her.

'Do you think your enquiries in the neighbourhood will take very long?' Arthur asked.

Jane knew he definitely wanted her, and Marmaduke, gone. 'Hopefully, I shall be able to return to London soon. I don't think I can be spared for many days.' She blew out a thin stream of smoke.

Arthur's expression brightened a little at this.

Jane telephoned the brigadier first thing the following day.

'Who is it you say? Jane, my dear, any news?' The brigadier bellowed in her ear, and she held the receiver a little further away.

She gave a crisp and concise report of everything she had discovered so far and outlined her plans for the day.

'Hmm, I see, and you say this George chappie may either be in danger or might be the culprit, eh?' the brigadier said.

'Yes, sir. It's imperative that we discover his present location. His file indicated he was being sent to the Low Countries. I asked Stephen to make enquiries.' Jane knew that the files were not always accurate since agents could have assignments switched if circumstances changed.

'Very well, my dear, leave it with me. I take it you are to stay at Half Moon Manor for a while longer? I presume there are people there you wish to speak to?'

'Yes, sir. I need to talk to these other people and then I shall probably return to the office. Unless I find anything else that might keep me here for longer,' Jane confirmed.

'Good show. Keep me informed and do be careful,' the brigadier said. 'And if I hear anything more about either Maura or Rose, then I shall let you know.'

'Thank you, sir.' Jane replaced the receiver on the handset.

She leaned back in Arthur's green, leather desk chair and lit a cigarette while she looked around his office. The shelves of the tall, oak bookcase were filled with obscure and ancient-looking tomes, mostly on science, astronomy and mathematics.

A large globe of the world rested on a stand in the corner and a portrait of a man she assumed must be Arthur's uncle hung above the small Portland stone fireplace. The top of the desk was neat and tidy with a clean blotter, brass pen tray and a green, shaded electric lamp. The ashtray was annoyingly absent, so Jane jumped up from her seat and headed into the sitting room to search for one.

Benson was present in the room tidying the already neat pile of newspapers beside Arthur's chair.

'Oh, Benson, I was looking for the ashtray.' She glanced around the room.

'Certainly, miss.' The manservant produced the one she had been using the previous evening. Now empty and sparkling clean. Jane managed to deposit the ash from the end of her cigarette just before it fell.

'What time is breakfast?' she asked.

'In about ten minutes, miss. Mr Cilento will be downstairs to join you shortly.' Benson placed the early morning paper, neatly folded, beside Arthur's chair on top of the ones from the previous day.

'Thank you.' Jane seated herself on the sofa where she had a view of the damp and windblown front garden.

Benson departed, no doubt to prepare the dining room for breakfast. As soon as he had gone, Jane picked up the morning newspaper and shook it open. She was keen to see if there was any mention of the body in the water.

There was nothing on the first two pages. It wasn't until she reached the third that she discovered a small paragraph near the bottom corner. To her relief it merely gave brief details of the discovery of a woman's body that was yet to be identified. No doubt tomorrow's edition would see the story of the murder moved onto the front page.

She had just closed the newspaper and was about to refold it when Arthur opened the sitting room door. He was dressed in his usual slightly rumpled grey trousers and tweed jacket. His hair already fighting whatever pomade he had used to try and stick his curls tidily to his head.

'Benson said you were in here. Breakfast is ready.' He caught sight of the previously pristine newspaper now slightly creased and untidy in her hands.

'Thank you.' She dropped the paper back down beside his chair and caught him pursing his lips. 'I was checking to see if your murder victim was in there,' she said.

'Polly Flinders is not *my* victim. I didn't kill her. She merely had the misfortune to be sent here by you and was then dispatched by a person or persons unknown,' Arthur remarked somewhat tersely as he led the way to the dining room.

Two places had been set with a small chrome-plated teapot beside one setting and a matching tall coffee pot beside the other place setting. A large chrome toast rack was in the centre, beside a very small dish of butter and a pot of home-made strawberry jam. A boiled egg in a white ceramic eggcup stood in the middle of a plate on each mat.

Jane's spirits had lifted at the sight of the coffee pot. A boiled egg and toast in her view was a most admirable breakfast. She had noticed the chicken run the previous day when she had gone down to look at the site of the murder. It had been placed beside the Anderson shelter in what must have been a rather nice garden before the war.

Arthur waited until she was seated before taking his place opposite her. He shook out a white linen napkin and placed it across his lap.

Jane poured herself a cup of coffee and sniffed appreciatively. 'I have spoken to the brigadier this morning. He will try to discover George's location. He will also inform us if he discovers more about Maura or Rose.'

Arthur nodded as he removed the top of his hard-boiled egg with mathematical precision. 'I think if we go to the Fenwicks' house after we finish breakfast, we should find Andrew at home. His sister, I believe, is engaged in war work in Exeter so may be absent.'

Jane assumed this information had probably been acquired from Mrs Mullins. 'It would be good to speak to the sister as well if we could.' She opted to do without butter on her toast and hoped her egg yolk was still runny.

Arthur was now engaged in cutting his toast into small triangles of identical size, before applying minute scrapings of butter to each piece. Jane refrained from commenting as she smashed the top of her egg with her spoon, pleased to discover her egg was nice and soft.

'I suppose we could also call on Major Hawes. He was a friend of my uncle's and may well have seen Polly at church,' Arthur suggested, wincing as Jane plunged a slice of toast into her egg to dab at the rich, yellow yolk.

'Excellent,' Jane replied approvingly, before biting into her breakfast. The egg was really wonderful. At least the food provided some compensation for her present companion.

She finished her toast and picked up her coffee cup. Arthur was still arranging his plate to his satisfaction. Truly, he was a peculiar creature.

'It will be time for lunch before you've eaten any of that. I'm sure it must be stone cold by now with all your faffing about.'

Arthur looked up from his plate. 'I assure you, I shall be ready to call on my neighbours in good time. Food should be savoured. It is a feast for the eyes as well as the stomach.' He gave a disapproving look at the remnants of shell scattered on her plate and the dribble of yolk drying on the side of the eggcup.

Jane resisted the temptation to roll her eyes and topped up her cup with the last of the coffee from the pot. 'We shall need an explanation for my presence.'

Arthur nibbled delicately on the edge of one of his tiny toast triangles. 'The news will have gone around the village I expect about the car bringing you here. I suggest we say that you are a cousin of Miss Trevellian's. Although I will leave it to you to explain the presence of your cat.'

'Very well,' Jane agreed.

* * *

Arthur could see that Miss Treen was champing at the bit to get going by the time he had finished his breakfast and donned his outdoor things. He refused to allow her impatience to hurry him through his morning routine. It had been vexing enough that she had destroyed his newspaper before he'd even had a chance to peruse the front page.

It wasn't far to the vicarage, but he still begrudged having to wrap his woollen scarf over his nose and mouth to trudge along the cold and muddy lane.

The vicarage was a handsome rendered house opposite the stone square-towered church. Built in the Georgian style, it had stone doric columns on either side of the black painted front door. There was a very short frontage to the road which still contained the previous incumbent's prize-winning rose bushes, now bare of leaves and hunkered down close to the red-brown soil.

The back garden had been given over to fruit and vegetables, which had included sacrificing what had once been a rather fine croquet lawn to the planting of potatoes and winter cabbage. He pressed the unpolished brass doorbell and waited beside Miss Treen on the front step.

'Oh, Mr Cilento, what a surprise. Do come on in,' Diana

greeted him as she opened the door. 'You just caught me, I'm off to woman the tea room at Central Station in Exeter in a bit. My contribution to the war work, feeding the troops as they pass through on their way to camp.' She opened the door wider to allow Arthur and Jane to enter the house. He could see she was dressed in her WVS uniform.

'Jane Treen, I'm a relative of the lady found in the river.' Miss Treen offered her hand to Diana in between briskly divesting herself of her outdoor hat, coat and gloves.

'Oh, I'm so sorry. I take it that we know who she is then now? There seemed to be some confusion when we called at the manor,' Diana asked, shaking Jane's hand.

'I'm afraid we do. Is your brother at home?' Arthur asked as he passed Diana his hat. She took their things and hung them on a fumed oak hallstand near the front door.

'Yes, come through to the drawing room and I'll go and haul him out of his study,' Diana said cheerfully. 'He won't want to miss this, I'm sure.'

Diana left them to wait in the large shabbily furnished drawing room while she fetched her brother. The fire in the hearth was low and the room looked neglected and untidy. Crumpled newspapers lay abandoned on the end of the sofa and a fine layer of dust coated the side tables.

Jane sat herself down primly on the edge of the chintz-covered armchair closest to the fire and a glass ashtray. Arthur took the clear end of the sofa. He would have preferred to be nearer to the fire, but he suspected that Jane would start smoking as soon as their hosts returned.

Diana bustled back into the room, her brother following behind her. Miss Treen introduced herself once more and the vicar and his sister took a seat, Andrew on the chair opposite Jane, and Diana moved the pile of old newspapers to sit beside Arthur.

'My condolences, Miss Treen, on your loss. Diana said you were related to the mystery lady,' the vicar said.

'This must all have been the most dreadful shock to you. We knew her as Miss Trevellian you see, we have no idea of her real name.' Diana's large hazel eyes were bright with curiosity.

'My cousin was engaged on war work and had been placed at Mr Cilento's house with a companion while she recuperated. She had been unwell. The family had no idea where she was until this happened.'

Arthur could only marvel silently at Miss Treen's ability to blend the truth into fiction without giving anything away that was not already known.

'Golly, so you didn't know that she wasn't using her real name?' Diana said.

'Polly's work was top secret. I only discovered what had happened to her when her employers contacted me,' Jane said. 'Mr Cilento was kind enough to suggest I stay for a couple of days at Half Moon Manor. I wanted to speak to anyone who saw her while she was here. My mind won't let me settle unless I know what happened to her during her time here.'

'Of course, that's quite understandable,' Reverend Fenwick agreed. 'I'm not sure how much assistance Diana and I can give, however, as we only saw your cousin and her companion on a few occasions.'

'I do understand. I have spoken to the chief inspector already, and he was very kind,' Miss Treen said. 'He said that my cousin had a visitor over Christmas?'

'That's right, a gentleman called Richard Trent, I don't know if you know that name?' Reverend Fenwick asked. 'We understood he was also a cousin.'

'I'm afraid I don't. He certainly wasn't related to me or Polly. Was Polly pleased to see him, do you know?' Jane asked.

'I think so. Surprised, but not overly unhappy. Miss Perez,

her companion, appeared a little less pleased I thought,' Diana said.

'Forgive me for asking, but do you think this Mr Trent may have been a boyfriend? Perhaps this Miss Perez felt she was playing gooseberry.' Jane looked at the Fenwicks.

Diana seemed to give the question careful consideration. 'No, they didn't seem to be on those kinds of terms. It was more, well, almost brotherly affection I suppose. He was a very good-looking man though.' A faint hint of colour crept into Diana's cheeks at this observation.

'It seems unlikely then that he was the person who killed her. I mean, if they seemed on good terms. If he was her boyfriend or something, I must try to let him know what has happened to her.' Miss Treen fumbled in her handbag for her cigarettes and a lighter.

Diana hastened to push the glass ashtray in her direction. 'Well, they certainly appeared to be friendly. As I said, I don't think your cousin's companion was so pleased to see him. It was just a feeling I had about the way she looked at him a couple of times.'

'But you think Polly was expecting him?' Miss Treen asked.

'Yes, I rather think she was.' Reverend Fenwick looked thoughtful. 'I got the impression he was a pilot or something. I don't know if that will help you to track him down.'

Diana jumped to her feet uttering a squeak of alarm as she caught sight of the time on the wooden clock on the mantelpiece. 'Golly, I must get off or I shall never get to the station in time for my train. Do forgive me.' She kissed her brother on the cheek and hurried out of the door.

'Diana, take your umbrella, more rain is forecast,' the vicar called after her.

A few seconds later they heard the front door slam, followed by the crunch of gravel under the tyres of Diana's bicycle as she pedalled past the window.

'She won't be back until later tonight. I do worry about her being out in the blackout, still, the work she does is so important for morale. She tried to join the women's land army, but she has a heart murmur and the doctors said she wouldn't be strong enough,' Reverend Fenwick explained.

Arthur felt inside the breast pocket of his tweed jacket and produced the photograph of George, the agent Mrs Mullins had recognised. 'We found this in one of the upstairs rooms.' He was quite pleased with his subterfuge. It would be good to get George's identity confirmed by a second witness.

'That's the chap who was here at Christmas. That Richard Trent fellow, I'm sure he said he was on leave from the air force.' Andrew Fenwick's eyebrows rose as he studied the picture. 'He must have been important to your cousin if she had his picture.' He looked at Miss Treen.

'Yes, that was my thought too,' Jane said.

It seemed there was little more information to be gained from the vicar and it was clear the offer of a cup of tea was not forthcoming. Jane caught Arthur's gaze, and he could tell she was of the same mind.

'Thank you, Reverend, you've been most kind. I don't suppose you know the name of the priest at the Catholic church, do you? The one Miss Perez attended while she was here?' Miss Treen asked as she gathered her patent leather handbag ready to leave.

'Yes, indeed. Father Dermott, a very pleasant fellow. We have supper together sometimes. Shall I give you his telephone number?' Reverend Fenwick disappeared off to his study and returned with a slip of paper. 'Here's the address and telephone number for you. He lives in the village nearer the station.' He passed the paper to Miss Treen who tucked it away inside her bag.

'Thank you. I'm not sure if he ever met Polly, but I shall

simply feel better knowing that I've spoken to everyone who may have had some contact with her.'

'Yes indeed, you must have been very close?' the vicar said as he showed them to the hall where they put on their outdoor things ready to venture back out into the cold.

'We were. Polly used to tell me everything. I had a Christmas card from her and thought perhaps I might see her in the new year, that's why this is such a terrible shock.' Miss Treen tugged on her brown leather gloves.

'Well, I wish you well, and, of course, if you decide the funeral is to be here then my services are at your disposal.' The vicar shook hands with Miss Treen before doing the same with Arthur.

Arthur had not considered the funeral. He fell into step beside Miss Treen as they made their way back into the lane.

'Polly had no family left according to her file. I suppose it probably would be better to have her laid to rest here,' Miss Treen said.

Arthur nodded. It seemed a sad end for poor Polly Flinders.

CHAPTER NINE

Arthur had hoped that Miss Treen might suggest returning to Half Moon Manor. Instead, she asked for directions to the home of Major Hawes.

'We may as well kill two birds with one stone as we are already out and about,' she said as she quickened her pace.

Arthur could have quite cheerfully killed her. His chest was sore, and his feet were numb with cold. He also thought that Mrs Mullins would not be pleased with the mud splashes on the hem of his second-best pair of trousers.

Major Hawes lived further along the lane just past the centre of the village in a large, white-painted Devon longhouse with a thatched roof. As they neared the thatched porch roof that was supported by two venerable tree trunks, small icy bullets of hail began to ping down from the leaden sky.

Arthur grasped the brass fox's head door knocker in the centre of the front door and gave it a sharp rattle.

'Why, Mr Cilento, whatever brings you out in this weather?' A pleasant-faced young maid had answered the knock and ushered them into the small, red-tiled hallway. Somewhere in the depths of the house Arthur heard the major's dog bark.

'Is the major at home?' he asked the girl as he and Miss Treen attempted not to drip slush onto the tiles.

'Oh yes, sir. He's in the sitting room with Miss Darnley, working on his memoirs. You can go on through, sir. I expect he'll be glad to stop. He generally has a cup of tea about now,' the maid assured them.

They handed their coats to the girl and walked through the door at the end of the hallway. A welcome blast of heat met them as they opened the sitting room door. A fire blazed in the inglenook brick fireplace, the rosy glow reflecting off the polished horse brasses that decorated the black wooden beams of the low ceiling.

'Arthur! What the devil brings you out on such a foul day?' Major Hawes was seated in his favourite leather armchair beside the fire. His black Labrador, Nero, at his feet and his cherrywood pipe in his hand. He jumped up as Arthur entered the room, his hand extended in welcome.

'And with a pretty young filly with you, eh?' Major Hawes nudged him in the ribs and winked.

Arthur half expected Miss Treen to bridle at the major's greeting. Instead, he was surprised to see a faint blush appear on her cheeks as she shook hands and accepted an invitation to sit on the sofa.

'Jane Treen, it's a pleasure to meet you, sir.'

The major beamed at her before turning to a woman seated at a desk on the far side of the long narrow room. 'Georgette, be a good girl and ask Sarah to bring us a tray of tea. Bit early for something stronger, eh?' Major Hawes resumed his seat beside the fire.

A rather stern-faced young woman in a plain grey frock set aside her work and rose from her seat to go and pass on the request.

'We're frightfully sorry to disturb you while you're working.' Miss Treen sat primly on the edge of the leather chesterfield sofa and smoothed the tweed material of her skirt across her knees.

'What, heavens above, my dear, no need to apologise. I've always time for a good-looking gal.'

Arthur watched in bemusement as Miss Treen's blush deepened. He hadn't thought of her as being pretty until the major had mentioned it. In fact, he rarely considered her looks at all. She was simply Miss Treen. Now, though, he realised that she did have a nice figure, her shiny brown hair suited her slim features, and he supposed she could be considered an attractive woman.

'Sarah will bring a tray through in a few minutes.' Georgette returned to the sitting room and took her place back at the desk by the leaded pane window.

'Miss Darnley works at the library and very kindly gives me a few hours on her day off to assist me with my memoirs. She also runs various errands for me.' The major beamed at Georgette.

'It's nice to meet you.' Jane inclined her head in greeting.

'Pleasure, I'm sure,' the girl said.

Arthur had met Miss Darnley on a few occasions before. She always made him feel slightly uncomfortable. He wasn't sure quite why that was. She was always perfectly pleasant.

'Arthur and I know each other, of course.' She smiled at him. 'It's nice to meet a friend of Arthur's.' She gave Jane a curious look.

'Yes, well I take it you have both probably heard about the poor woman we found dead in the river at the end of my garden?' Arthur began.

'Oh yes, jolly bad show, eh? Heard it was a murder. Sarah said it was that woman who was staying at your house while you were in Scotland. A Miss Trevellian?' The major waved his pipe in the air and spilled a fragment of ash onto the hearth rug, just missing his dog. 'I met the lady a few times at church, along with her friend, the Spanish girl.'

'Polly was Jane's cousin,' Arthur interjected quickly.

The major gave Miss Treen a shrewd glance. 'Polly, eh? I thought her name was Kate?'

'She was working undercover for the War Office,' Miss Treen said. 'Her real name was Polly. Forgive me, this has all been such a dreadful shock.'

Georgette Darnley had swivelled on her seat and was perched side on now to face them. 'Gosh, how exciting. Well, that is, I mean, I'm very sorry for your loss, of course. Were you and your cousin close?' Miss Darnley appeared to suddenly recall that Jane was related to the deceased woman. 'Her other cousin was here at Christmas.'

'Yes, good-looking fella, pilot or something. Trent, that's it, Richard Trent; never forget a name. Pleasant fella.' Major Hawes looked pleased with himself.

Sarah rattled her way into the room pushing a small wooden trolley laden with crockery and a plate of biscuits. The smell of the biscuits seemed to rouse Nero the dog from his slumbers, and he sat up and yawned.

'Did you speak to my cousin or her companion at all during their stay at Half Moon Manor?' Miss Treen asked as Miss Darnley served them all with a cup of tea.

'Invited them all round for drinks a few times. It being Christmas and all.' Major Hawes helped himself to a biscuit. 'They always declined until Trent arrived.'

'Oh?' Arthur stirred his tea and wondered if it would be rude to add a cube of sugar to his cup. Rationing had turned the usual social niceties into a minefield.

'Then they accepted the invitation?' Miss Treen asked, waving away the milk jug.

'Yes, they came around one evening just for an hour, Kate, or rather Polly, and the chap, Richard. Christmas drink and a few nibbles.' Major Hawes brushed a couple of biscuit crumbs from his regimental tie and Nero immediately picked them up from the floor with his tongue.

'Anna wasn't with them?' Miss Treen asked.

'No, she had gone to something or other at her church.' Major Hawes looked thoughtful. 'Got the impression that she didn't know they had come out. They seemed keen to get home to the manor before her.'

Arthur glanced at Miss Treen. This was some new information.

'Did my cousin seem in good spirits?' she asked.

'Oh yes, she was quite bubbly. Said that she would be leaving in a few days as her lease was up and she was going home to Cornwall for a spell. Something about some work that had been done on her house. That was why she was here, it had affected her health. Trent said his leave was almost up and he was off the next day. Georgette, my dear, that was right, wasn't it?' Major Hawes turned to Miss Darnley.

It sounded as if Polly had kept to the script she had been given in her guise as Kate Trevellian.

'Yes, that's right. Obviously, Mr Trent couldn't say where he was based but I got the impression it was in the Cotswolds somewhere. Miss Trevellian said she was eager to get home. Something about her pets.' Georgette set down the teapot.

'Her pets?' Arthur asked.

'Yes, Mr Trent seemed to find it amusing. Something about, oh dear, what did she say?' Georgette's brow creased in concentration as she attempted to recall the conversation.

'She said, Winston would be missing her. I assumed it to be a dog or cat,' Major Hawes said.

'Yes, of course. Polly was very fond of her animals. She named them all after political figures.' Miss Treen bent her head to take a sip of her tea.

Arthur suspected it was to avoid Major Hawes's sharp eyes.

'I wonder what brought her back here?' Miss Darnley remarked in a thoughtful tone.

Miss Treen shrugged. 'That's part of the puzzle. We don't know if she had left something behind at the house or, perhaps, she had arranged to meet someone. It's all rather a mystery. It's partly why I wanted to talk to any friends she may have made here.'

'Of course.' Georgette blushed slightly as she helped herself to a biscuit.

'And your cousin, Richard? Does he have any idea? I assume he *is* your cousin?' Major Hawes asked, looking at Miss Treen.

'Unfortunately, I've not even been able to contact him to tell him of Polly's death. You know how things are at the moment. It's all very difficult.' Miss Treen neatly sidestepped the question.

'Operational stuff I expect. Bad show. Perhaps he might be able to help you when you do get to speak to him.' Major Hawes's tone was thoughtful.

Arthur suspected that he knew full well that Richard Trent was no more Miss Treen's cousin than Polly had been.

'I suppose we should get back to the manor,' Arthur suggested as he finished his tea. 'We called at the vicarage on the way here to see what they could tell us about Polly's stay.'

'Good idea, they attended the church regularly. The Spanish girl went to the Catholic one, of course,' Major Hawes said.

'I shall try and speak to the priest there before I go back to London. I feel that I should talk to everyone who may have known my cousin while she was here,' Miss Treen said again.

'Of course,' Major Hawes agreed. 'It's a terrible thing to have happened.'

'It makes one feel quite unsafe.' Georgette shivered. 'I'm surprised the vicar's sister still feels able to be out and about on that bicycle of hers. Diana keeps very late hours. I should feel quite unnerved at returning in the dark down these lanes.' She looked at Arthur as if expecting him to agree. 'I always try to get my errands done and get home before the blackout.'

'Nonsense, Georgette, Diana is a strapping lass and quite used to fending for herself. Although I agree the blackout does make things awkward,' Major Hawes declared briskly.

Miss Darnley's blush deepened at the slight rebuke. 'Of course, Diana is very independent.'

Miss Treen set down her cup and saucer. 'Thank you so much for the refreshments. It was most kind of you, Major.' She rose and extended her hand for her host to shake.

They said their goodbyes to Miss Darnley and collected their outdoor things from the maid before stepping back out into the drizzle.

Miss Treen appeared quiet and thoughtful as she set off at a cracking pace through the puddles back towards Half Moon Manor. Arthur lagged behind her, his chest burning as he attempted to keep up.

'I don't understand. What was Polly playing at?' she declared as she suddenly halted at the stone gateposts that marked the entrance to the driveway of the manor.

Arthur panted to a stop and attempted to catch his breath. 'In what way?' he gasped, wishing the wretched woman would just go inside so he could collapse into a nice, comfortable armchair.

'This business with Trent and agreeing to go for drinks at the major's house once Anna was safely out of the way.' She shook her head and marched up the gravel path to the large, oak front door.

She fidgeted impatiently on the stone front doorstep while Arthur fumbled in his coat pocket for his key. He had scarcely put the key in the lock when Benson opened the door, almost pulling him into the hall.

'Begging your pardon, sir. I thought I heard someone outside.' The manservant assisted Miss Treen and Arthur with their outdoor clothing.

Arthur was delighted to see that the fire had been banked up in the drawing room. He sat down gratefully in his favourite chair and waited for his breathing to settle. Miss Treen continued to pace up and down on the rug in front of the fire.

'What are we missing? There is something we're not seeing in this lot, isn't there?' she demanded.

Benson re-entered the room to place a glass of water at Arthur's elbow, before discreetly withdrawing once more.

'I agree.' Arthur was relieved to see his hand wasn't shaking when he picked up the glass for a reviving sip of his drink.

'Well? You're the ideas man.' She whirled around to face him.

'There are a few things that struck me from our visits today.' Arthur frowned as Miss Treen produced one of her inevitable cigarettes.

'Such as?' she demanded, as she struck a match.

'Did you think it odd that Polly and Trent only accepted the major's invitation behind Anna's back?' Arthur asked. He felt better now that he was sitting calmly in his own front room once more.

'You mean that they didn't trust Anna?' Miss Treen took a seat, her face thoughtful. 'That they had something else in mind beyond a simple social visit?'

'It would provide useful cover if Anna found out where they had really been, that is if we assume they had an ulterior motive. Either another secret meeting close by or perhaps they needed to hide something.' Arthur took another sip of water.

'They may have been trying to protect Anna from whatever was going on. What could they have been hiding? Or who could they have been meeting?' Miss Treen exhaled, thankfully blowing the smoke away from Arthur's chair.

'Polly returned here for a reason. It had to be either to recover something she had left here, or to meet someone,' Arthur said.

Miss Treen seated herself opposite him and stubbed her cigarette out in the ashtray Benson had left close by for her. 'What about that comment she made about Winston?'

'Do you think that was really about a pet? Or just her way of referring to the prime minister?' Arthur asked.

'It was a strange remark from Polly. She wasn't a facetious girl and from the major's description it sounded as if it was some kind of in-joke between her and Trent.' She leaned back in her chair. 'A hint that she had something that was important to the government? A gift? Some kind of knowledge?'

Arthur could see what she meant. It was a slim clue, but they really had very little else to go on so far.

'Anna has been parachuted abroad now so we have no chance of obtaining anything useful from her.' Miss Treen appeared to be thinking hard. 'Trent is also abroad, I believe, although the brigadier or Stephen has yet to confirm that theory.'

'Then we appear to be at something of an impasse. Perhaps you should return to London and see if any more information has turned up on Maura?' Arthur suggested. His spirits lifting slightly at the idea of his troublesome house guest and her blessed cat departing.

Miss Treen gave him a sharp glance. 'Yes, maybe you should return with me, Arthur. A change of air might do you good.'

Arthur was saved from a response to this outrageous suggestion by Benson announcing that lunch was ready.

CHAPTER TEN

Jane stirred the lumpy mashed potatoes on her plate with the tip of her fork and stifled a sigh. She knew that Arthur's cook was doing her best with the limited supply of food, but breakfast had been so good her expectations had been falsely raised. She supposed that if she stayed any longer, then she would need to contribute her own rations to those of the household.

She couldn't help feeling that they had missed something important about Polly's death. Something that was right under their noses. It really was extremely irritating. She placed her cutlery down on her plate and declined the dessert of stewed apples. With the shortage of sugar, she suspected they would be rather tart.

There was only the Catholic priest left for her to see. From what they had gleaned this morning, it appeared as if Anna had been kept in the dark about Polly and Richard Trent's plans. She thought it was unlikely that the priest would be able to tell her anything useful but at least she would have followed every trail.

Arthur announced his intention of taking a rest in the afternoon, so Jane was left to her own devices. The weather appeared to have brightened somewhat and the drizzle from the morning had dissipated.

She took the paper Andrew Fenwick had given her with Father Dermott's details and settled herself in Arthur's study to telephone the presbytery. A female voice answered the telephone and Jane assumed it was probably his housekeeper.

'Hullo, is it possible to speak to Father Dermott?' Jane asked.

'One moment, please.' There was a rustling from the other end of the line before a male voice with a soft Irish accent answered.

'This is Father Dermott. How can I be of assistance?'

Jane gave the priest her story about Polly being her cousin, and how she was trying to discover anything at all about her last days at Half Moon Manor.

'I see, Miss Treen, my deepest sympathies on the loss of your cousin. Her companion, Anna, did attend the church here during her stay. Perhaps you might care to call for tea this afternoon if you are free?' Father Dermott suggested.

'That would be very kind of you.' Jane thought the priest had sounded vaguely troubled when he had mentioned Anna's name.

There must be something he felt he had to say, or the conversation would have concluded on the telephone. Jane leaned back in Arthur's office chair and took out a cigarette. She was running rather low and disliked the idea of asking Benson to nip out to the local shop to get her some more. She suspected that Benson's view of her smoking habit concurred with that of Arthur.

Father Dermott had given her directions to his house, which he had assured her was a mere twenty-minute walk to the far end of the village on the opposite end to the Fenwicks' house and Half Moon Manor. Not that she objected to walking, but she could see why everyone else in the village appeared to have a bicycle. Still, she supposed she could call in the village shop for more cigarettes on her way. At least that was one thing that wasn't being rationed, even if sometimes the shops seemed to be low on supplies.

Jane placed another call to Whitehall only to have Stephen answer the telephone.

'I'm afraid the brigadier is unavailable; he's been called to a meeting with the top brass. Anything I can help you with?'

Jane could picture Stephen lounging back in his chair, smirking to himself with that stupid supercilious smile.

'No, I don't think so, unless you have any information for me on those requests I made. I'll call him again later.' She had no intention of telling Stephen anything.

'Nothing as yet, I'm afraid. Well do carry on enjoying your little holiday, while we all crack on here with the real work.'

Jane gritted her teeth knowing he wanted her to rise to the bait. It was typical of his misguided idea of banter. 'I rather think that you would struggle to identify real work, Stephen, but I'm sure your best will be adequate until I return.'

His low chuckle tickled her ear. 'Touché, Jane, dear heart, toodle-pip for now.' He ended the call.

Still feeling annoyed, Jane put on her thick woollen winter coat and warm hat before informing Benson that she intended to go and call on Father Dermott and would not be in for tea.

'Very good, miss. I shall inform Mrs Mullins.' Benson gave a slight bow and vanished back towards the kitchen.

Jane tugged on her leather gloves and tucked one of the umbrellas from the hallstand under her arm. It looked as if the rain from earlier had cleared but one could never tell. She called in at the village shop and purchased more cigarettes on her way to the presbytery.

Georgette Darnley passed her as she was walking, giving her a cheery wave as she pedalled along through the wet streets. By the time the small red-brick home of Father Dermott loomed in front of her, Jane was hot and tired from her exertions.

Unlike the faded grandeur of the Fenwicks' home, Father Dermott's abode was simpler and more modern. It was closer to the station and the marketplace, so the streets were busier. She tugged the black cast-iron bell pull and waited on the nicely scrubbed front doorstep to be admitted.

'Miss Treen?' A plump elderly woman dressed in faded black, wearing a crisply starched white apron, opened the door.

'Yes, Father Dermott is expecting me.' Jane looked about her with interest as the housekeeper let her into a small square hallway.

'Of course, miss.' The woman took her coat and umbrella and showed Jane into a comfortable lounge. A fire blazed brightly in the grate, piles of newspapers were stacked neatly on a side table and a large ginger cat was curled up on the broad windowsill.

Father Dermott stood to greet her as she entered. A small round man with sparse grey hair and shrewd blue eyes.

'Miss Treen, welcome. Do come and take a seat.' He shook her hand and directed her to the faded chenille-covered armchair opposite his own seat.

'Thank you for agreeing to see me, Father.' Jane was acutely aware of the priest's assessing gaze as she settled into her seat. 'I do appreciate it.'

'Not at all, Miss Treen. I'm very sorry to hear about the death of your cousin. That must have been a great shock.' Father Dermott leaned back in his chair.

'It was. The police believe that she was murdered, and I have so many questions about what she was doing back here that day and if she had come to meet someone or to collect something. I know that her friend, Anna, attended Mass at your church so I thought perhaps she may have said something to you. Something that might help me find out what happened.' Jane looked at the priest.

Father Dermott's expression seemed to indicate that he was turning something over in his mind. 'Your cousin was from Cornwall, I believe?'

The housekeeper clattered into the room with a small wooden trolley laden with tea things and a plate containing slender slices of some kind of plain cake. She left the trolley near to Father Dermott and returned to the kitchen.

'Yes, that's correct. Shall I be mother?' Jane asked, applying herself to the white china teapot.

'Thank you. And you yourself are from London?' Father Dermott asked.

'Yes, from Kent originally but I live in the city now. Do you take milk and sugar?' Jane poured the tea.

'No sugar, thank you, and a small spot of milk.' Father Dermott accepted the cup from her.

Jane poured herself a drink and resumed her seat, wondering what lay behind the priest's questions.

'This may sound like a very strange question, and I don't wish to be rude or embarrass you in any way, Miss Treen, but do you have any identification on you at all?' Father Dermott's question took her by surprise.

'Yes, of course.' Jane opened her handbag and produced her ration book and her library card. This was a strange turn of events.

Father Dermott inspected them carefully and handed them back to her with a satisfied nod. 'Thank you, Miss Treen. I'm sure you are wondering why I asked to see your papers?'

Jane surveyed him levelly. 'I am and I can only assume, Father, that Anna has said something to you that has made you wary about what you say about her and Kate's stay at Half Moon Manor.' She placed her documents back inside her bag.

Father Dermott picked up his tea and took a sip. 'Another

young lady called at the house only yesterday. It was shortly after we had learned of the murder. She too gave her name as Jane Treen.'

Jane blinked in astonishment. She had not been expecting this revelation at all. 'I see, and this other Jane Treen, what was she like?'

Father Dermott took another sip from his drink before continuing. 'Young, mid-to-late twenties with dark hair; a pretty girl. She said she had come from London and was asking about Anna.'

'That is deeply troubling, Father.' Jane's mind raced through the possibilities for who the imposter might have been. And why someone had been impersonating her.

'I just had a feeling that there was something not quite right. I had heard from my housekeeper that a young woman was staying at Half Moon Manor and initially I thought this other young lady might be you. However, when we were talking she didn't mention Mr Cilento. She said she had come on the train from Exeter that day. I understood from my housekeeper that you had arrived by car.' Father Dermott drained his cup and placed it back on the saucer.

'I wonder who she was and why she came straight here?' Jane said. This was very troubling.

'I presume she may have intended to ask in other places, but she must have gathered that you were already on site, so to speak. I asked her, you see, if she was staying long and if she had seen the police yet. Obviously, Pennycombe being a small village, one hears all of one's neighbours' activities. She was very vague in her replies and seemed eager to be off once I asked her a few things. I don't think she would have wished your paths to have crossed.' Father Dermott set down his crockery and helped himself to a thin slice of cake.

'How very peculiar.' Jane was confused. What had this imposter hoped to discover?

'So, Miss Treen, I accept that you are Miss Jane Treen. Anna spoke of you as being her employer. Forgive me, but who was Miss Kate Trevellian? I assume that she was not your cousin? And indeed, from what I've heard just lately her name was almost certainly not Kate?' Father Dermott licked a tiny crumb from the corner of his mouth with the tip of his tongue.

Jane fixed him with a glance. 'You realise, Father, that I cannot say very much, but no, Kate was in fact a woman called Polly, and she and Anna were staying here temporarily at the manor for their protection.'

'I understand, Miss Treen. I did not say very much at all to the other young lady. I expressed my sadness at the death of the woman discovered in the water, and that I believed Anna had returned to London.' Father Dermott finished his cake and placed his plate back down.

Jane nodded. 'Thank you. Did this other woman ask about anything in particular?'

'She wanted to know if Anna had entrusted anything to me for safe keeping,' Father Dermott said. 'She claimed that Anna had asked her to collect a package.'

'And did she?' Jane asked. Was this what Polly had returned for? Was she intending to collect something?

The priest rose from his seat and took a few steps across the room to a small oak bureau in the corner. He unlocked the lid and extracted a small parcel wrapped in brown paper and tied up with string.

'Anna left this with me. She said that if anything happened to her or Kate, or if you were to come, that I was to give it to you.' He passed the parcel to Jane. 'She impressed upon me that I was to tell no one that this was here.'

Jane could tell from the shape of the package that it seemed to be a book of some sort. She longed to open it but determined that would be better done back at Half Moon Manor.

'Thank you, Father.' She placed the package inside her

handbag. 'I appreciate that you cannot share anything that Anna may have said within the confessional, but is there anything you can tell me about Anna and Polly's time here?'

'Anna said very little really. She found her faith to be a source of great comfort and support. I had the impression that while she and the other young woman were friendly, they did not confide in one another. Anna did not say so, but I felt that on some level she distrusted her friend. That Polly was keeping something from her.' Father Dermott's brow crinkled as he spoke.

'Did she say anything about the man who visited at Christmas?' Jane asked.

'Anna was not expecting a visitor, but she thought that her friend had arranged it without her knowledge. She was upset and worried about it. I think she was relieved when he departed.'

A log on the fire slipped, releasing a cloud of fiery sparks.

'When did she ask you to look after this package?' Jane glanced at her handbag.

'Before the young man left. She was very worried, I felt, but she didn't say why. She said she would be glad to leave Half Moon Manor to return to London. The other young woman was to go to Cornwall I believe.' Father Dermott picked up a poker and stirred the fire, before adding another piece of wood from the basket beside the fireplace.

Cornwall again. Jane knew they had arranged the cover story that Kate was from Cornwall but was there a connection there that she was unaware of? Where had Polly been after leaving Half Moon Manor until her return?

'Did Anna say anything else to you?' Jane set her cup and saucer aside.

Father Dermott shook his head. 'I'm afraid not, Miss Treen. I am very sorry that the young lady was murdered, and I hope that Anna is safe wherever she may now be.'

'Thank you, Father, you have been most helpful.' Jane gathered her bag and said her farewells to the priest.

Jane's mind was busy all the way back to Half Moon Manor. Who had impersonated her and why? She was itching to get back to open the package to see what was inside.

Benson answered the front door on the first ring of the bell.

'Is Arthur up?' Jane asked as she divested herself of her hat and coat, thrusting them into the manservant's arms before making her way into the drawing room.

'In the sitting room, miss,' Benson replied as he hung her hat on the hallstand.

Arthur was seated in his usual place next to the fire, a large tome of some description open on his lap. He looked up as she entered the room and Jane thought she detected a flicker of irritation at being disturbed.

'We have a development!' Jane seated herself opposite him and held her hands out to the flames to warm herself up. The light was beginning to fade now, and the curtains would soon have to be drawn for the blackout.

Arthur inserted a leather bookmark to hold his page and reluctantly closed his book. 'You went to see Father Dermott this afternoon I gather?'

'While you were resting upstairs like a Victorian gentlewoman, I discovered some very curious facts. And, there is this.' She delved into her handbag and brought out Anna's parcel. 'Anna left this in Father Dermott's care.' She gave him a succinct report on everything she had gleaned from her visit to the presbytery.

'Very interesting. So some brave soul impersonated you?' The corners of Arthur's mouth twitched as if he found the idea amusing.

'Yes, the question is who and why? I know that is technically two questions before you start with your pedantry.' Jane held up a hand to cut him off before he could correct her.

'The most likely candidate must be Maura Roberts,' Arthur suggested. 'She knew of your connection with Operation Exodus and must have discovered you had placed Polly and Anna here.'

Jane nodded. 'That was my thought too. I don't see who else it could be. But why?'

'Perhaps if you open Anna's parcel, we may discover more.' Arthur looked at the unopened package on her lap.

CHAPTER ELEVEN

Arthur had to admit his curiosity was piqued by the information Miss Treen had uncovered. He passed her the small ivory-handled paperknife he kept on the table next to his chair. She slit the string holding the brown paper covering the package.

There was no writing on the paper, no address or name. She carefully folded back the paper to reveal the contents. As the shape had suggested, it was a book.

'What is it?' Arthur leaned forward to look at the slim volume.

Miss Treen frowned. 'A guidebook to Cornwall.' She opened the cover as if she expected to discover a note or message tucked inside. 'Nothing.'

Arthur reached over and plucked the book from her lap before she could stop him. There had to be a reason Anna had left the book with Father Dermott. He carefully leafed through the book, pausing when he discovered a corner of a page turned back near the centre of the volume.

'Well?' she asked, peering at his discovery as he opened the book at the dog-eared page.

'Trelisk House lies in a pleasant valley in the heart of the

Cornish countryside. While the house is now a private residence, visitors are welcome to view the outstanding gardens and to visit the ancient private chapel.' Arthur read directly from the page in the guidebook.

'The real Kate Trevellian's house?' She stared at him for a moment, before pulling out her cigarette case and lighting up another of her infernal cigarettes.

'It seems we keep being directed towards Cornwall,' Arthur said, trying to resist the urge to waft away the smoke that was inevitably drifting his way.

Benson entered the room and drew the curtains before switching on the table lamps.

'Benson, what do you know of Cornwall?' Arthur asked.

'A most charming place, sir. I believe, however, they suffer under the misapprehension that jam is applied to one's scones before the cream.' The manservant raised his brow.

'And Trelisk House, home of Miss Kate Trevellian?' Arthur continued.

'From my research on the matter at the library this afternoon, sir, I understand that there is a twelfth century chapel in the grounds which is open to visitors and a sub-tropical garden. There are several small guest houses in the village should one wish to take a holiday. How this has been affected by the war I cannot say,' Benson said.

Miss Treen fixed Arthur with an icy glare. Arthur suspected she would have said something about him and Benson being one step ahead of her, but the sound of the telephone ringing in the study interrupted them.

Benson vanished to answer the call only to reappear a second or two later.

'Chief Inspector Thorne for you, sir.'

Arthur followed the manservant out of the room.

'Chief Inspector, how may I help you?' Arthur sat down on his office chair and noticed with a frown that the items he kept on the top of his desk had been rearranged. A doodle of a cat now adorned his previously clean blotter. No doubt Miss Treen had been meddling whilst making her own telephone calls.

'Good afternoon, Mr Cilento. I thought I should update you and your guest on the progress of the investigation so far.' The chief inspector's voice sounded tinnily in his ear.

'Thank you, Chief Inspector, that's most kind of you. Miss Treen and I are both keen to see the matter resolved as speedily as possible.' Arthur was careful with his phrasing. One never knew who might be eavesdropping on a telephone call.

'The young woman found in the river came into the village via a train from Exeter. My enquiries there suggest she alighted at Exeter from the Penzance train,' the chief inspector said.

'I see, and was she travelling alone?' Arthur asked. So, Polly had gone to Cornwall after parting from Anna.

'It would seem so,' the chief inspector said. 'There is another matter pertaining to this enquiry that I would like your advice on, sir.'

'Oh.' Arthur wondered what this might be.

'Mr Bendigo Mullins, I believe he is your gardener and the son of your housekeeper?' The chief inspector's tone was hard to read.

'Yes, that's correct. He was ruled medically unfit to enlist. As you may know he is non-verbal.' Arthur wasn't sure where this conversation was leading.

'We have a witness who says that the woman found in the river was seen with Mr Mullins after she got off the train in the village that day.'

'I see. No doubt you wish to speak to Bendigo? He is quite capable of answering questions, although he writes his replies down,' Arthur said.

'I have some concerns about why he has not already come forward to say he saw the victim on the day of her murder.'

Arthur could see why the chief inspector might be suspicious. 'I suppose he may not have realised the relevance. He is a little slow to take in information sometimes, Chief Inspector. I would suggest that his mother accompanies you when you talk to him. He can be apt to panic if he feels pressured.'

Arthur had known Bendigo all of his life. The older man was a stolid individual who had been non-verbal from birth. He was a shy man and didn't mix easily with other people, preferring to spend his time outdoors, at one with his natural environment.

'Thank you, Mr Cilento. Could you ask Mrs Mullins if she and her son would be available to speak to me tomorrow morning?' Chief Inspector Thorne asked.

'Certainly, would you like to use my study?' Arthur offered. It would cause less disruption to the routine of the household if the interview were conducted at Half Moon Manor. He also knew that Miss Treen would be eager to discover what Bendigo might reveal.

'Thank you, that would be most helpful. You are, of course, welcome to sit in for the interview. It sounds as if having someone else familiar in the room may assist the questioning.'

Arthur thanked the chief inspector and ended the call before asking Benson to inform Mrs Mullins of the arrangements. When he returned to the drawing room, Miss Treen was peering at the page in the guidebook.

She had the book open and was holding it close to the table lamp to allow the light to shine through the thin page.

'Anything interesting?' Arthur asked as he retook his seat opposite her.

'I think that the paragraph about the chapel has been underlined in pencil. It's very faint but it's there.' Miss Treen passed the book back across.

Arthur delved inside his waistcoat pocket and took out his magnifying glass. 'Yes, I believe you're correct. An indication of where to look perhaps?'

'Maybe, but what are we looking for? Clues to the murderer? Something else? Something from Operation Exodus that the department was unaware of?' She frowned.

'Or something that Maura knew about and desperately wants to recover? If we assume it was her who attempted to impersonate you,' Arthur suggested.

Jane nodded. 'That makes sense. What did the chief inspector want?'

'He asked me to arrange a meeting tomorrow morning here with Mrs Mullins and her son. He has a witness that alleges Polly was seen with Bendigo near the station on the morning of her murder.'

The small crease in the centre of Miss Treen's forehead deepened into a frown. 'Mrs Mullins's son?'

'Yes. Bendigo is my gardener. He was born unable to speak and was ruled unfit to enlist. He labours for a nearby farmer and helps look after the garden here,' Arthur explained.

'And he was seen with Polly, hmm.' Miss Treen looked directly at Arthur, and the back of his neck prickled under his shirt collar. She had a way of making him feel he had done something wrong. 'I presume you told him that we would also be present at this interview?'

'Ah, well, since Bendigo struggles with strangers I said I would be present. To avoid overwhelming him. It will be a tricky thing anyway as he responds to questions by writing his answers down and he gets flustered sometimes.' Arthur didn't try to explain that, for those who knew Bendigo well, he had a range of sounds and hand movements that he used to express his feelings.

Miss Treen didn't look entirely happy with this but gave her consent to the arrangement. 'Did the chief inspector mention if he had information about anyone else alighting from the train that day?'

'He didn't say. We can always ask him tomorrow. I presume

you are thinking of the woman who impersonated you?' Arthur said.

'Well, if whoever impersonated me is Polly's murderer, then she must have arrived that day or the day before. If she was here the day before she would have stayed in lodgings somewhere local.'

'Have you ever lived in a village, Miss Treen?' he asked.

She glared at him. 'Your point is?'

'A stranger lodging in a village, especially at a time when a murder has taken place? We would have heard about it already. The only place in the village that lets rooms is the Swan near the church,' he explained. It was clear that Miss Treen had little experience of living in a small community. He wondered if she had always resided in towns or in London.

'Then she must have arrived and left again on the same day as Polly came back here. If Polly had arranged to meet her, then she couldn't have been far behind her. It wasn't the kind of weather you could hang around in out of doors for very long.' Miss Treen threw him a triumphant glance.

'That's if Polly came to meet a woman. It could have been a man she came to meet. When the imposter turned up at Father Dermott's to claim the parcel, Polly was already dead,' Arthur countered.

She drummed her fingers on the arm of the chair. 'If what you're saying is correct then surely any stranger in the village would have attracted notice?'

'Normally yes, but this was a market day, just after New Year. The village would have been busier than usual with people coming and trying their luck to see what they could get.' Arthur knew that market days were always busy. As shortages had become more intense, people tended to try and acquire something extra for the table in all kinds of places.

'I see what you mean. There is also the possibility that Polly was killed by someone here in the village,' Miss Treen suggested.

'I suppose so.' Arthur was forced to concede that she was right. Perhaps whoever killed Polly was already someone he knew.

'Then our plan is to see what we can learn tomorrow from Bendigo, and then we set off for Cornwall to follow up this clue from Anna. I presume Mrs Mullins will be happy to look after Marmaduke for me.' She looked at him.

Arthur shifted uneasily in his chair. He was not happy that Miss Treen seemed to be using the 'we' word again. Quite frankly, interesting though this puzzle was, he really had no desire to head off on what could be a wild goose chase to Cornwall. Especially since it would mean being chivvied along by Miss Treen the whole time.

Unfortunately, she appeared to read his mind. 'And, if you are thinking of trying to get out of this, remember we are at war. Polly's death and everything that goes along with it could be vital to the security of our nation. Plus, someone impersonated me!'

* * *

Jane woke early the following morning. It was typical of Arthur to try to weasel out of accompanying her to Cornwall. The clue Anna had left in the guidebook had to mean something. Why else would the girl have gone to so much trouble?

She would have liked to sit in on Chief Inspector Thorne's interview with Mrs Mullins and her son. The impertinence of someone trying to pass themselves off as her had stung her deeply. Whoever it was had known her name and had been aware of her connection to Polly. It had to be Maura. First with the murder of her agents and then Polly's reluctance to telephone the department and now the temerity of someone impersonating her! Everything seemed to indicate that deep in their department there was a mole.

It confirmed something that she and the brigadier had suspected for a while. It also meant that talking to the brigadier was risky. She could only hope that if the brigadier learned more about Maura Roberts's whereabouts, he would contact her here at Half Moon Manor. Hopefully without alerting whoever might be behind the deaths of the agents from Operation Exodus.

Chief Inspector Thorne arrived shortly before ten and went straight into the study with Arthur. Jane stationed herself in the lounge with the door open, so she had a view into the hall. Mrs Mullins, apron clad and rosy cheeked, emerged from the direction of the kitchen. A sturdy dark-haired man in his late thirties dressed in labourer's clothes accompanied her.

The two of them entered the study and the door closed behind them. Jane listened to see if she could hear any voices but disappointingly found the doors of Half Moon Manor were very solid. She was about to steal into the hall to position herself closer to the door when Benson arrived to thwart her plan. The door to the sitting room was firmly closed and now she could neither see nor hear anything.

* * *

Arthur had permitted the chief inspector to take the seat behind the desk. He stationed himself on a wooden chair in the corner so his presence would hopefully reassure his housekeeper and her son. Mrs Mullins and Bendigo entered promptly, and he guessed they had probably been looking out for the chief inspector's arrival at the house.

They seated themselves on the chairs from the dining room that Benson had thoughtfully placed in front of the desk. Mrs Mullins appeared slightly flustered with an anxious look in her eyes. Bendigo was solid and unmoving. The only indication of any possible concern was the way he was nervously twisting his cloth cap in his hands as he took his place beside his mother.

The chief inspector took out his small black notebook and set it on the desk next to another slightly larger notebook and a pen. 'Thank you both for agreeing to this interview this morning. You are both aware that this is in connection with the murder of the woman discovered in the river at the end of the garden?'

Mrs Mullins nodded and nudged her son who also inclined his head in agreement.

'Mrs Mullins, we already have your statement regarding the young women who were renting the house.' The chief inspector looked at the housekeeper. 'The reason I've asked to see you both today is that we have a witness who has stated that she saw Mr Mullins with the murder victim on the day of her death.'

'Bendigo? You understand what the chief inspector is saying to you? Did you see Miss Trevellian when she came back to the village that morning?' Mrs Mullins turned to her son.

Bendigo glanced up at the chief inspector briefly and nodded his head.

'I have provided a notebook and pen for you to write your replies, Mr Mullins. Your answers to my questions could be very helpful in discovering who may have wished to harm Miss Trevellian and why she had decided to return to the village.' Chief Inspector Thorne pushed the spare notepad and pen towards Bendigo. 'Where did you meet Miss Trevellian that day?'

Mrs Mullins gave her son another nudge with her elbow. Bendigo set his cap aside on his knee and picked up the pen. Arthur leaned forward slightly in his seat so he could see what the man was writing.

Bendigo held the pen awkwardly, his brow furrowed in concentration as he scratched at the notebook with the pen.

'Saw her at the station in the morning. She just off the train,' Chief Inspector Thorne read Bendigo's writing aloud. 'Was this on the morning she was killed? You hadn't seen her in the village before this, after she had given up her tenancy at this house?'

Bendigo picked the pen up again and poked his tongue out of the corner of his mouth as he painstakingly wrote out his answer to the chief inspector's questions.

'Took delivery to station for Farmer Larkins. Saw Miss Kate in her blue coat. She say she just back to pick up something she forgot.' Chief Inspector Thorne read out Bendigo's words once more. 'Did she say where she was going? Or who she was meeting?'

Bendigo resumed writing. 'Didn't say much else. Her seemed nervy, looking about.'

Arthur couldn't help but feel frustrated that yet another seemingly promising lead was petering out.

'Where did you leave her? Did she accompany you to Half Moon Manor?' the chief inspector asked.

Bendigo shook his head and wrote a little more. 'Left her at market. Had to get back to farm. Didn't see her no more after.'

Arthur sensed the chief inspector shared his feelings of frustration. The policeman asked Bendigo a few more questions about if he had seen Miss Trevellian talking to anyone or in which direction she might have been headed. Bendigo appeared to have no more information on the matter.

'Thank you, Mr Mullins. If you do recall anything else about the meeting or that morning, then please let me know.' Chief Inspector Thorne dismissed Mrs Mullins and her son and replaced his notebook in his pocket.

'What next, Chief Inspector?' Arthur asked.

'To be frank, Mr Cilento, I'm not certain. My manpower is depleted as you know, because of the war, and in this case there is very little to go on. I've had enquiries made in the village and amongst the market stallholders, but no one seems to have noticed our victim.' The policeman gave Arthur a keen glance. 'There is also the added complication of the victim living under a false identity. I presume that you and Miss Treen are pursuing your own lines of enquiry?'

Arthur bowed his head in acknowledgement. 'We shall, of course, pass on anything we discover that may be used to capture the person responsible.' He didn't need to say that this would only be the case if the security of the nation were not compromised. He also didn't mention the woman who had impersonated Miss Treen.

He was sure Chief Inspector Thorne was fully aware of the difficulties that might be caused by a public trial should an arrest be made. The coroner had already opened and adjourned the inquest and arranged for it to be held behind closed doors.

'Thank you.' The chief inspector rose from his seat and shook Arthur's hand. 'I must be off, I'm afraid.'

'Of course, Chief Inspector, please allow me to see you out.' Arthur opened the study door and was unsurprised to discover Miss Treen lurking near the hall table attempting to appear innocent.

'Good morning, Chief Inspector.' She extended her hand to the policeman. 'Off already?'

'Indeed, Miss Treen. We are rather busy at the moment so I must be away.' Chief Inspector Thorne shook hands with her and continued towards the front door where Arthur opened it ready for the policeman to depart.

'We will be in touch if we discover anything useful,' Arthur said as the chief inspector donned his overcoat and hat.

'Thank you, Mr Cilento.' The chief inspector turned to Miss Treen and raised his hat slightly. 'Miss Treen.'

The door had barely closed behind the policeman when her questions began.

'Well? How did it go? Did Bendigo know anything?'

'It went well but there was very little Bendigo could add to what we knew already.' Arthur headed back into the sitting room and his chair beside the fire. The cold air from the front door was irritating his chest and making him cough.

Miss Treen followed behind, seating herself opposite him, an impatient expression on her face.

Arthur cleared his throat and took a sip of water from the glass Benson always left beside his chair. He explained what Bendigo had told them.

'Pah! Useless, *she seemed nervy.* That was it?' Jane drummed her fingers on the arm of the chair. 'Hopeless. There is nothing for it, we shall have to go to Trelisk as soon as possible and see if we can find anything there,' she declared.

'Really? Do you still think we both need to go?' Arthur protested.

He shrank back a little in his seat when she looked at him.

'Of course we both need to go. We have already discussed this. The brigadier has given his instructions. Two heads are better than one and this whole case is a riddle. *You* are supposed to be the expert at solving puzzles and riddles.'

Arthur didn't like the way she emphasised the *you* in that sentence.

CHAPTER TWELVE

Benson was dispatched to organise train tickets and then to book rooms at a guest house within easy walking distance of Trelisk. He also organised Arthur's packing. Jane preferred to pack her own small assortment of clothes into her compact suitcase unaided.

Mrs Mullins, a trifle reluctantly, agreed that she would be responsible for Marmaduke while they were gone. He promptly rewarded her for her munificence by presenting her with a decapitated mouse. This was not appreciated, judging by the shrieks of dismay emanating from the kitchen.

Jane took the time to send a telegram to the brigadier to inform him of their intentions. She was reluctant to telephone, fearing that the conversation could be overheard. A letter too was risky. It could be intercepted before reaching the office and, indeed, could be read by someone other than her intended recipient.

Instead, she fell back on an arrangement she and the brigadier had used in the past when communications had been at risk of going astray. Consequently, the brigadier received a telegram that read,

Dear Uncle,

Away for couple of days.

Look after Em.

Affectionately,

J

Benson had arranged for them to travel into Exeter Central station where they would then have to change trains in order to continue into Cornwall. The station was busy with soldiers when they pulled in. There seemed to be a sea of khaki and olive green teeming like ants.

'Troops heading for training on Dartmoor, and others heading off to the front line,' Arthur murmured in her ear as he and Benson assisted her onto the platform.

Jane nodded, feeling somewhat swamped by the volume of uniformed men surrounding her. She was used to the hustle and bustle of London, but this had a different feel. Wives and sweethearts were bidding farewell to loved ones, waving hand-kerchiefs, and smiling bravely as a train departed. Some of the women were accompanied by confused-looking small children, other women were older, mothers and grandmothers wearing stoic smiles.

Benson went to get their luggage and arrange a porter.

'I think we have time for a cup of tea before our train gets in,' Arthur suggested, leading her towards a bustling tea room.

Jane spotted Diana Fenwick looking smart in her uniform. She was occupied dispensing drinks and smiles to the soldiers from behind a trestle table laden with crockery. Jane took a seat at one of the few vacant tables while Arthur looked for Benson.

'Hello, what a surprise to see you and Arthur here, Miss

Treen.' Diana appeared at the table a moment later. A tray laden with dirty cups and plates in her hands. 'Are you off back to London?'

'No, not quite yet. We are taking a couple of days away,' Jane replied just as Arthur returned to join her.

'Miss Fenwick, it looks as if you are being kept busy.' Arthur looked around at the hustle and bustle surrounding them.

'Tell me about it. My feet are red hot by the time I've finished my stints.' Diana laughed. 'Miss Treen was just telling me that you were going away for a few days?'

'Doctor's orders for both of us.' Jane cut Arthur off before he could say anything. 'The shock of my cousin's death for me and obviously Arthur has chest problems. A couple of days' peace and quiet in milder air.'

'Oh dear, I hope you will both feel better when you get back.' Diana shifted the tray in her hands causing the crockery to clink together.

'I'm sure we will. It's all been very distressing. I've been recommended to take a short break before returning home. My area has been badly affected by bombing; the sirens apparently are going off quite frequently. Arthur has kindly agreed to accompany me since his doctor also felt he needed a more temperate climate. Travel these days is so difficult for a woman travelling alone,' Jane explained further as Benson joined them carrying a tea tray.

'It's always good to have company when travelling. Are you going somewhere nice?' Diana asked as Benson took his seat at the table.

'Just to a small guest house in Cornwall.' Jane smiled her thanks to Benson as he passed her a cup.

'Coffee, Miss Treen.'

'Thank you, Benson.'

Diana smiled at them all again. 'Well, have a jolly good rest.' She turned her gaze directly on Arthur. 'I suppose I shall see you when you get back. You must call round to the vicarage and tell us all about it.'

'Of course, that would be delightful,' Arthur agreed as Diana disappeared back to her station behind the table.

Jane sipped her drink and wished it tasted more of coffee and less like dishwater. Still, it was warm and wet, and they had a couple of hours' journey at least ahead of them.

She was relieved to find that Benson had managed to secure seats in a first-class carriage for herself and Arthur. The train, like the station, was so full of people, she had been dreading the prospect that they might have had to stand all the way to Cornwall.

The train exited the station in a cloud of smoke and steam. Jane wasn't absolutely certain, but she thought she saw Georgette Darnley, Major Hawes's secretary, talking to Diana Fenwick as they pulled away from the platform. The two women were standing to one side and Georgette seemed very agitated, waving her arms around as she conversed with Diana.

* * *

Arthur settled himself in his seat opposite Miss Treen. His space was somewhat compromised by a large, older lady squashed into the seat next to him. To add to his discomfort, the bag on the woman's lap seemed to contain several very knobbly packages, all of which poked into him at some point.

Miss Treen appeared to be unaffected by any such woes as the seat next to her was occupied by a rail-thin older man dressed in a shabby black suit. Arthur managed to fish his book from his pocket and started to read. He had always found carrying a book a good defence against random strangers attempting to force him into conversation whilst travelling.

'Are you going very far?' The woman seated next to Arthur addressed her question to Miss Treen.

'Only to Trelisk,' she replied.

'Oh, it's a lovely place there. Very quiet, mind you. I'm on to Penzance to my daughter's. She's had a little one so I'm going to help her with the other kiddies.' The woman shifted the bag on her lap and managed to nudge Arthur again. 'Got a couple of presents in here for them.' She tapped her bag.

'How lovely.' Miss Treen's reply sounded polite, but Arthur suspected she was as uninterested in the woman's grandchildren as he was.

'How about you, lovey?' The woman addressed the man next to Miss Treen. 'You on till Penzance?'

The man appeared somewhat startled by the question. 'No, I too will be leaving at Trelisk.'

Arthur raised his book in front of his face. He had no desire to be dragged into the conversation. He caught Miss Treen's gaze and could tell she knew what he was doing.

'You off at Trelisk too?' The woman jogged him with her elbow.

He saw Miss Treen trying to hide a smirk when his ploy failed.

'Yes.' He kept his reply short hoping that now her curiosity about her fellow travellers' destinations had been satisfied the woman might leave him alone.

His wish was not to be granted, however, and the woman kept up a stream of conversation, mostly as a monologue, virtually all the way to Trelisk. Something that seemed to afford Miss Treen great amusement whenever she caught his eye.

The station at Trelisk was tiny and he, Miss Treen, Benson and the man in the black suit were the only people to disembark. Benson commandeered a spotty youth and a porter's cart to take their luggage.

'I am informed by the boy that the guest house is a short walking distance away, sir, miss,' Benson informed them as the lad hovered close by attempting to look important in his over-sized jacket and cap.

'Very good, Benson.' Arthur fell into step behind his manservant and the young lad pushing the cart.

Miss Treen sauntered along at his side. 'I presume you are relieved to have lost our garrulous friend?' she asked.

Arthur gave her a sour look. 'It's a good thing she is not responsible for any national secrets.'

He wondered where the man in the black suit had gone. He presumed that he must live locally. He had disappeared from the station very quickly and didn't appear to have any luggage with him.

Benson and the boy rumbled their way out of the station and along the road past several stone-built cottages, before turning off down a quiet lane. They proceeded on before finally halting outside a cream-painted Victorian villa. A stone tub of winter pansies was beside the front door, lifting their yellow and purple faces to the weak wintry sunshine.

'Here you am, sir,' the boy said as he hefted Arthur's bag from the trolley and trotted towards the front door.

The dark-blue front door opened immediately to Benson's ring on the well-polished brass doorbell.

A tall, thin woman in a floral-print frock and dark-green woollen cardigan peered out at them.

'Miss Thomas? I believe you are expecting us? Mr Cilento's party?' Benson asked.

'Yes, yes, do come inside.' She beckoned to them. 'You, lad, wipe your boots before you carry those things in.' She fixed the boy with a steely gaze.

Arthur and Miss Treen were shown into a comfortable, if somewhat over furnished, sitting room. A small fire had been lit in the hearth and the room smelt of polish. Benson finished overseeing the unloading of the luggage and tipping the boy from the money Arthur had supplied for just such a purpose.

'Welcome to Trelisk, Mr Cilento,' the landlady simpered at Arthur. 'I have put you and your man on the first floor and Miss Treen, you are on the second floor next to my own quarters. I hope this arrangement is satisfactory? I run a respectable business here, so I'm sure you understand that proprieties must be observed.' Their landlady turned the same look she had given the young porter in Miss Treen and Arthur's direction.

'Of course, Miss Thomas.' Arthur shifted uncomfortably at the mention of impropriety. Miss Treen, however, looked mildly amused at the suggestion.

Benson dealt with the business of handing over ration coupons while they signed the register. Miss Treen then accompanied Miss Thomas to inspect her room, while he went with Benson to look at their accommodation.

Miss Thomas had allocated him a large, pleasant room overlooking the town with a distant glimpse of a large house surrounded by gardens. He assumed that must be Miss Trevellian's house, named after the small village that shared its name. A bathroom was across the landing and Benson had a smaller single room nearby.

Satisfied that all was well, he left Benson to unpack their bags and went back downstairs. Miss Treen joined him a few moments later, followed by Miss Thomas bearing a tray of tea.

'Normally, of course, I expect my guests to be out of the house between ten and four during the day. However, since Mr Benson has told me of your infirmities, Mr Cilento, I shall make an exception for you and Miss Treen to use this room during the day. You must, however, be quiet, and I shall not provide any extra meals or refreshments unless given prior notice.' Miss Thomas set the tray down on one of the many small, dark-oak tables cluttering the room.

'Quite so, Miss Thomas. We very much appreciate your kindness,' Arthur murmured, ignoring Miss Treen's raised eyebrows at their landlady's rules.

Miss Thomas smiled graciously at him. 'Dinner will be served in the dining room promptly at six thirty.'

'Thank you.' Arthur breathed a small sigh of relief once the landlady had gone, leaving them to their tea.

Miss Treen lifted the lid of the china floral teapot and dispiritedly poked a spoon at the contents. 'I hope we are able to find what we need here quickly.'

'Is your room satisfactory?' Arthur enquired mildly.

She gave him a look much like the one Miss Thomas had given the young porter. 'I have a view of the bins and if I stretch out my arms, I can probably touch the walls on both sides of the room with my fingertips.'

Arthur decided it was probably wise to say nothing about his own quarters, but instead waited patiently for Jane to decide that the tea was strong enough to pour into the cups. Benson came to join them having completed the unpacking.

'Permit me, Miss Treen.' He promptly took command of the teapot, placing the metal strainer over the top of her cup.

'What are our plans for the rest of today?' Miss Treen asked once the rather weak tea had been served. It seemed that no amount of standing would have improved the strength of the brew.

Arthur glanced at the wooden clock on the mantelpiece. 'It's four o'clock already and it will be dark soon. I think any chance to explore will have to wait until morning.' He had no wish to traipse about in the cold and the dark. Especially as they had no idea what they were after or where it was likely to be.

'I can ascertain from Miss Thomas if she has any guides or information about Trelisk House and the opening hours and arrangements of the gardens and the chapel,' Benson suggested.

Arthur could see that Miss Treen was thinking. 'I wonder if Polly, Anna or Richard stayed here, or were observed visiting the village? It's an even smaller place than where you live,

Arthur, so at this time of year perhaps someone may have seen them?' she suggested.

Arthur nodded. 'Yes, that's true. We shall have to be careful though, about how we ask. We don't wish to arouse any suspicions. If there is something here, then there may well be others searching for the same thing.'

Miss Treen sighed. 'Whatever this wretched thing might be.'

* * *

Dinner was a lacklustre affair of cheese and potato pie, followed by tinned prunes and custard. Jane couldn't decide which had more lumps, the potato in the pie or the meagre portion of custard.

Miss Thomas did, however, consent to providing coffee after dinner after Benson made a politely worded request. Their hostess also produced a small number of pamphlets about the village, Trelisk House and its local environs.

With dinner concluded they escaped to the sitting room where Jane promptly lit up a cigarette while she studied the information Miss Thomas had supplied.

'Trelisk House is within walking distance.' Jane frowned as she looked through the information in the leaflet. 'The gardens are on winter opening hours, so between eleven and three.'

'And the chapel?' Arthur asked.

Miss Thomas entered the room bearing the coffee tray. She set it down and promptly placed a large, pressed-glass ashtray in front of Jane.

'Please do be careful of the soft furnishings.'

'Of course, thank you, Miss Thomas.' Jane barely glanced up from her perusal.

'Which is the quickest way to Trelisk House from here?' Arthur asked the landlady.

'Oh, it's only a short step away. You go along the lane here until it joins with the main road, then you cross over and carry on into Tregowan Lane, and it will take you right there,' Miss Thomas said. 'There's not much to see, of course, this time of year. The house is private, but the grounds are open, and you can apply for a key to see the chapel should it be locked.'

'Thank you. It was recommended to us by some friends who had been there. They suggested that the snowdrops were particularly good,' Arthur said.

Miss Thomas sniffed dismissively. 'I don't know about that. We get quite a few visitors interested in the chapel though, because of the frescoes. There was a gentleman here a couple of weeks ago came especially on his leave to see them.'

Jane lifted her gaze from the leaflet. 'They must be very good for someone to do that.'

'Yes, a young man too, nice-looking boy. In the air force, I think. I hope he stays safe. It's such a worry, isn't it, these days, with our brave young men and women.' On that note, she departed back to her own quarters.

Benson rose quietly from his seat. 'If you'll excuse me, sir. I think I may have left something in the hall.'

Jane suspected that whatever Arthur's manservant may have lost would probably be located near the guest house register.

CHAPTER THIRTEEN

Breakfast was served promptly at eight o'clock. Jane was relieved to see that at least there was toast and eggs. She had slept poorly in her room and consequently was quite out of sorts with the world. The mattress felt as if it had been stuffed with rocks and the neighbouring cats seemed to enjoy yowling in the small courtyard below her window.

Arthur and Benson both appeared to have had no such troubles and greeted her cheerfully when she took her seat at the table. Evidence of their uninterrupted night's sleep only served to increase her irritation. Benson's investigation of the guest house register the previous night had confirmed their suspicions. An R Trent had indeed been signed into the register on December 29th.

Benson had also made a note of other names who had signed in both before and after Richard Trent's stay. There was no one else who seemed to stand out in any way. Jane couldn't help wondering if the whole trip would end up being a giant wild goose chase.

They agreed over breakfast that Jane and Arthur would go to Trelisk House to view the chapel and grounds. Benson was to occupy himself in the village, ostensibly running errands while he made discreet enquiries about any recent visitors in various establishments.

Arthur joined her in the hall of the guest house wrapped up as if about to head out on an expedition to the North Pole. His felt hat was pulled well down on his head and a large mustard-coloured cashmere muffler covered his mouth and nose.

'Good heavens, are you certain you can walk under the weight of all that wool?' Jane asked crisply as she tugged on her own leather gloves.

'I need to avoid cold air,' Arthur replied in a somewhat huffy tone as he opened the front door for her.

'I don't think it's that cold today.' Jane set off at a brisk pace in the direction Miss Thomas had suggested.

Arthur muttered something indistinguishable and fell into a leisurely stride behind her. She was forced to stop and wait for him to catch up with her when she reached the main road.

The row of cottages had petered out by this point and no vehicles had passed them as they had walked down the lane. The main route too was empty. Jane had not expected to see many cars since petrol was scarce, but she had thought there might be a few farm carts.

'Do slow down, Miss Treen. We are not in a race,' Arthur remarked as they crossed the road together to follow the lane that Miss Thomas had said led to Trelisk House.

'I wasn't aware that I was rushing. If you didn't dilly-dally we might get this done more quickly.' Jane was busy looking over the bare hedgerows and dry-stone walls for a sight of the house.

'The gardens aren't open until eleven, we have plenty of time,' Arthur retorted.

Further along the lane they came to the main gates to the house. Large wrought-iron affairs that had not yet been surrendered in the increasing drive for metal. A long, gravel driveway extended through the grounds towards the cream-painted Georgian house nestling in the green valley.

To the side of the main entrance, a smaller, white-painted arch-topped door was set into the grey stone wall. A black iron bell pull hung above a sign advising that visitors to the gardens and chapel should pull the bell for attention.

Jane tugged on the bell and waited for Arthur to catch her up.

'Purely out of interest, how did Polly end up taking Miss Trevellian's identity?' Arthur asked as they waited for the bell to be answered.

Jane gave him a speaking look.

'Oh, I see. She is also part of one of your teams,' Arthur interpreted her response correctly. 'Did you say you had spoken to Miss Trevellian since Polly was killed?'

'Yes, she is currently working in Wales.' Jane didn't expand.

'Interesting,' Arthur murmured.

Before Jane could ask him what he meant the gate in the wall opened. A man, who she assumed must be one of the gardeners, stood before them dressed in old brown moleskin trousers, an ancient tweed jacket and a battered flat cap. He appeared, however, strangely familiar.

'May I help you?' he asked.

'We wondered if we might see the gardens and the chapel.' Jane tried to work out where she had seen the man before.

'Of course, miss, sir. Would you be wanting a guidebook at all?' he asked as he stood aside to allow them to enter the grounds.

'No, thank you. We have one already.' Arthur tapped the pocket of his jacket before paying the two shillings admission fee to the man.

'Right you are then.' The man turned to issue them each with a ticket and Jane recalled where she had seen him before.

'Excuse me, but weren't you on the train with us yesterday?'

Previously he had been wearing a black suit and travelling in the first-class carriage, but now it seemed he was a gardener on the estate.

'That's right, miss. I'd been to Exeter on a fool's errand.' The man started to lead them along a narrow path across the grounds towards a small stone building in the grounds.

'Oh dear, how so?' Jane asked.

They reached the door of the chapel, and the gardener produced a large iron key from his trouser pocket.

'I had a letter come with two train tickets to go to Exeter. I was supposed to learn something from a solicitor there to my advantage. An inheritance or something.' The man paused and scratched his head, knocking his cap slightly askew. 'It was my day off and the train were paid so I didn't see the harm.'

'What happened?' Arthur asked. He was clearly as eager as Jane to learn more.

'I went to the address like they said but they didn't know anything about it. Said as I were mistaken. I showed them the letter and all and they were proper surprised, said it must have been a prank. But who spends money on first-class train tickets for a prank?' the gardener asked. He appeared most affronted at the idea.

'That's certainly very peculiar,' Jane agreed. This sounded suspiciously as if someone had wanted the man out of the way for some reason. Were they too late? Had whatever they had come to find already been claimed?

'I reckon as how they had made a mistake and got me confused with somebody else and didn't want to admit it,' the man said.

Arthur nodded. 'That could well be the case, I suppose. What a waste of your time.'

'Got myself all gussied up for nowt. Waste of a day and wear and tear on my best suit.' The man unlocked the wooden door of the chapel. 'I'll come and lock up again later.'

'Thank you, that's most kind.' Jane hoped they weren't wasting their time on a fool's errand too.

It sounded to her as if someone had lured the gardener out of the way for the day, presumably so they could search the chapel and grounds. She could see no other reason why someone had gone to so much trouble with train tickets and a forged solicitor's letter.

The gardener touched his cap and returned to his duties, leaving Jane and Arthur at the door of the chapel.

'That was quite a story,' Arthur remarked as he followed Jane inside the building.

The air in the chapel was cold and smelled faintly musty, like old books and damp. The interior was, however, surprisingly light due to the leaded-glass windows inset in the thick stone walls. Fresh greenery was placed on either side of the altar in two lovingly polished copper jugs and dust motes whirled in the air as they ventured further along the aisle.

'It definitely sounded as if someone wanted him out of the way for the day.' Jane paused and looked around. 'Let's hope we are not too late.'

The walls were painted with the frescoes mentioned in the guidebook. The paintings were said to date back to the Middle Ages. One wall depicted St Peter with his boat and nets. The other showed St Christopher with the Christ child on his shoulders. The colours, although slightly faded with age, were surprisingly well preserved.

'I agree. These are rather magnificent, aren't they?' Arthur too had halted to admire the artwork.

Jane estimated the chapel would probably hold between sixty to eighty people seated on the polished oak bench seats topped with embroidered cushions. At the rear of the room a small oak table held copies of hymn books beside a wooden box for donations.

The floor consisted of engraved stone slabs, worn with age,

marking the final resting places of various members of the Trevellian family and the priests that had served the household.

'I wish I knew what we were looking for.' Jane could see there didn't appear to be many hiding places within the interior of the church. She sat down on one of the nearby pews and looked ahead at the front of the church.

The small wooden altar was covered with a simple white embroidered cloth, topped by a pair of brass candlesticks. A heavy stone font was on one side and a wooden lectern holding a large open Bible on the other side.

Arthur continued to survey these objects curiously. His head tipped slightly to one side like an inquisitive bird.

'What are you—' She stopped mid-question when he held up his hand to silence her.

Annoyed, she stayed quiet, and waited for him to finish whatever he was doing. Arthur swivelled around and looked carefully at their surroundings before walking to the back of the chapel where they had first come in.

Jane folded her arms and waited, trying not to tap her toes impatiently on the stone floor while Arthur continued his silent ponderings. He halted again, his hand on his chin while he stared at the altar.

'Well?' Jane asked, unable to stay quiet any longer.

Arthur pulled the guidebook from his coat pocket without answering her question. Jane knew it was the one that Anna Perez had left in the parcel with the priest. Frustrated at being inactive, she jumped to her feet and went to the neat stack of hymn books and started methodically searching each one.

She wondered if sending them to the chapel had any connection with the words left with the bodies of the agents murdered in London. Both notes had contained the same biblical quote: Exodus 21, *an eye for an eye.*

Arthur ignored her, continuing to scan the pages of the guidebook as he made his way along the wall depicting St Peter.

From time to time, he stopped to look down at the floor as if checking the inscriptions.

Jane drew a blank with the hymn books and started to feel under the table in case something had been secured to the underside. Again, finding nothing, she took a quick peep outside to make sure no one was likely to enter the church while they were conducting their search.

The garden remained empty. The only life appearing to be a robin who watched her curiously from his perch on the branch of a nearby holly tree. She re-entered the chapel to discover Arthur peering intently at a spot on the wall in between the two stained-glass windows that punctuated the fresco of St Peter.

'There's no one outside. What have you found?' Jane asked as she went to see what he had discovered.

'I think it's an old offertory box. You know, where people would have made donations to the chapel in the past.' Arthur frowned as he studied a dull brass plate set flush into the wall. The slot where people would have once posted money had been sealed.

He handed her the guidebook. 'Hold this.'

Jane took the book while Arthur extracted a small, wooden-handled screwdriver from the inside pocket of his coat.

'What are you doing?' Jane watched as he started to unscrew the two brass screws holding the plate to the wall. 'Are you mad? If you damage anything here...' Her voice trailed to a halt as he removed the plate exposing the box set into the wall. Inside the box lay a small bundle wrapped in paper and tied up with string.

Arthur moved swiftly to tuck the package inside his coat pocket before hastening to replace the brass plate.

'How did you know where to look?' Jane asked as he took the guidebook back from her.

'The clues were in the book. Very faint marks on the page. I spent a long time in bed last night with my magnifying glass.'

Jane's eyebrows raised at his response. 'We need to get back to the guest house so we can take a look at what's in that parcel.'

'I would suggest that we return to Half Moon Manor as soon as Benson can arrange travel for us. I think it would be safer to consider the contents there.' Arthur placed the guide-book back in his pocket before adjusting his scarf.

A shiver ran down Jane's spine. 'What do you think is in that package?'

Arthur shrugged. 'Maybe a book, documents, whatever it is, several people have been killed for them.' His tone was sombre.

Jane supposed he was right. 'My feet are turning to ice now, we should start back to the guest house.'

As she spoke the door to the chapel which she had left slightly ajar, closed with a sudden bang, startling them both.

'How odd. There was no breeze out there.' Jane hurried down to the door and turned the ancient wrought-iron handle.

'It's locked. Someone has locked us in.' She twisted the handle without any success. The door refused to budge. They were trapped.

CHAPTER FOURTEEN

Arthur strolled up to join Jane. 'Perhaps the gardener thought we had gone,' he suggested.

Jane paused in her attempts to open the door and glared at him. 'Really? If you believe that you'll believe anything. Someone has locked us in here on purpose.'

Arthur took a seat on a nearby pew as she resumed her attempts to open the door. Jane gave up with the handle and pounded on the wooden door with her gloved fist.

'You're wasting your time,' Arthur said.

'At least I'm trying something,' Jane snapped before proceeding to call for help at the top of her lungs.

Arthur merely covered his ears and winced as she yelled.

There was no response from outside the chapel. After a few minutes, she took a seat next to Arthur. 'All right, clever clogs. What do you suggest?'

He stood and went to examine the lock. 'There's no key in the keyhole. We could try picking it, I suppose. It appears to be a fairly simple lock.'

Jane rolled her eyes behind his back. She hadn't much personal expertise at picking locks, and besides which, she didn't have anything on her person that might be useful for such a task. It wasn't as if many women used hatpins any more.

Arthur patted the pockets of his coat as if feeling for something before delving into one of them. He extracted something that looked suspiciously exactly like a hatpin with a cork on the sharp end.

'Do you have an entire toolbox in there?' Jane asked incredulously as he removed the cork.

He ignored her again as he began to delicately probe the inside of the lock with the pin.

'I was a boy scout. Be prepared and all that,' he remarked presently. 'Ah hah!' He replaced the cork and put the hatpin safely back into his pocket.

She shook her head in disbelief as he twisted the handle and opened the chapel door before standing to the side.

'Shall we?' he asked.

'Unbelievable,' Jane muttered as she marched through the doorway back out into the garden.

* * *

Arthur saw the garden appeared deserted as they stepped outside. Whoever had locked them in the chapel had long gone. There were no signs of any footprints in the damp soil to offer a clue as to who may have been there. Maybe it had been a mistake on the part of the gardener, but surely he would have checked the building before locking up?

He was more inclined to believe Miss Treen's theory that it had been done deliberately, but who by and for what purpose? The chilly air rasped at the back of his throat as he followed Miss Treen through the grounds towards the gate where they had entered the garden.

The sooner they left Trelisk and returned to Half Moon Manor the better. He was keen to know what had been hidden inside the old offertory box. It had to be something that Polly and Richard had felt could not be sent through the usual channels. Once he had examined the package they had retrieved from the chapel, perhaps Miss Treen might be persuaded to return to London.

Miss Treen as usual was marching ahead of him, while he followed at a slower pace. Her reaction to his picking the lock had amused him. Fortunately, the lock had been old and simple as he was rather out of practice.

Since the ground was more uphill on their return journey, he could feel the ill effects of the unaccustomed exercise in his lungs. He would need Benson's aid with his inhalations once they got back. Hopefully, Benson would have everything ready in anticipation of his requirements.

It was Benson who opened the front door to the guest house when they arrived.

'I saw you approaching, sir, miss,' the manservant explained as he assisted Arthur with the many layers of wool in which he had enveloped himself to keep the cold from affecting his chest.

'Thank you, Benson,' Arthur wheezed the words out.

'I have set your equipment up in the parlour, sir.' Benson guided him to an armchair next to the meagre fire and within a few minutes he was breathing in the medicines which opened his air passages. Once he no longer felt as if he were drowning, he directed Benson to retrieve the parcel from his coat.

Miss Treen returned from powdering her nose and took her seat opposite Arthur.

'Benson, have you been upstairs at all since you returned from town?' she asked.

'Only to collect Mr Cilento's medical equipment, miss,' the man replied, passing the paper-wrapped bundle to Arthur.

'My room has been searched. On the surface it looks the same, but I can tell my things have been moved,' she explained in a low voice.

'I shall go and take a look upstairs.' Benson bowed his head and disappeared on his mission.

'That could be why we were locked in. To prevent us from returning here too quickly.' Miss Treen drummed her fingers on the arm of the chair.

Arthur sensed she probably would have liked to light a cigarette but since he was clearly still recovering from his exertions, was refraining.

'Was anything missing from your room?' he asked.

She shook her head. 'I am always very careful. I made sure the files I had from the office were all hidden away back at the manor before we left.'

Benson rejoined them. 'Everything appears to be in order, sir, but Miss Treen is correct, the room has definitely been searched.'

'Where is our landlady?' Jane asked.

'I saw her in the village, miss. She was engaged in what seemed to be a lengthy conversation with the postmistress,' Benson said.

'Did she leave the house at the same time as you?' Miss Treen looked at the manservant.

'A trifle before me, miss. She was already in the village when I arrived. I passed her on several occasions whilst completing my errands,' Benson said.

'That would seem to exclude Miss Thomas as a suspect. Was the house locked, Benson, when you went out?' Arthur asked as he finally put down his mouthpiece.

'I'm afraid not, sir. Miss Thomas did not appear to feel it necessary.' Benson gave an apologetic cough.

'Then it could have been whoever mysteriously locked us inside the chapel.' Miss Treen frowned as she spoke.

'I beg your pardon, miss?' Benson asked, raising one silver-streaked eyebrow.

Arthur realised Benson hadn't been told about the chapel

lock-in. He explained what had happened and about the discovery of the parcel that he had in his lap.

'I see, a most unsatisfactory development, sir.' A slightly troubled expression ruffled his servant's usually placid exterior.

'Did you have any success in the village with your own enquiries?' Miss Treen asked.

'I visited several establishments. It seems that the gentleman who visited Half Moon Manor at Christmas was seen here also. It would also seem that there have been several visitors over the festive period and the New Year,' Benson confirmed as he busied himself with tidying Arthur's medical apparatus.

Miss Treen leaned forward slightly in her seat. 'Anyone that we may be interested in?'

'It would appear that a young woman with a London accent visited a few days ago. She was only here for the day, taking in the gardens and having luncheon at the local hostelry. She claimed to have been fulfilling the wish of her late aunt to visit the village whilst on her way home to London.' Benson placed the rubber tubing back inside the wooden travelling box.

'Did you get a description?' Arthur asked. He had his own suspicions of who this woman might be.

'Yes, sir. Mid-twenties, smart appearance, dark hair, respectable,' Benson replied.

Miss Treen leaned back in her seat, her brow furrowed. 'It could be Maura, the description fits. That would be after the time the last big raid started in London. The time she was supposed to be missing. After Polly's murder?'

'We know she was unsuccessful in her visit here since she didn't recover this parcel. She must have another contact here though, who has instructions to look out for us. That must be the person who locked us in and searched our rooms. Whoever it was, and we still cannot be absolutely certain yet that it is Maura, knew you were searching, presumably, for this package,' Arthur said.

'Because of them impersonating me to Father Dermott?' Miss Treen asked.

'Precisely.' Arthur could breathe much more easily now and the tightness in his chest had eased. He tried to work out the timeline. 'Polly was killed, and they didn't find anything. Then they impersonated you and talked to Father Dermott. We booked to come to Trelisk after finding the guidebook.'

'Whoever this woman is, she was here a few days ago, so probably around the time she impersonated me?' Miss Treen looked at him.

'They must have worked out there was a Cornish connection somehow and followed a hunch to Trelisk. But then didn't find anything.' Arthur frowned.

'Or they were unable to search properly until they lured the gardener away.' Miss Treen leaned back in her chair.

'Then we booked train tickets and the guest house, so they thought they'd try again.' Arthur didn't like where all of this was leading. He hoped that their poking about had not placed them in danger.

'We had better look at that parcel. I suspect there are papers or documents that will shed light on this whole thing,' Miss Treen suggested, her gaze landing back on the battered package lying in his lap.

Before either of them had a chance to examine the parcel for documents, they heard the front door of the guest house open and footsteps in the hall.

Benson acted swiftly and moved the package, collecting it up with Arthur's medical supplies, ready to take them back upstairs. The lounge door opened, and Miss Thomas appeared.

She was still dressed in her outdoor clothes, the shoulders of her brown woollen coat damp from the drizzle that had sprung up again since they had returned to the guest house. She had a large wicker basket on her arm filled with vegetables and a package of her own wrapped in brown paper tied with string.

'Good afternoon, Miss Thomas. I trust your shopping was successful?' Benson asked smoothly.

'Yes, thank you, Mr Benson. I managed to get some sausages for supper.' She inclined her head towards the basket. The small wet brown feather in the band of her dark-green hat drooping sadly in the same direction.

'Excellent news. I'm sure we shall all enjoy them,' Benson said.

Miss Thomas appeared slightly mollified by his approbation. 'I suppose you'd all like a pot of tea?' she offered with a begrudging sniff. 'The weather has turned quite nasty.'

'If it's not too much trouble, Miss Thomas, we would be most grateful,' Arthur said.

'Hmm.' The door closed, and she disappeared presumably in the direction of the kitchen, leaving Arthur uncertain if that meant tea would be forthcoming or not.

'The parcel will have to wait,' Miss Treen said. 'Benson, can you ensure it is secured in a safe place? Not that I expect that whoever searched our rooms will try again in a hurry, but I do think we should return to Half Moon Manor as soon as possible tomorrow.'

Benson bowed his head to acknowledge her request. 'Very well, miss. Shall I make arrangements?'

'Please, Benson. I think Miss Treen is right. Much as I wish to examine the contents of that parcel, I feel it would be unwise to do so at the moment,' Arthur agreed.

The package and its contents would have to wait for now. He might get a chance once he was in his room later. Then he could pass any information about what was inside on to Miss Treen. It was too risky to look at it immediately, however much they both wanted to see what was contained in the parcel.

Benson carried the apparatus and the package away, before setting out with his large black umbrella in the direction of the station.

Miss Thomas carried in a wooden tea tray just after Benson had set off.

'Is Mr Benson not joining you?' she asked as she set the tray down on the low table in front of Arthur.

'He'll be back shortly. Unfortunately, it seems we may have to return home tomorrow. He has gone to see if he can arrange transport,' Arthur explained.

Miss Thomas raised her eyebrows at this information. 'I see, well I hope as you're not unhappy with your stay here,' she said.

'Oh no, Miss Thomas, you have been a wonderful hostess. Arthur has become unwell again so we feel he should return to see his doctor sooner rather than later,' Miss Treen explained as she placed the metal tea strainer over the cup ready to pour.

Miss Thomas looked at Arthur. 'I shall add the cost of the tea to your bill. He does look rather peaky.' She peered at Arthur again before returning to the kitchen and leaving them alone.

'I hope you have a good hiding place in your room.' Miss Treen covered her conversation by noisily stirring the spoon against the side of the teacup.

Arthur winced at the clatter. 'There is a false bottom in the medical bag. Benson has packed the gun so he will place the parcel there too. He keeps that bag with him all the time whilst we are travelling.'

Miss Treen sniffed suspiciously at the top of the chipped floral-patterned china milk jug, before adding a splash of milk to each teacup. 'The sooner we can get back to Half Moon Manor the better.'

'I agree. I presume once we know what it contains you will be returning to London?' Arthur asked. He tried not to sound too hopeful about this prospect. He was longing for a return to a quiet, Miss-Treen-free life.

She raised an immaculately arched eyebrow at him. 'That depends on the contents of that package and if the inspector has made any progress into Polly's murder.' She took a sip of tea and pulled a face.

Arthur suppressed a sigh. It seemed he would have Miss Treen and her wretched cat as his guests for a while longer.

Benson returned just as Arthur was finishing his drink. Miss Treen had abandoned her cup after a couple of sips and was smoking one of her cigarettes when his manservant entered the sitting room.

'I have tickets for tomorrow morning, sir, miss. The ten past ten train.'

'Thank you, Benson. Do sit down. Miss Treen, is there more tea in the pot?' Arthur asked as the older man somewhat reluctantly took a seat.

Jane added more hot water to the teapot from the small chrome jug that had accompanied the rest of the accoutrements. 'I'm afraid it's not terribly hot.'

'No matter, miss, it's most welcome.' Benson accepted the tea once she had poured it through the strainer and added milk. 'Do you wish me to call the house, sir, and apprise them of our expected arrival tomorrow. I daresay the staff will wish to plan supper?' Benson asked.

'Yes, I suppose so. What time will we reach Exeter?' Arthur asked.

'Around lunchtime, sir, then we have to make the connection to the village.' Benson drained his cup.

'Very good.' Arthur settled back in his chair as his manservant went to ask Miss Thomas if he might use her telephone.

The events of the day and the exertion of climbing back up the hill had quite exhausted him. It would be nice to return to Half Moon Manor tomorrow. Then they could find out what was in that parcel, and he could rid himself more quickly of Jane Treen and her wretched cigarettes.

CHAPTER FIFTEEN

Miss Thomas grudgingly provided an early breakfast so that they had time to pay the bill, take back their ration books and pack. The young boy came from the station with the trolley for the luggage and they set off for the station into the damp, cold morning.

Benson kept the large, brown leather bag with Arthur's medical supplies with him as the lad loaded the rest of their luggage onto the train. They had the carriage to themselves this time, at least for the start of the journey. Although more passengers joined them at the next few stops.

Jane was eager to return to Half Moon Manor so they could examine the package from the chapel in the relative safety of Arthur's study. She was a little surprised that Arthur had not already peeked at the contents in his room after he had retired for the night.

However, she had noticed that he still seemed exhausted after yesterday's exertions, and she could hear his breathing still sounded rattly even now. He spent the journey with his head back against the train seat, and his eyes closed. Much as she longed to light up a cigarette to pass the time she decided to wait until they arrived back at the station in Exeter.

By the time they pulled into Exeter Central their carriage was as crowded as it had been on the outward journey. They kept their seats until everyone else had left before stepping down onto the platform. Arthur assisted her from the train and Jane looked along the line of green-painted carriages for Benson's black bowler hat and coat.

The station was busy as before with khaki-clad troops boarding the train and sweethearts waving off their loved ones. It took her a few minutes before she spotted the manservant supervising an elderly porter with their luggage.

'Over there, Arthur!' She tugged the sleeve of Arthur's coat and pointed towards Benson.

She started along the platform to go to Benson's aid when someone cannoned hard into her, knocking her off balance and almost pushing her over.

'Oof, be careful...' She started to remonstrate with whoever had bumped into her when she realised that her handbag was being tugged from her shoulder.

Jane grabbed onto the leather strap in an effort to hold on to it, but it was wrenched from her grasp, twisting her wrist as the thief got away. She set off in pursuit but was forced to abandon the chase when she couldn't get through the crowd of people on the platform.

After a moment Arthur caught her up, wheezing and puffing from the unexpected exertion.

'What happened? Are you all right?' he asked, peering anxiously at her.

'Some wretched little toerag just stole my bag. I need to find a policeman.' Jane scanned the crowd trying to see both where the thief might have gone and also for any sign of someone who might be in authority.

'Perhaps the ticket office might be able to help,' Arthur suggested. 'Did you see who it was?'

Jane shook her head. 'I didn't get a look at their face. It looked from the back like an urchin of some kind.' Her injured wrist had started to throb, and she was forced to support it with her other hand.

'Come, let's go and report it.' Arthur led her to the ticket office where he explained to the kind-faced woman in the booth what had happened.

'Oh, dear me. I'll get the first aid box. Take a seat just over there and I'll ask for a call to be put out. There's usually a policeman around somewhere nearby these days.' The woman indicated a vacant wooden bench near the ticket booth.

A moment later they heard the crackle of an announcement over the hubbub of noise within the station asking for a police officer to attend the ticket office. Jane nursed her wrist, moving it gingerly. She winced as she flexed her fingers.

'Is anything broken?' Arthur asked as he sat down beside her. He took her hand in his, his long, clever fingers gently probing her wrist.

'I don't think so. I think it was wrenched when I tried to keep hold of my bag.' Jane flinched when Arthur inadvertently touched a sore spot.

'It's a little swollen, perhaps some strapping would help,' he suggested. He collected the first aid box from the booth and returned to apply some strapping to her wrist. He smoothed the bandage down carefully and sealed it with a strip of plaster.

While ministering to her, a policeman arrived at the booth and the woman pointed him in their direction. Arthur appeared to recollect that he was still holding her wrist and released it suddenly.

Jane had little time to collect herself before she had to give the constable details of what had happened and a description of her bag and its contents.

'Thank you, miss. I'll keep an eye out. Chances are it was an opportunist thief and once they've had the contents of your purse your bag will no doubt be dumped somewhere close by. 'Tis a pity as you didn't get a better look at whoever took it.' The constable tucked his black notebook back inside the breast pocket of his uniform.

'Well, if you could let me know if you find it or the thief, I should be most grateful.' She gave Arthur's address and her own as points of contact if anything should be recovered.

'It really is extremely vexing. My ration book, my cigarettes and my best lipstick were in that bag,' Jane grumbled as the policeman strolled away. 'Not to mention my gas mask.'

'Let's hope no one asks you where your mask is until you can get one reissued. There's Benson with the rest of our luggage. He's no doubt wondering where we've been. We had better hurry, I daresay our connecting train is due at any moment.' Arthur rose from the bench and offered his hand to help her up.

'Thank you.' Jane accepted his assistance before using her good hand to brush any stray pieces of lint from the back of her skirt and they went to meet Benson.

The connecting train was due to go, and they had to hurry to the platform in order to secure a seat. Arthur and Benson were both forced to stand, and Jane was crushed between the carriage wall and a large lady and her shopping. She was glad it was only for a few stops before they could disembark and sort themselves out.

Benson had arranged for Mrs Mullins's son to collect their bags with the local farmer's horse and cart so at least they had a ride back to Half Moon Manor. By the time they reached the house Jane was longing for a strong cup of coffee and a cigarette.

Her wrist was still painful despite the strapping, and it occurred to her that perhaps the theft of her bag had been intentional. She could have been targeted, and the thief may not have been after money. They may have suspected that she was carrying the mysterious parcel they had found in the chapel.

A large black car was parked outside the house when Bendigo pulled the cart to a halt near the front door.

'Isn't that Chief Inspector Thorne's car?' Jane asked as Arthur and Benson assisted her down from the cart.

'It certainly looks like it.' Arthur frowned as he walked towards the front entrance to the house.

The door opened as soon as he was on the step and Mrs Mullins appeared with an agitated expression on her face. She twisted her white apron between her hands as she came to greet them.

'Oh, Mr Cilento, sir, I'm ever so glad as you'm come back.'

'My dear Mrs Mullins, whatever is the matter?' Arthur asked as Jane hurried up behind him.

'I've had to call the police, sir. Someone has burgled the house,' Arthur's housekeeper explained.

'Burgled the house? Has much been taken? My uncle's silver?' Arthur asked as he stepped past the distraught woman into the hall.

'Not as far as I can tell, sir. It was just everything was such a mess. I'd been to the fishmonger as I'd heard as they had some hake. With you all coming back, I thought I'd try and get some for dinner. I weren't away from the manor all that long and when I came back, the door to the scullery had been forced.' Mrs Mullins followed after him as Arthur headed for the kitchen to see the damage for himself.

'Chief Inspector Thorne, I just heard what has happened.' Arthur stopped in the scullery and spoke to the inspector who was crouched down looking at the damaged lock on the back door.

'They seem to have forced this lock. Made quite a mess, I'm

afraid.' The policeman's expression was troubled as he straightened up.

'Arthur, you should check your study. The safe,' Jane said as she entered the kitchen behind him. She scanned the room looking for Marmaduke and relaxed when she saw he was placidly cleaning his paws in front of the range. She had been afraid he might have run away or been hurt in the commotion.

'I only got here a few minutes ago. Your housekeeper said the silver was all still in the butler's pantry and she had already been upstairs and seen that your cufflinks and such are still in their boxes. It's just the house itself that has been turned upside down,' the chief inspector said.

'I see. I'll go and look in my study.' Arthur brushed past Jane as he went to check.

'Now then, Mrs Mullins, perhaps if you could put the kettle on while Mr Benson brings in the luggage. I'm sure we could all do with a cup of tea.' Jane could see the older woman was on the verge of tears at the upset in the house.

'Yes, miss.' The housekeeper moved to do her bidding.

'Perhaps if we go through to the drawing room if you have finished in here, Chief Inspector,' Jane suggested.

The drawing room was also in disarray. The cushions had been thrown from the chairs and drawers left pulled out of the bureau in the corner.

'It seems the burglars were in a hurry. Do you think they were disturbed?' Jane asked the inspector as she quickly tidied the chairs and replaced the seat pads.

She winced as she tried to use her injured hand.

'Please, allow me to assist you, Miss Treen. Have you hurt yourself?' The chief inspector took over straightening the room. He eyed the strapping on her wrist.

'My handbag was snatched at Exeter Central on my way home and I've jarred my wrist,' Jane explained as she took a seat on the chair beside the fire.

'I see.' The chief inspector's eyebrows rose. 'And now you've returned to this burglary.'

'Quite.' Jane could see what he meant.

'My study is a complete mess; all the drawers open in my desk and everything pulled out. The safe is untouched it seems. Although there is nothing in there that would have been of any value to a thief. Just my will, a few share certificates and the house deeds.' Arthur looked around at the now much more orderly drawing room.

He took his usual seat beside the fire on the chair opposite Jane.

'So, nothing of value appears to have been stolen?' the chief inspector asked.

'It wouldn't appear so. Whatever the thieves were searching for, it clearly wasn't money or valuables. The petty cash is still in my study and the silver is untouched.' Arthur was wheezing slightly, Jane presumed from both the shock and his exertions.

The chief inspector took out his notebook and made a note as Benson carried a tray of tea into the room. 'May I commence straightening up your study, sir?' He looked first at Arthur and then to the inspector for permission.

'Chief Inspector?' Arthur asked.

'Very well, if you do discover anything has been taken, please let me know,' the chief inspector said.

Benson placed the tray on the table and left to begin clearing up.

Arthur took on the task of pouring the tea as Jane continued to nurse her injured hand. The chief inspector accepted a cup and sipped it gratefully.

'In view of the earlier incident here, when your house-keeper called to report a robbery, I felt it best to attend myself. Now Miss Treen also tells me that her bag was taken on her way back here today.' Chief Inspector Thorne set his cup back on its saucer and looked at Arthur and Jane.

'Thank you, Chief Inspector. I think we can all agree that these incidents are not a coincidence,' Arthur said. 'Not unless you can tell us that there has been a spate of burglaries in the village or a rise in thefts at the station.'

'The only crime in the village locally is, I believe, the theft of a bicycle from outside the library, some washing gone from a line and a fight at New Year's Eve outside the local hostelry,' Chief Inspector Thorne confirmed.

'Then I think we may safely assume that these issues are all probably connected with Polly's murder.' Arthur stirred his tea.

Jane surveyed her own beverage gloomily and wished it were coffee. She could also very much have used a cigarette.

'I take it that whatever the thief or thieves were searching for was not here or in Miss Treen's bag?' the chief inspector asked.

'No,' Jane replied.

The telephone in Arthur's study rang out. A moment later Benson entered the room. 'That was the police at Exeter, miss. Your bag has been recovered from a hedge not far from the station. It seems the contents are all intact apart from your purse.' He paused. 'Oh, and your cigarettes.'

'Thank you, Benson. I take it I shall need to go to the police station in Exeter to retrieve it?' Jane asked.

'I'm afraid so, miss,' the manservant confirmed before returning to the study.

'At least your bag has been recovered,' Arthur remarked.

'I shan't have the awful faff of sorting out a new ration book or identity card I suppose,' Jane remarked gloomily.

'I can speak to my colleagues and see if someone could drop it off here. It would save you the bother of having to go back into the city,' Chief Inspector Thorne offered.

'That's very kind of you, thank you.' Jane hesitated for a moment. 'We learned just before we went to Cornwall that someone had been impersonating me here, in the village, a few days after Polly was killed.'

The chief inspector's brow lowered. 'I see, and you are only making me aware of this now?' he asked.

Jane could tell by his tone that he was cross. 'There was a matter of some urgency in Cornwall that we had to follow up. I do apologise, Chief Inspector, it slipped our minds.'

She saw Arthur look at her when she used the collective term.

'Then perhaps, Miss Treen, Mr Cilento, you might oblige me by filling in that omission for me now.' The chief inspector took his notebook out once again.

Jane told him what they had learned from Father Dermott.

'I see, and you think you may know who this woman might be I take it?' Chief Inspector Thorne looked thoughtful.

'There is someone from our department in London who has gone missing. She was thought possibly killed in one of the bombing raids at the start of the new year.' Jane explained about Maura and her possible connection to Polly.

'You can see our dilemma, Chief Inspector,' Arthur said when Jane had finished. 'As you know this is all tied in with national security.'

The policeman sighed and scratched a spot behind his ear with the end of his pen. 'During this jaunt over the county border, did you learn anything there that might be relevant to the murder?'

'Only that the man who stayed here at Christmas had also visited Trelisk,' Jane said. She wished she knew exactly what had been going on between her agents. She also wished she knew where Richard Trent, or Georgie Porgie as he'd been in Operation Exodus, was now. She was still waiting on the brigadier for information.

'I take it that this burglary and the taking of your bag at Exeter are all connected with this Richard Trent and the murder. Presumably the murderer is attempting to retrieve something and believes you possess it?' The chief inspector's keen gaze rested on Jane's face.

'We think that is so, yes,' Jane replied.

'I shan't ask what this item might be. My only request to you is that if anything comes to you at all, be it information, physical evidence, etcetera, that you inform me. Immediately,' the chief inspector emphasised.

'We will,' Arthur promised as the policeman returned his book to his pocket and finished his now almost cold cup of tea.

CHAPTER SIXTEEN

'I think it is high time that we took a good look at whatever was concealed inside the chapel at Trelisk,' Jane said as soon as the chief inspector was gone.

'I agree.' Arthur went out to speak to Benson and returned a few minutes later with the package.

Jane closed the curtains and turned on the lights. The daylight was almost gone, and she had no wish for them to be fined for showing a light in the blackout. Arthur moved the tea tray to one side of the coffee table so there was room for them to empty out the contents of the battered brown-paper parcel.

He used his paperknife carefully to cut the string and folded back the paper. A small black notebook and a bundle of what seemed to be blueprints lay inside the wrapper.

'What on earth?' Jane looked at Arthur.

He picked up the plans first and opened them up fully so they could both see what they were.

Jane sucked in a breath. She really could have used a cigarette right now if those were what she thought they were.

'Are those the plans for a new aircraft?' Arthur frowned at the blueprints.

'Not so much new, as some important modifications to our current aircraft.' Jane's tone was clipped.

She had heard whispers around Whitehall that there were problems with one of their planes. The best engineers had been working on a way to reduce the incidents of breakdowns and fatalities.

'Then how and why did they end up inside a disused offertory box? Have these gone missing, do you know?' Arthur's brow creased in perplexity.

'I have no idea. Are they copies, do you think, or originals?' Jane asked. If originals, then whoever had taken them must have stolen them with a view to delaying the installation of the improvements. If they had been concealed by her own agents, then a wish to delay made no sense to her. Surely, if her agents had recovered them, they would have sent them back to the ministry. Jane couldn't imagine that one of her agents would betray their own country like this. There had to be another reason.

'I'm not sure. I suspect they must be copies. There are hand-written annotations of some kind here, look.' Arthur looked closely at the documents.

'Were they taken to give to the enemy?' Jane asked. Surely Anna had not been complicit in such a terrible betrayal, or why had she left a clue to help Jane find them?

'Probably, but then why would our own people have hidden them away?' The lines on Arthur's brow deepened as he voiced Jane's own thoughts.

'Unless, someone else stole them and then Polly or one of the others recovered them and needed to place them somewhere safe. If they couldn't find a way to get them back to the office.' Jane tried out a theory.

'They could have simply destroyed them,' Arthur said.

'Not if they believed them to be the originals,' she

suggested. 'That notebook, what does it say? There may be an explanation in there.'

Arthur folded the blueprints in half and picked up the notebook before Jane could get it.

'It seems to be a diary from last year.' Arthur squinted at the pages covered with a spider-like scrawl of black ink.

'Whose diary? What does it say?' Jane tried to get closer so she could see the contents more clearly. Honestly, Arthur was so slow with this kind of thing.

'It's in code.' Arthur continued to examine it carefully.

'Well, you can crack it, surely? That is what you are good at.' Jane was aware that she sounded a little peevish, but it was so tantalising to have got this far to hit yet another stumbling block.

'It isn't that simple. It may take me a little time. It all depends on whether it's a pattern that I'm already familiar with.' Arthur glared at her.

'Right, of course, I apologise,' Jane said.

Arthur appeared a little mollified by her apology. 'There's no name at the front of the book and it seems it was only started from February last year.'

'What date in February?' Jane asked.

'The twentieth.' Arthur leafed through the pages.

'That would be around the time problems started occurring with Operation Exodus,' Jane said. 'This book has to contain details about the murders.'

The drawing room door opened, and Benson entered. 'Your study is now in order again, sir.'

'Thank you, Benson. Can you bring me my notebook, a pencil and the red-covered notebooks from the bottom drawer of the desk, please?' Arthur asked.

'Of course, sir.' Benson withdrew and returned moments later with the items Arthur had requested.

Jane could see Arthur was about to start attempting to

decode the diary. She couldn't help but feel somewhat surplus to requirements. She also desperately needed a cigarette and a cup of coffee, and it seemed that neither of those things were to be immediately forthcoming.

'Right, well I'll go and telephone the brigadier, shall I? See if he has anything he can tell me about Maura?' She looked at her watch. Stephen had probably left for home by now and the brigadier would be at his desk for at least another hour. It surely should be reasonably safe to call.

'Hmm, yes, feel free.' Arthur had opened his notebooks and was busy comparing the code in the diary to the samples he already had.

Jane rolled her eyes and went off to his study to make her telephone call. Benson had drawn the curtains, so the room was in darkness as she entered. She turned on the green shaded desk lamp and took a seat on the office chair.

She dialled the number for the office and waited for the switchboard to connect her. After a moment the brigadier's familiar booming tone reached her and she moved the receiver a fraction away from her ear.

'Good evening, sir. Are you free to talk?'

'Jane, my dear, I received your telegram. Where are you?'

'I'm back at Half Moon Manor. We have recovered certain items from Cornwall which may be of interest.' She kept her conversation general just in case there might be someone lurking at the brigadier's end who could overhear the conversation.

'Jolly good show.'

'Arthur is working on the one part of our discovery now as coding is involved,' Jane explained.

'I see. What is the other part?' the brigadier asked.

'Blueprints for a modification to aircraft,' Jane responded, keeping her reply succinct.

There was a moment's silence and she wondered if the connection had dropped.

'Do you have a number on the bottom right corner of the plans?' the brigadier asked.

'One moment.' Jane rested the receiver on the desk and hurried across the hall to the drawing room. She whisked the plans up from the coffee table and scuttled back. 'Yes, sir. 129B.'

'Thank you. I take it you have a safe place to keep hold of those until I give you further instructions?' he asked.

'Yes, sir. Arthur can lock them in his safe. There was a burglary here at the house today and my bag was snatched when I got off the train at Exeter. There have also been other worrying incidents.' She explained about the woman who had impersonated her.

'That is most troubling. I fear you may be right to think the woman is Maura Roberts. You were not injured when your bag was stolen, I hope, my dear?' The brigadier sounded concerned.

'My wrist was jarred but other than that I'm fine. Nothing was taken from the manor.' Jane allowed this piece of information to speak for itself.

'Hmm, I take it the police have been? That chap, Thorne, is it?'

'Yes, sir. Has there been any news on Richard Trent or Maura's whereabouts?' Jane asked.

'Nothing as yet on Maura. Trent is overseas. As soon as I know something more I'll be in touch. I take it you intend to remain in Devon for now?' the brigadier asked.

'Yes, sir.' Jane thought she could hear the distant sound of explosions and the tinny wail of a siren at the brigadier's end. The line began to crackle ominously.

'Be careful, Jane. I must go.' The call ended abruptly, and Jane hoped her superior would leave his office in time to reach the safety of a shelter.

She replaced the receiver on the handset and picked up the

blueprints. The number on the corner presumably must mean something to the brigadier. Had they made several copies with different numbers so they could trace who had each one?

She took the plans back through into the drawing room where Arthur was busy scribbling in his notebook, while frowning at the diary.

'I've updated the brigadier. He's asked that these are secured in the safe until he gives us new instructions,' Jane said. 'Trent is abroad. There's no news on Maura, although he agrees with our theory that she is the one who impersonated me.'

'What? Oh yes, of course.' Arthur didn't bother to look up from his work.

'Have you solved it yet?' She tried to see what he was doing.

'Sort of. I'm just, yes, that could be, hmm,' he muttered crossly, clearly annoyed by the interruption.

Frustrated, Jane seated herself back on the chair opposite Arthur's and relieved her feelings by drumming the fingers of her uninjured hand on the arm of the chair.

'Do stop that, Miss Treen. It's a very annoying habit of yours.' Arthur glanced up at her after a few minutes.

'Arthur, as we have been working together for a few days now, do you not think it is time you called me Jane rather than Miss Treen?' she said.

Arthur looked up at her distractedly, then with a half-smile nodded his head.

'Dinner will be served in thirty minutes, sir, miss.' Benson had appeared silently in the room. He turned to Jane. 'I've taken the liberty of acquiring these for you.' He offered her a packet of cigarettes.

She pounced on them joyfully. 'You are a lifesaver, Benson. Thank you.'

'Not at all, miss.'

She noticed Arthur didn't appear to be very pleased by his manservant's gift, but Jane could have hugged the man.

'Mrs Mullins said to tell you that she has restored order to the kitchen, and nothing is missing.' Benson inclined his head towards Arthur and left the room once more.

Jane helped herself to one of the paper spills from the small Benares brass jar on the mantelpiece. She lit one end from the fire and used it to light a cigarette before dropping the burning shred of paper onto the coals.

'That feels better,' she declared after taking a few puffs from her cigarette.

Arthur rolled his eyes and gave a pointed cough.

Jane contented herself with enjoying her cigarette. Even her wrist had started to feel less sore, no doubt because she was more relaxed. She watched Arthur as he continued to mutter to himself, flicking back and forth between the pages in one of his red notebooks.

It was all very annoying that she wasn't able to help him. She was impatient to know what was in the diary and who it had belonged to. After watching in silence for several minutes she couldn't help herself after he made yet another pencil squiggle in his notes.

'Well?' she asked.

'I'd be quicker if you didn't keep interrupting me,' Arthur snapped irritably.

'Well, is there something I can do?' she asked.

He lifted his gaze from the notes and glared at her. 'Yes, stop annoying me. I need to focus.'

'In that case, I am going to dress for dinner and add more strapping to my wrist,' Jane declared. Perhaps by the time Benson sounded the dinner gong Arthur might have some answers for her. If he took much longer, she might have to take up decoding herself!

* * *

Arthur scarcely noticed Jane's departure from the drawing room. The code wasn't especially complex, but it seemed to be a combination of a couple of things he'd seen before. Whoever had written the diary had clearly known what they were doing.

He continued to work without any regard to time until Jane reappeared in the drawing room having changed from the tweed suit she had travelled in, to a more formal dark-blue velveteen dress.

'Have you anything nicer for a pre-dinner aperitif than this disgusting sherry?' She rattled the few bottles and decanters on the small drinks trolley in the corner of the room.

He frowned, ready to tell her off, when Benson called them through to the dining room.

'Dinner is served, sir, miss.' The manservant raised his silver eyebrows at the pile of scribbled notes surrounding Arthur's chair and the large schooner of sherry in Jane's now re-bandaged hand.

'Thank you, Benson.' Jane followed the manservant into the cool and dimly lit dining room, leaving Arthur to bring up the rear. He rather resented having to stop working to eat, when he had just started to reach some interesting entries in the diary. Miss Treen, or Jane as he now thought of her, might be a nuisance but she had brought him a wonderful puzzle.

CHAPTER SEVENTEEN

Dinner, in Jane's opinion, went on for far too long. She was impatient for Arthur to return to his task of decoding the diary. Having the work interrupted by an indifferent fish course, some tinned peaches and a glass of quite frankly diabolical sherry was most inconvenient.

It didn't help that Arthur had to be one of the slowest diners on earth. His insistence on seemingly chewing every morsel of food for what felt like forever had her half wishing he would choke on a fishbone.

Eventually they were done and able to return to the drawing room. Benson at least managed to produce some coffee. With a cup of her favourite beverage and an after-dinner cigarette, Jane settled down to wait for Arthur to continue his work.

She watched him for a while as he continued to scribble and search in his books.

'Interesting.' Arthur paused in his work and looked at Jane. 'This diary is in two parts. The first, earlier part has been written by a different hand to the second part.' He showed her what he meant.

She could see immediately that the earlier writer had neater handwriting. The second section was written in a more crabbed and untidy style without the loops and flourishes in the first half.

'Do you know who the writers were yet?' Jane asked.

'I believe the first writer was the man you said had been killed during Operation Exodus. Peter Piper, the radio operative?' Arthur looked at her for confirmation.

'Yes, that was his code name. He was shot during a raid on the house where he was staying. We believe someone betrayed his whereabouts to the enemy.' Jane sighed, her gaze lingering on the worn and battered diary. 'Then who retrieved this and why did they continue writing in it?'

'I've managed to decipher the first part. It started off just as a record of activity from February. Who was where, messages, code names I assume of personnel who had passed through the line and had made it out.'

Jane frowned. 'All highly irregular, even if he did record it all in code. That kind of information would be jolly useful in the wrong hands.'

'As I said, it started off like that but then the entries changed. They started to refer to problems with the operation.' Arthur flicked forward several pages. 'This passage here, for instance,' he said, and handed her the notebook.

Since Jane had no idea how the code worked, Arthur showing her the page was of no consequence. 'What does it say?'

'He mentions that he thinks something is wrong. They have had a couple of near misses, only avoided because they had changed their plans right at the last minute. He talks of being fearful that they are being betrayed.'

'Does he say who by?' Jane leaned forward in her seat. It would have been helpful to have a name.

'No, just that he is certain that the root cause of the problem is not on the ground, but is coming from the instructions they are receiving from command in London,' Arthur said.

'Peter was the wireless operator. He would get the messages on who was to be collected from Berlin and the route they were to take. He would liaise with the resistance movement, and I think Lucy Locket was his immediate other contact. She spoke several languages fluently.' Jane could see that so far everything Arthur had decoded seemed to tally with what they knew already. Lucy's murder later on back in London had been a bad blow.

'These are almost the last entries in his handwriting,' Arthur continued. 'There seems to have been another operation planned. He writes that he is concerned that this may be a set-up.'

A shiver ran along Jane's spine. 'And there is definitely no mention of anyone in particular? No name that has cropped up at all?'

'No, he says he has discussed his concerns with "LL" and they are of the same mind,' Arthur said.

'That must be Lucy Locket then, who was the second agent who was killed. I was right then; she was his immediate contact on the ground. I had assumed that whoever was committing these murders was trying to avenge Peter in some way,' Jane said. 'Those notes with the biblical quotes referring to Exodus left with the bodies in London all seemed to point in that direction.'

Arthur nodded slowly. 'My mind was on the same track as yours until I started to decode this diary. The "eye for an eye" reference in the notes seemed to point to vengeance of some kind. However, that doesn't seem to be true. I think those quotes may all have been a clever ruse to steer us away from the real purpose of the murders. A smokescreen.'

'And what purpose do these deaths serve? Why these

agents?' Even as she asked the question Jane suspected she knew at least part of the answer.

'All these incidents, everything that's happened so far, it can't just be the work of one person. There is something about Operation Exodus in particular that is behind it all, but I don't know what that is yet. I do think there is a tangled web here of people who wish to see us lose this war.' Arthur's tone was grave.

'Where there is a web there is usually a big, fat spider at its centre. We need to find the spider.' Jane shuddered. 'Do you know who the second author is?'

'I haven't a name, but I think it may be Georgie Porgie, the man who has been calling himself Richard Trent. There are not many entries in his hand, but they finish just before the diary was stashed at the church. He ran out of pages. It's a one-year diary so the very last entries are hard to decipher as he has squashed them onto the back couple of end papers.' Arthur frowned and picked up his magnifying glass to get a better look at the writing.

'It says he recovered the diary from LL. It was given to her for safe keeping with instructions to pass it to him if anything happened to Peter. The code was one he and Peter developed when they did basic training together before they left for their various postings. No one else knew of it. It's clear that LL had no idea what the contents of the book said. Peter just warned her to be very careful.'

'That at least explains how the diary came to be in England and how it ended up in the chapel. What else does it say?' Jane asked.

Arthur squinted at the crabbed writing through the lens. 'He collected the diary from LL in London, after she said she thought she was being watched. Two days after he took it, she was killed. He heard that everyone involved with Operation

Exodus was being moved. He was sent on a short mission abroad, returning back to England just before Christmas.'

'That's true, Polly and Anna came here. He would have been sent abroad I think at around the same time. I had no instructions to place him in a safe house. Then he found out where they were. Does it say anything about that?'

Arthur turned back to the earlier, pre-Christmas entries. 'He got a note from Polly. Lucy's death had scared her, and she thought she was in danger here at the manor. She wasn't even certain if she could trust Anna.'

'So, he arrived here for Christmas, and they hatched this plan, presumably as a kind of insurance of some sort?' Jane speculated, wishing there was more information in the brief entries.

'Your placing Anna and Polly here, was that just down to the murders? Or did something else influence your decision?' Arthur peered at her, blinking myopically after adjusting his gaze from the magnifying glass.

'I was worried by the murders and the notes. I discussed the matter with the brigadier, and we arranged the safe house, this house, without telling anyone else in the department. As I said, Georgie Porgie who we believe to be Richard Trent, was being posted and the other agent was abroad already.' Jane shifted uncomfortably in her seat.

'But was that all?' Arthur persisted.

Jane blew out an exasperated sigh. 'Very well, I also had an anonymous tip-off. A telephone call claiming the agents were in danger.'

A gleam entered Arthur's eyes. 'A male voice?'

'Yes, and it sounded as if it were coming from a telephone booth. Somewhere noisy. At a guess I would have thought a busy street or possibly at a train station.' Jane sighed again. 'I keep thinking there was something more I should have done. I placed Anna with Polly to protect her and give her some company. I'm certain Anna is completely trustworthy and she wasn't known to any of the Operation Exodus people. Her leaving the guidebook with Father Dermott was the only safe way she felt she could get information to me.'

'Plus Anna couldn't have murdered Polly as she was already overseas when Polly was killed. Maura Roberts was not involved in these decisions?' Arthur asked.

Jane took out one of her precious cigarettes and used another of the newspaper spills from the mantelpiece to light it. 'No, the decision was above her level. The brigadier and I were keen to try to shut down any possibility of a leak. As few people as possible were informed of our plan.'

'What about the brigadier's secretary? What did you say his name was?'

Jane blew out a thin plume of smoke, taking care to direct it away from Arthur. 'Stephen? No, Stephen was also not involved. I don't like Stephen much, but he works closely with the brigadier and if there was any hint at all of him being unreliable, he would not be in that office. The only people who made any of the arrangements were me and the brigadier.'

Arthur leaned back in his chair, the diary temporarily forgotten. 'Yet, the man calling himself Richard Trent came here and Anna thought that Polly had invited him. Why would Polly do that? She presumably knew how perilous her situation was? Diana said she thought Anna was uneasy and Polly was nervous.'

Jane frowned. 'Yes, she did, and Polly wasn't stupid. She was an experienced agent as you know. A love affair perhaps? She clearly trusted him. Is there anything more in the diary that tells us of their relationship?' She looked at the book still resting on Arthur's knee.

Arthur picked up his magnifying glass once more and peered at the entries. 'PF contacted me sent a note. Worried her safety breached and not sure if can trust A. Can't contact Uncle as leak in office may be MT.'

'Uncle is the brigadier. MT? Did she mean me?' Jane shot forward again, aghast at the idea that Polly might even have considered that she was the traitor.

Arthur looked reprovingly at her. 'You can't blame them for not being certain. Especially since you say only yourself and the brigadier knew of the arrangements.'

Jane dropped back in her armchair and extinguished her cigarette, stubbing it out fiercely in the chrome ashtray that had mysteriously reappeared next to her seat whilst they had been at dinner.

'What does Richard have to say about these blueprints? Where have they come from and why were they with the diary?' she asked.

Arthur held the glass and diary closer to the lamp. He turned the pages back to the end papers of the diary. 'I'm struggling to make this out. Hold on for a moment.'

Jane fidgeted as Arthur made notes in his book as he tried to decipher the cramped, coded writing.

'The last entry is the day he went to Trelisk between Christmas and New Year and left the book in the church. He says Polly recovered the blueprints here in the village.' He looked at Jane.

'Here? But who here would have access to these?' She picked up the plans and waved them at him. 'Who is it?'

'He doesn't say. He says he is leaving them in the church for safe keeping. He has a new assignment and Polly and Anna are being sent away again. This is the only record of what has happened.' Arthur closed the diary. 'That's it, I'm afraid. I don't know if he believed he was going to be able to retrieve these or if the clue that Anna left in the guidebook was some sort of insurance policy. You said there is one more agent from Operation Exodus out there?'

'Yes, but they are in deep cover as far as I know and not in this country. I have a high level of security clearance but that doesn't mean that I am party to everything that goes on at Whitehall.' She desperately wanted to light another cigarette to help her think but was mindful that the small packet might have to last her for some time.

She put her head in her hands. 'How did Polly get those blueprints? Who from? From the context of the words in that diary it sounds as if she removed them from someone who shouldn't have had them. Then, with no secure way to get them back to their rightful owner because of everything that was happening, she and Richard hid them at Trelisk. Is that right? Is that what you think has happened?'

Arthur nodded slowly. 'I think they would have given them to you, but with Polly feeling unsafe they couldn't trust that you were not part of whatever we have stumbled upon. There wasn't time to give them directly to the brigadier.'

'We know that Anna and Polly kept to a limited social circle here. They attended church, met the major and presumably went to the shops. Where else could they have gone? Does that mean that someone we have visited was the source of the blueprints?' Jane asked.

'I'm rather afraid that may well be the case. It would also mean that it may not have been a stranger who killed Polly.' Arthur looked tired, fine lines around his mouth gave him a drawn appearance.

Jane was suddenly aware that for her, these people she had met were strangers, but Arthur had known several of them for many years. 'We cannot exclude members of your household from involvement in this I suppose?'

'I think we have to be mindful of the possibilities. It was well known in the village that we were away from the manor, and it would be easy to determine our destination,' Arthur said.

'And the potential purpose of our visit there since other

people had clearly noted Richard Trent's visit to Trelisk,' Jane said.

A bone-heavy weariness settled over her as the events of the day finally made themselves felt.

'I think I should lock everything away in the safe for now. After breakfast tomorrow we can look again and think about what our next course of action should be.' Arthur began to gather everything together.

'Very well,' Jane agreed.

Arthur locked the papers in the safe. He had half expected Jane to put up more of an argument or to insist on burning the midnight oil while trying to work out who could have had the blueprints and where it all fitted in with the agents from Operation Exodus.

Unsurprisingly, he slept badly that night. A recurring dream where Jane Treen's face merged with that of Polly Flinders lying on the mortuary slab had him waking up several times bathed in a cold sweat.

The ever-faithful Benson clearly heard him on the second occasion and knocked softly on the door of his bedroom.

'Are you all right, sir? Do you require any of your medication?' Benson asked, his long, thin face illuminated by the candle he was carrying, presumably to avoid disturbing the household by snapping on the lights.

'I'm fine, thank you, Benson. A bad dream.' Arthur sat up in bed and switched on his bedside lamp before wiping his brow with the palm of his hand. 'I'm sorry, I didn't mean to disturb you.'

'May I get you some hot milk from the kitchen, sir?' his servant asked, a concerned frown creasing his brow.

'Thank you, yes.' Arthur watched Benson depart and pulled his pillows up more comfortably behind his head.

He was wide awake now and he could only hope that a hot, milky drink might prove effective.

Benson was back a few minutes later, candle in one hand still and a blue-and-white striped mug in the other. He placed the mug on the bedside table and produced two biscuits from his dressing gown pocket.

'I thought perhaps a digestive, sir, might help.'

'It's this business of the diary we found in the church,' Arthur confided.

Benson closed the door and stood beside the bed as Arthur crunched on a biscuit. He told his manservant of the contents of the package they had retrieved from Trelisk. He knew if there was anyone he could trust it was Benson. They had worked together for many years, since Arthur had been a boy.

'I see, sir, it is most disturbing. I assume the inference must be that someone you know well in the village is an enemy agent?' Benson's face was grave.

'I think that conclusion is inescapable, but who and why?' Arthur finished his biscuit and brushed some of the crumbs from his counterpane.

'I expect Miss Treen and her cat will be staying with us for a while longer then, sir?' Benson asked.

'What? Oh yes, I expect she will. This whole business suggests that there is quite a network of people involved. She will need to investigate it further before reporting back to the brigadier,' Arthur said unhappily.

At this point, having Jane stay longer was the least of his concerns. Benson bade him goodnight and Arthur tried to go back to sleep.

CHAPTER EIGHTEEN

Jane woke the next morning with a new sense of purpose. The decoding of the diary had been shocking and the extent of what lay before them was quite daunting. It was awful to discover that her own agents had not trusted her. She was, however, determined that she was going to bring Polly's killer to justice and to ensure that no possible cloud could besmirch her own good name. It was bad enough that someone had already tried to impersonate her.

A knock at the front door of the manor shortly after breakfast restored her handbag so she was at least able to give Mrs Mullins her ration book. It also meant she had her lighter, her gas mask and her treasured fountain pen and lipstick back. The theft of her purse and her cigarettes, however, was quite frustrating.

Arthur did not appear at the breakfast table, so she took the opportunity to share a few titbits of her breakfast with Marmaduke in the dining room. Benson informed her that his master had not slept well so would be rising later. Jane decided to put her time to good use, telephoning the local branch of her bank to arrange to go and collect some money from there later in the day.

The delivery of her handbag was followed shortly after breakfast by the arrival of a rather breathless and windswept Georgette Darnley.

'Golly, it's brass monkeys out there this morning,' the girl exclaimed as Benson showed her into the drawing room, where Jane was enjoying her post-breakfast cigarette.

'It does look rather bleak,' Jane agreed, glancing out at the grey, dull scene outside the sitting room window.

Georgette advanced towards the fire and held her hands out appreciatively to the blaze. 'I'm so sorry to arrive unexpectedly like this but the major asked me to call in and invite you and Arthur to tea this afternoon.'

'That's most kind of him. I'm sure Arthur will be delighted. He isn't downstairs yet so I shall answer for both of us,' Jane said. Some colour seemed to be returning to the girl's pale cheeks as she began to warm up.

'Bendigo told me that you'd had your handbag stolen at the station in Exeter.' Georgette looked at her, clearly hoping for a little more information.

Jane considered that for a man who was non-verbal, Bendigo Mullins certainly had a way of spreading gossip.

'Yes, the police have recovered it. They actually dropped it off this morning, although obviously my purse and my cigarettes were taken.' Jane gestured towards her bag.

'What beastly bad luck,' Georgette sympathised. 'I say, did you hurt your hand too?' She looked at the strapping on Jane's wrist.

'I jarred it a little trying to keep hold of my bag,' Jane admitted.

'Gosh, such a shocking thing to happen. I suppose with the station being so busy these days with the troops moving through on their way to and from Dartmoor and Exmoor for training, these things will happen from time to time,' Georgette said.

'I suppose so.' Jane, however, was quite sure this was no random attack. 'Although, the police didn't seem to know of any other incidences there recently.'

Georgette's cheeks flushed a deeper shade of pink. 'Perhaps there will be more now. I do hope not.'

'So do I. Do you go to the station often?' Jane asked. She was curious about her sighting of Miss Darnley and Diana Fenwick together there the day they had left for Trelisk. They had appeared to be arguing.

'I have to go into Exeter from time to time on library business.' Georgette had averted her gaze now and was looking at the fire.

'It was very busy. Still, I suppose it gives you the chance to catch up with your friend, Diana. We saw her working at the station.'

Georgette looked uncomfortable. 'Yes, she works on the tea stall. Diana and I are not particular friends though.'

Jane's eyebrows rose slightly at this. Perhaps her impression that the girls had been arguing that day was correct.

'Will you be staying at Half Moon Manor for long, Miss Treen?' Georgette asked. 'It's all been rather awful for you really, I expect, what with your poor cousin and now this.'

'Arthur has kindly said that I may stay here as long as I wish. The bombing has been quite severe near the area where I live, and I must admit I am concerned about returning home straight away.' Jane wondered at how her ability to lie so easily was developing.

'Oh, of course, and it will be company for him too, I expect.'

'He has been most kind. Although with my bag being stolen and the break-in here yesterday, well, I'm starting to think London might be safer after all.' Jane waited for Georgette's reaction. If Bendigo Mullins had told her of the stolen bag, he would have also mentioned the break-in. He had dropped them off while the chief inspector had been at the manor.

'Oh yes, Bendigo did say something about the police. I thought it was about your cousin. Gosh.' Georgette looked really flustered by Jane's mention of the burglary.

The girl glanced at the plain, brown wooden-cased clock on the mantelpiece and emitted a small squeak of alarm. 'Oh, look at the time. I really must dash. I'll see you and Arthur later at the major's house.' Georgette hurried out into the hall and Jane heard her murmuring her thanks to Benson as he handed her things to her.

By the time Arthur emerged downstairs, Georgette was pedalling past the house, presumably either on her way to the library or to the major's house. Jane wondered what had caused the girl to run off so quickly. Did she know something about the break-in?

'You just missed your lady friend,' Jane announced as Arthur entered the drawing room. 'She came with an invitation to the major's house for tea.'

'Oh, right.' Arthur looked confused.

'Georgette Darnley,' Jane expanded, guessing that Arthur hadn't a clue who she was talking about. Honestly, the man had no idea about the social norms.

'Miss Darnley, right, yes of course. She assists him with various matters, as you know. I take it you accepted?' he asked, frowning slightly.

'Well, of course. I fully intend to get to the bottom of where those blueprints came from and why my good name is being somehow besmirched.' She couldn't help sounding upset.

'Right, yes, of course. Good idea. I suppose we shall have to start somewhere.' Arthur took a seat in his favourite armchair, his gaze alighting on Jane's now slightly scuffed patent leather handbag. 'I see the police have returned your bag,' he said.

'Yes, and I've already arranged to call at the bank this afternoon for some money. We can stop off there on our way to the major's house,' Jane explained. 'Now, our other suspects—'

'Stop for a minute. Suspects? You mean the Fenwicks, I suppose?' The furrows deepened on Arthur's brow, illustrating his distaste for having to consider his neighbours as possible traitors and murderers.

'Well, yes, amongst others. We know they had contact with Polly and Anna. Then, of course, there is Mrs Mullins and her son, although I am inclined to believe them not to be involved. I don't see how they could have obtained confidential military blueprints.' Jane paced about the Turkish carpet.

'I'm glad to hear you have at least ruled a few people out. Especially as they are my household staff,' Arthur said.

'I didn't say I'd ruled them out. Just that they were very low on my list of suspects.' Jane ignored Arthur's horrified expression.

'Who else is on this list of yours?' Arthur asked. 'Benson?'

She ignored his sarcasm. 'I suppose Father Dermott has to be considered. He could have already opened the package Anna gave him and seen the clue for himself,' Jane said thoughtfully. She didn't really wish to consider the kindly priest as being suspicious but in the interests of fairness she had to take him into account.

'And then he tipped off someone who was at Trelisk when we went there and whoever looked for the diary and blueprints before?' Arthur said. 'Yes, I suppose it is possible. He could have killed Polly too. She may have known Anna had given him the guidebook and arranged to meet him to get it back.'

A shiver ran along Jane's spine. Everything they were considering was perfectly plausible. 'But how would he get hold of the blueprints?' she asked.

'He didn't. Don't you see? That was why he would have wanted someone to go to Trelisk to retrieve them.' Arthur blinked at Jane. 'He could have murdered Polly thinking they had it in the bag, and she would be unable to give them away.'

'With Anna having gone overseas you mean?' Jane said.

'Then, when whoever he is working with was unable to locate the blueprints, he gave you Anna's parcel knowing that we would follow it up.' Arthur leaned back in his chair.

Jane perched herself down on the edge of the seat opposite Arthur. 'But didn't the diary imply that Polly had discovered the papers somewhere here? If it was Father Dermott who had the documents, then how and where did he get them from? And it was Anna who knew him, not Polly. As far as we know Polly had no contact with him at all while she was here. It was Anna who went to his house with the parcel and attended his church.'

Arthur templed his hands together as if considering her points. 'Hmm, I suppose so. We could make a case for Andrew Fenwick too, couldn't we.'

'Yes, he knew Polly well. Again, she attended his church, and both he and Diana were friendly with her. Suppose someone gave Diana those blueprints? She works at the station, so she is in contact with a lot of military personnel. It would be easy for them to give her a parcel to pass on.' Jane was troubled by the thought, but she could see how it would work.

'Then Polly found it at the vicarage and stole them?' Arthur asked.

'Yes, she could have asked Anna to ensure they were safe since she knew her own life was potentially in danger,' Jane said.

'But then why would she have returned here to meet someone she didn't trust? Polly was too experienced an agent for that,' Arthur countered.

'The message could have reached her from someone pretending to be someone she trusted. Tricked her into meeting. Also, remember those Bible quotes in the messages,' Jane said, although those could be applied to Father Dermott too.

'Very well, we will allow that as a possibility,' Arthur agreed, although Jane could see he really didn't care for any of her ideas so far. She knew he would like her next suggestion as a suspect even less.

'Then we have your old friend, the major,' Jane said.

Arthur frowned. 'Seriously?'

'We have to consider everyone, however unlikely, you said so yourself. He's a retired military man. He has the contacts and could have managed to lay his hands on those plans. He was friendly with both Anna and Polly. Whoever is behind all of this is good at planning. You know yourself that he was a military strategist.' Jane hated having to even imply that Arthur's old friend was a possibility, but he did fit all the criteria to make him a plausible suspect.

'I suppose then we also have to lob Miss Darnley into the frame too since she is a regular visitor to the major's house?' Arthur's distaste for this line of discussion was writ large on his face.

'She also goes to the station in Exeter regularly. I saw her there the day we left for Trelisk talking to Diana Fenwick. She behaved very strangely this morning when I suggested she and Diana were friends.' Jane jumped to her feet again, too restless to remain seated.

'And I suppose your theory is that she could have received the papers from someone at the station?' Arthur asked.

'Or she could be working with either the major or with Diana Fenwick,' Jane said.

'Hmm, there is a case to be made for all of them, although at the moment Father Dermott stands out in my mind. He is Irish after all and you know the history between Ireland and England has always been troubled,' Arthur said.

'True, but it doesn't feel right. I've always found that hunches can carry almost as much weight as anything else when working in the field.' Jane fiddled with the Staffordshire porcelain dogs on the mantelpiece.

'I much prefer scientific evidence over a hunch,' Arthur remarked drily.

'Well seeing as we have neither, what shall we do now? Obviously, we have our invitation to tea this afternoon, but what about the others? We need to find out who is behind all of this.' Jane turned around to face him once more.

'I agree, but it will take a little thought. We need to know more about the blueprints. You said the brigadier was looking into that?' Arthur said.

'Yes. If we can trace where they came from, we might be able to work out how they came to fall into Polly's hands.'

'Then we might get to unravel who is behind all of this. My concern is, if we go blundering about, we could end up netting the small fry and let our bigger fish escape.'

Jane smiled. 'With our talk of fish and spiders we shall have a veritable zoo on our hands.'

'True. You said you had an appointment at the bank?' Arthur asked.

'Yes, we can call on our way to the major's house. My appointment is for two o'clock. What are your plans for this morning?' Jane eyed him curiously.

'I shall finish decoding the diary, just in case there is anything in there that we may have missed last night. What about you?' He looked at Jane.

'Annoyingly I am at somewhat of a loose end until after lunch. I want to revisit Father Dermott, but before you say anything, I know that wouldn't be terribly prudent just yet.' She held her hand up to prevent him from speaking. She could see the warning trembling on the end of his tongue. 'Actually, I rather think what I might do is take a stroll into the village. If I am to be here for a little longer perhaps a library book might help me pass the time.'

Arthur sighed. 'And you will do a little digging about Georgette whilst you are there, no doubt.'

Jane left Arthur to lock himself away inside his office, and put
on her hat and coat to walk to the library. She had noticed the
building the day before when they had ridden through the
village on Bendigo Mullins's borrowed pony and cart.

It was a modern, square red-brick single-storey building
with cream-coloured Portland stone steps leading to heavy
wooden and glass doors. Jane stepped smartly up the steps and
pushed on the ornate brass plate to open the door. The wind
was quite nippy, and she had no desire to dawdle on the steps.

An older woman with her hair in a low roll at the nape of
her neck glanced up from behind the desk as she entered.

'May I help you?' she asked as Jane approached the desk.

'Good morning, yes. I'm staying at Half Moon Manor in the
village and wondered if I might get a library membership?' Jane
asked.

The woman pursed her lips. 'Will you be a permanent resi-
dent here?'

Jane decided to fudge the truth a little since she had a
feeling she would be denied membership if she said no. 'I'm not
certain.'

'I see. Hmm, we have been issuing some temporary cards.
The evacuees, you know, and some other displaced persons. It
only permits you to loan two books.' She lifted the glasses which
were dangling from a chain around her neck and placed them
on the bridge of her nose to study Jane's response.

'Oh, I quite understand, that would be marvellous, thank
you.' Jane waited as the woman delved in a drawer below her
desk to produce a form.

'Do you require a pen?' the woman asked as she set the form
in front of her.

'No, thank you.' Jane had been pleased to find that whoever had snatched her handbag at the station had left her trusty fountain pen behind. It had been a gift from her late father, and she was quite attached to it.

The woman watched as Jane completed the form.

'Half Moon Manor, that was where that young woman was killed?' the librarian said as Jane finished and replaced the cap on her fountain pen.

'Yes, my cousin.' Jane felt she should continue the subterfuge that Polly was related to her.

'A very nice young woman. Sad business. She used to call in with her companion to borrow books,' the woman said as she started to fill out a library card.

'She was fond of reading. I think she was friendly with a girl who works here, Georgette Darnley?' Jane said. She had no idea at all if there was any truth in this statement, but she was keen to see if there was a connection they were unaware of.

'Georgette? Oh yes, I believe they were quite friendly at one time, very chatty.' The woman clicked her tongue in disapproval and Jane guessed that chattiness was not necessarily a desirable trait in a library.

'You say they were friendly? Did they have a falling out?' Jane kept her tone casual as the librarian stamped her library card and slid it across the counter towards her. This was a new discovery. It seemed her question was bearing unexpected fruit.

'I don't know that falling out would be the correct phrase, but they went from being very pally-pally, to barely exchanging the time of day just before your cousin surrendered her card and gave up her tenancy at Half Moon Manor,' the librarian said, before launching into a list of rules which Jane was expected to now follow as an official library member.

'Oh dear, that sounds most unlike my cousin,' Jane said.

'Well, you know what young women today are like. I daresay there was a man in the picture somewhere. That's what

usually is behind things.' The librarian shook her head disap-
provingly.

Jane thanked the woman and drifted away to peruse the
library shelves deep in thought. She wandered up and down
between the bookcases. The library appeared to be fairly well-
stocked with a good array of books.

She paused in front of a section that appeared to be devoted
to local interest and folklore. It crossed her mind that it might be
interesting to discover what books Polly had borrowed. Or had
her library membership merely been some kind of cover to talk
to Georgette Darnley?

The librarian had said that Anna had accompanied Polly.
Had she too been a member? Jane selected a book on the
legends of Dartmoor and headed back to the counter.

'You have a wonderful selection of books,' she remarked in a
conversational tone as she slid her book across to be stamped.

'Oh yes. The library is fairly new, a donation from a wealthy
village member made it possible. He left money for it in his will.
His daughter laid the foundation stone,' the librarian informed
her, stamping her card and the paper affixed to the inside front
of the book.

'How very thoughtful.' Jane took back her new library card
and took her time placing it away inside her handbag. 'I didn't
know what to choose. My concentration has been so affected by
Kate's death.'

The librarian looked sympathetic. 'I do understand. I was
just the same when my dear mother passed. Your cousin always
enjoyed factual books too,' she remarked, glancing down at
Jane's selected book. 'Very interested in books on Cornwall she
was, oh and on London too.'

'She was always a big reader as a child.' Jane hoped a bolt of
lightning would not descend and strike her down with all the
tall tales she had been spinning lately.

'Yes, she was in here every week, sometimes her friend would be with her. The foreign lady,' the librarian said.

'Anna? Yes, I'm glad she had some company while she was here.' Jane finally finished tucking her ticket inside the pocket of her bag before picking up her book.

'Another nice lady. I expect she was very upset to hear about your cousin. She used to borrow books about Spain. She said it reminded her of her home.' The librarian tidied away her stamps, closing the lid on the small tin containing the ink pad. 'I hope you enjoy the book, and that it takes your mind off things.'

'Thank you, I'm sure it will.' Jane placed the book in her bag and made her way out of the library.

CHAPTER NINETEEN

Jane was in a thoughtful mood all the way back from the library. Benson answered the door at her first ring of the doorbell to let her into the house. The hallway felt pleasantly warm after the chill of the outdoor air. Arthur, she assumed, was still closeted inside his study looking at the diary.

As she removed her coat and gloves, she heard the telephone ring behind the closed door of the study, followed by a brief murmur of voices. The study door opened, and Arthur popped his head out.

'There is someone called Stephen asking for you,' he informed her in a stiff tone.

Jane placed her coat on the peg and followed him back inside his office.

She picked up the receiver from where Arthur had placed it down on the desktop amongst his papers and notebooks.

'Stephen.'

'Jane, dear heart, out gallivanting about the countryside?' Stephen's languid tones reached her, and she pictured him smirking lazily behind his desk in Whitehall.

'Trying to catch a killer,' she responded crisply. 'I assume you have information for me?'

'The brigadier asked me to telephone. There have been sightings of Maura Roberts.'

Jane's pulse quickened. 'Verified sightings?' She noticed that Arthur, who had gone to stand by the study window, ostensibly to look as if he were not eavesdropping, was obviously listening to the conversation.

'Yes. She has been seen around London at various train stations. We are hoping we can get someone on her tail if we can pick her up in time,' Stephen said.

'I see. That's very interesting. We shall stay alert here too,' Jane responded.

'We?' Stephen asked.

'Mr Cilento and me. I expect I shall be back in the office in a few days' time once this matter is concluded.' Jane ignored the inference in his question. She had no desire to rise to Stephen's rather obvious baiting.

'We have a couple of people watching the stations. The old man said to tell you we are trying to trace an address,' Stephen said.

'Thank you, that would be useful. We really do need to speak to her. We shall stay on the lookout.' Jane wished they could get hold of Maura.

'Jolly good. I'll pass that on and if we discover more, I shall be in touch. Toodle-pip!' Stephen rang off.

Jane replaced the receiver on its hook.

Arthur turned around to face her. 'I presume that was news from Whitehall?' he asked.

'Stephen is the brigadier's secretary. He was calling to say they have verified sightings of Maura at various railway stations around London. They are trying to nab her.' Jane surmised that he had been unable to hear Stephen's part of the conversation.

'Hmm, so she is definitely alive and is up to no good.'

Arthur retook his place behind his desk. 'It does rather confirm what we thought.'

'Yes, I keep feeling there is a connection here, closer to home, that we are missing somehow.' Jane sat herself down on the plain oak chair in front of Arthur's desk.

'I agree. I've been going through all the diary entries while you've been out but nothing more there, I'm afraid. How did you fare at the library?' he asked as he started to gather up his notebooks, stacking them neatly on the corner of the desk.

'It was quite interesting. It seems that your little friend Georgette may not have been entirely truthful about the extent of her friendship with Polly. It's rather worrying, especially as she has since been made aware that Polly was here under an assumed name.' Jane told him what the librarian had said about a quarrel.

Arthur's eyebrows raised as she spoke, betraying his surprise at the information. 'I wonder what they argued about? And how come Georgette never mentioned that she had seen her at the library. Or that they were friendly? I wonder if she knew at the time that Polly wasn't really called Kate?'

Jane shrugged. 'I don't know, but I find her omission rather odd, don't you? The librarian suggested they had fallen out over a man. Richard Trent, perhaps?'

'I'm sure she will be at tea this afternoon so we can always find out more then,' Arthur said.

After lunch, Jane prepared for her appointment at the bank. Arthur, whilst still not appearing very happy about it, agreed to accompany her since they intended to walk straight to the major's house afterwards.

Jane also intended to call and replenish her supply of cigarettes once she had some money. The packet Benson had kindly furnished her with was looking rather depleted, despite her careful rationing.

The sun was attempting to push through the clouds as they set off along the street towards the village centre. It was still bone-chillingly cold and Jane was glad of her gloves. Arthur, as usual, walked somewhat slowly so Jane was forced to curb her usual brisk trot to keep pace with him.

The bank was another modern building, but one which had been built to appear older with a nod to the arts and crafts movement which had been so popular when Jane's parents had been younger. Jane wondered if Stephen had seen her mother again recently. When she returned to London, she would have to bite the bullet and telephone her, much as she didn't want to.

Once inside the building Jane announced her appointment to the young woman teller at the counter and she went off to inform Mr Pegg, the manager, that they were there. The bank manager turned out to be a spritely, elderly gentleman who showed them into his large wood-panelled office with an air of old-world courtesy.

Jane and Arthur seated themselves in front of his desk and declined his offer of tea.

Mr Pegg opened a folder and removed the top from his fountain pen before peering at Jane over the top of his half-moon glasses.

'Now then, my dear, I have ascertained from the manager of your branch in London all the details of your account. It will unfortunately take a little while to be able to issue you with a cheque book, printing problems and paper shortages being what they are. However, I can advance you some money from your account.'

'Thank you, I'm most grateful. I've had a very trying time lately.' Jane was relieved that at least something seemed to be going her way.

'Not at all. I was most disturbed to hear of the death of the young woman at your home, Arthur.' Mr Pegg looked at him before returning his gaze to Jane. 'I understand she was a relation of yours, Miss Treen?'

'My cousin, yes,' Jane said.

'Terrible, terrible. My condolences.' The bank manager clicked his tongue sympathetically. 'Most unheard of in our small village. Then you had your handbag taken in Exeter, shocking. I cannot think what the world is coming to these days.'

'There was a break-in at the manor too,' Arthur said.

Mr Pegg looked horrified at this particular piece of information. 'Appalling. The level of lawlessness.' He shook his head in despair.

'It has all been very distressing. At least nothing was taken from the house, but with that and everything else, I felt the least I could do was assist Jane by inviting her to stay for a while,' Arthur responded.

'Of course, and a break from London too, my dear, with the events there I understand.' Mr Pegg looked sympathetically at her. Jane realised that even though the news was heavily filtered he must have heard of the terrible damage the constant bombardment had done to the city.

'Yes, one hears such bad reports,' Jane said.

'I only had the pleasure of meeting your cousin once during her stay. She came to the bank with a gentleman just before Christmas. A most personable young man.' Mr Pegg finished filling out a document and slid it across to Jane to sign.

'I expect that would be my other cousin. He stayed with her and Anna here for a few days.' Jane signed her name and filled in the amount of money she wished to withdraw.

'I believe he said he was going travelling to see other family members before his leave was up.' Mr Pegg took back the document and unlocked a drawer of his desk to give Jane the money she required. 'I do hope he is not too distressed by the news of your cousin. These young men are so brave, especially our airmen. It's a trying time for us all, isn't it?' He directed the latter part of his question to Arthur who hastened to agree.

Once the money had been counted and checked, Jane stowed it safely in her handbag. She would need to buy a new purse if the shop had any for sale. For now, she would have to use the small pocket in the silk lining to try and keep her money together.

She and Arthur shook hands with Mr Pegg and made their way out of the bank back onto the small high street. The air was even colder than when they had first left the house and tiny needles of ice spattered against the skin on their faces as they walked in the direction of the major's house.

Arthur immediately adjusted his woollen muffler to cover his nose and mouth, burrowing down into the many layers like a mole. Jane bit her tongue to avoid commenting and dived into the small shop that sold tobacco and sweets.

Arthur stood somewhat reluctantly in the doorway while Jane purchased two packets of cigarettes and some peppermints. Once her purchases had been added to her handbag they set off once more. The pavement, already damp, was growing slippery as the temperature dropped.

Despite her usually independent nature, Jane was glad to accept Arthur's offer of his arm as her shoes slid on the icy surface. His arm was surprisingly strong and reassuring.

'It struck me that Polly did actually venture to more places than we were initially led to believe,' Jane observed, hoping Arthur could hear her under his woolly layers.

'Yes.' Arthur's reply was rather muffled, but he nodded as he spoke. He adjusted his scarf a little before adding, 'By the way, when we get to the major's house I think I should lead on this, Jane. He is an old friend, and it needs a sensitive touch.'

Jane rather resented the idea that she didn't have a sensitive touch but decided to let it go. Arthur did know the major better

than she did, so he was probably right. Much as it might irk her
to admit it.

'Very well,' she agreed.

The lights were on in the major's house as they approached,
and Jane guessed the blackout curtains would be closed early
tonight against the weather and the fading light of the afternoon. In fact, she wouldn't be at all surprised if snow wasn't
expected.

Sarah, Major Hawes's maid, opened the door to them, her
cheery face wreathed in smiles. 'Come on inside out of this
terrible weather. I was just about to close up the curtains and
shut out the cold.' She ushered them inside the cottage and
relieved them of their coats and scarves.

'The major is just through here. You know where to go, Mr
Cilento, sir. I'll be along in a minute with the tea. Miss Darnley
will probably be a bit late; she went off on some more errands
for the major and hasn't returned yet,' Sarah informed them as
she stowed their things away.

'Thank you, Sarah.' Arthur looked rather pink cheeked now
he had taken off his woolly layers. His curly dark-blond hair was
rumpled and he reminded Jane of a rosy-faced cherub she'd
seen in one of the pictures in the art gallery when she had been
younger. Arthur led the way through to the comfortable sitting
room they had been in the last time they had called at the
house.

Major Hawes was seated beside the fire as before with
Nero, his dog, sprawled out at his feet.

'Arthur, Jane, I do hope I may call you Jane, my dear? Come
and get warm by the fire. Filthy weather out,' he said as he rose
to greet them.

'Of course. It is rather chilly out today,' Jane assured him,
blushing at the twinkle in the elderly man's eyes.

'I daresay Sarah told you that Georgette might be a bit late.
Sent her off to post some letters and run a few more errands.

Mind you, I don't know what the post is coming to these days. I expect it's the war, things delayed and going missing. Terrible, still, if that's the worst the Jerries can do, we mustn't grumble, eh?' He sat back down heavily in his chair after shaking Arthur's hand and kissing Jane's cheek. Nero opened an eye to look at his master as if checking that he was all right.

The room was warm and snug after the icy cold of their walk and the fire crackled in the grate. The lamps were on, and the room exuded a comfortable calm that felt like a balm to Jane after the last few days.

'Georgette told me you had your bag taken at the station in Exeter?' The major's gaze rested on Jane's bandaged wrist.

'Yes, sir. Fortunately, the police managed to find it. Whoever stole my bag took my purse and my cigarettes. We've just come from the bank now,' Jane explained.

'Dashed nuisance. Diana Fenwick works at the station, doesn't she? Serving tea or something?' the major asked.

'That's right, sir. It's a very busy place now, obviously with all the troops moving through it,' Arthur agreed.

Sarah clattered into the room with a small trolley laden with crockery and a tiered stand containing small slices of cake, sandwiches and tea things. She placed it next to the major's seat and bustled about drawing the curtains.

The room took on a more intimate feel with the curtains closed against the fading daylight. Sarah withdrew and closed the door behind her.

'Jane, my dear, are you able to do the honours?' the major requested.

She applied herself to the teapot and set out the dainty floral china cups on their saucers.

'I've also heard you had a burglary at your house? Georgette was all of a twitter about it when Bendigo told her.' Major Hawes looked at Arthur.

'I'm afraid so. It seems that nothing was actually taken.

Whether Mrs Mullins returned home in time to scare them off, or if they were looking for something more specific, I'm not sure.' Arthur accepted a cup from Jane and added milk.

Major Hawes helped himself to a slice of cake, studying it carefully before adding it to his plate. 'Sarah tells me this was made with beetroot,' he remarked thoughtfully, before returning to the conversation with Arthur. 'By specific, I take it you mean something other than an object of monetary value?'

'It seemed a likely supposition to both of us given what happened to Polly,' Arthur agreed, avoiding the cake and selecting a meat paste sandwich instead.

Jane poured herself a cup of tea, wishing it was coffee, and asked the major if she might have a cigarette. He raised one eyebrow looking at Arthur but gave her permission and offered her a light.

'No one else locally has had a burglary. Mrs Pegg, the bank manager's wife, had some of her underwear stolen from her washing line, I believe, but hardly the same offence.' Major Hawes surveyed them both keenly.

'No, sir. You mentioned earlier having problems with the post? You said things had gone missing?' Jane had caught the mention as they had been settling into their seats and was curious to know what he had meant.

Major Hawes set his cake plate aside on a small table on the other side of his chair and stroked his chin thoughtfully. 'Yes, on a few occasions now I've either not received items I've been expecting or items I've sent back have not been received.'

'Is there any pattern to the missing items, sir?' Arthur asked. He had obviously noticed the purpose behind Jane's questions.

'Sarah usually gets the post and brings it in here for me. Or on the days Georgette is here she does the same thing. Obviously, I don't get out so much in this weather. Gout, terrible affliction, so Georgette takes my post for me. Dashed embarrassing when important stuff doesn't arrive. I've told her not to use the box at the end of the lane but to go directly to the post office,' the major said.

'Personal mail or items which may pertain to the war effort?' Arthur asked.

The major's eyebrows rose slightly, and he gave Arthur a sharp glance. 'Hmm, now you mention it, mainly government documents. I do some consultancy work for various departments. I still have my uses, you know. Some personal material too has gone astray.'

'Forgive me for asking this, sir, but since all of us here are bound by the Official Secrets Act, was one of the missing items a set of aeroplane blueprints?' Jane ignored Arthur's pointed glare.

The major's brow crinkled. 'Yes, I may be too old and decrepit to do much now, but I do have certain areas of expertise that are useful to the country. I had been asked to look at some engineering modifications, a speciality of mine.'

Jane looked at Arthur. It seemed that they may have found where the blueprints had originated from.

'Now, how on earth did you come to that conclusion, my dear?' asked the major.

CHAPTER TWENTY

Arthur could tell by the gleam in Jane's eyes that she had come to the same conclusion he had just drawn about the blueprints. It also explained the cryptic annotations which must have been made by the major. He also knew that they would have to tread very carefully now if he wished to clear his uncle's old friend of any wrongdoing.

'Some information has recently come into our possession,' Arthur said.

'I take it then that if you know something of this matter, either the plans have been found or, worst-case scenario, have been intercepted and fallen into the wrong hands?' Major Hawes's hand trembled slightly as he absent-mindedly picked up his slice of cake.

'The plans for the modifications are safe, sir. They have been recovered,' Arthur assured him.

'Thank goodness for that.' The major took a small bite of cake and pulled a face as he chewed. 'Not enough sugar,' he muttered.

'When did you last see the blueprints?' Arthur asked.

The major swallowed and considered. 'Hmm, just before

Christmas. I was anxious to get them returned and in the post. My understanding was there were three copies, and I was one of those entrusted to offer an expert opinion on the safety modifications.'

'Who took them to the post office, sir?' Jane asked, leaning slightly forward in her seat. She had abandoned her cup of tea.

'Let me think, it was the day before your cousin and her companions came, so it would have been Georgette who took them to the post office. I remember telling her to be sure not to miss the post or the things would be stuck for ages. I felt the sooner my thoughts were received the better.' Major Hawes frowned as he recollected the events.

He set down his plate and rose from his chair to hobble over to the desk in the window nook where Georgette usually sat. The dog lifted his head as he passed, only to resettle when the major hobbled back with a small book in his hand.

'Here, take a look for yourself, Arthur, my boy. Georgette puts all the postage receipts in here so the petty cash can be tracked. She is most conscientious when it comes to money matters.' Major Hawes passed the book to Arthur.

Arthur pulled a pair of wire-framed spectacles from his jacket pocket. He slipped them on and opened the book. The pages were set out in months with neat entries written in one column and expenditure in another.

'You are certain of the date, sir?' he asked as he started to examine December's entries.

The major gave an emphatic nod. 'Yes, thinking about it now, I remember Georgette being all of a dither that day as she had a lot of errands to run before the shops closed. With rationing, shortages and queueing, everything takes so much longer these days.'

Arthur traced the entries with the tip of his finger, being careful to examine the dates either side of the one they were interested in. There were a lot of things listed just before Christmas but no post office entry for that date.

'I can't see any postage for that date, sir. Does Georgette keep a supply of stamps?' Arthur asked.

'She does, but she had used them all on the Christmas cards, so she intended to buy more.' Major Hawes shifted agitatedly in his seat and Nero immediately sat up as if sensing his master's concern.

The brass clock on the mantelpiece struck the hour, startling them all.

'Georgette is very late.' Major Hawes rubbed his chin and Arthur could see he was distressed by their discovery as well as his assistant's tardiness.

Jane exchanged a look with Arthur. However, before either of them could speak there was a knock at the front door. They heard a murmur of voices in the hallway, then Sarah opened the sitting room door. Her face was pale, and her usual cheerful smile had vanished.

'Begging your pardon, sir, but the police are here to see you.' She stood aside to allow Chief Inspector Thorne to enter the room. He was still in his outdoor clothes and the shoulders of his coat were damp. He seemed unsurprised to see Jane and Arthur.

Sarah closed the door and the major and Arthur rose to shake hands with the policeman before he was invited to sit down.

'I'll stand, sir, my coat is rather wet. I hope you will forgive the intrusion, but I have just come from an accident on the road outside the village.' The chief inspector's expression was grave, and he had his hat in his hands, fiddling with the damp brim as he spoke. 'I believe a Miss Georgette Darnley was in your employ, Major Hawes?'

Arthur had a terrible feeling that he knew what the

policeman was about to say. It would seem from Jane and the major's expression that they too guessed what was coming.

'She is. We were expecting her to join us for tea. She should have been here an hour ago. You said there had been an accident?' Major Hawes asked, his face pale.

'I regret to inform you that Miss Darnley is dead. Her bicycle was hit by a motor vehicle which failed to stop. Visibility is very poor outside now with mists coming off the field, the rain and the time of day. It may be that whoever struck her simply didn't see her. She was found by Mr Mullins as he was on his way home from work.' The chief inspector looked weary. 'I believe Miss Darnley lived alone?'

'Yes, her mother died in the spring. I can't believe it. I always warned her to be careful on that bicycle.' Major Hawes pulled a handkerchief from his pocket and blew his nose loudly. Nero rested his head on his master's knee in silent sympathy.

'You are certain it was an accident, Chief Inspector?' Jane too looked shaken by the news.

'There were no witnesses and conditions are bad. The driver may have assumed they hit a badger or a fox,' the policeman said.

Arthur doubted that Georgette's death was an accident. It would be too coincidental when it seemed that they were once again closing in on who may have murdered Polly and the other agents.

He also guessed that Chief Inspector Thorne was also unconvinced. The news of Georgette's death was both distressing and frustrating. The policeman declined the offer of tea and said that he needed to get going. He took details from the major about Georgette's nearest relations and departed, presumably to break the sad news to them.

'We should really start back to the house,' Arthur said. He sensed his old friend needed time alone to process what had just happened.

'Yes, my boy. I need to go and break the news to Sarah. She'll be most upset. They were at school together, although I believe Sarah was a few years younger than Georgette.' The major seemed to have aged with the news. The lines around his mouth were more pronounced and he had lost his former vim and vigour.

'It is truly awful.' Jane rose from her seat and collected her bag. 'Thank you for tea, I'm so sorry about Miss Darnley.'

'Thank you, my dear.' The major saw them to the door of the sitting room and once they had gone through the front door, they heard him calling for Sarah.

The chief inspector had been correct about the weather closing in. The air was grey and smelt of smoke from the chimneys of the nearby cottages. Arthur had once again wound his scarf to cover his nose and mouth as they made their way carefully along the garden path and out through the wooden gate in the privet hedge onto the road.

Jane was conscious of tiny ice crystals glistening on the footpath as Arthur shone his dimmed-out torch onto the path immediately in front of their feet. Once again, she was glad to take his arm for support as they navigated their way back to Half Moon Manor. The rain turned to sleet as they entered the driveway.

Benson opened the door and ushered them inside, closing it quickly behind them so no flicker of light could escape.

'Miss Darnley has been killed,' Arthur informed his manservant as he was assisted with his coat. He looked ghostly pale in the light from the hall lamp.

'Yes, sir, Mr Mullins called here a few minutes ago to see his mother. An accident with her bicycle, I believe. He was most distressed.'

Despite the welcome warmth of the hall, Jane shivered.

Arthur seemed to pick up on her mood and ushered her into the drawing room.

'I think perhaps a drop of brandy might be beneficial,' he suggested.

Benson immediately moved to comply, pouring them both a glass before retiring from the room. Jane had slipped off her shoes in the hall and curled up on the armchair, tucking her stocking-clad feet beneath her.

'It's been quite a day, today.' She took a sip of brandy. The warm sensation of the spirit slid down her throat and into her stomach. Arthur sat opposite her in his usual space, nursing his goblet whilst staring glumly into its depths.

'Poor Georgette,' he said eventually.

'It seems that the major received the blueprints for his comments, and then gave them to Georgette to post on. What do you think happened then? Did she retain them, and Polly found them in her bag? Or did something else occur?' Jane mused.

'You mean, someone else could have offered to post every-thing for her? I suppose if, as the major said, she was worried about all of her errands, fitting everything in that day, someone could easily have said they were already going to the post office and intercepted the package.' Arthur's expression lightened. 'It makes more sense to me that way.'

'It's so frustrating. I wish we knew what caused Polly and Georgette to fall out.' Jane rubbed her hand against her fore-head in an attempt to stave off her incipient headache.

'It's hard to say. I suppose it could be the blueprints?' Arthur suggested.

'You think Polly may have challenged Georgette?' Jane took another sip of her brandy. 'I don't know about that. Polly wouldn't break her cover in that way, I'm sure of it.'

'Hmm. But why kill Georgette? And why now?' Arthur asked.

Jane hadn't really considered this aspect of Georgette's death. 'I see what you mean. You think someone saw her come here, and then with my visit to the library and us going to call at the major's house, the murderer thought she was going to lead us to them?'

Arthur took a gulp from his glass and coughed. 'It does look as if that is a possibility.'

'Who has a vehicle who could have killed her? Because she was murdered, wasn't she? We are both convinced of that. I think the chief inspector also feels the same way but, of course, it would be impossible to prove.' Jane shivered as she spoke despite the heat from the fire.

'It would have to be someone in the village. With petrol shortages and everything, I can't see it being someone travelling in. They would have to have been tipped off in some way. No, this was quite a bold move. The car could have been recognised. They could have been seen.' Arthur set his almost empty glass down on the table beside his chair.

'Who then?' Jane asked.

'The Fenwicks have a car. They don't use it much, obviously. Diana cycles usually, but they both can drive. Andrew uses the car to visit distant parishioners and to take people to the cottage hospital, that kind of thing. Doctor Redfern has one and Mr Pegg, the bank manager,' Arthur said.

'Father Dermott?' Jane asked.

Arthur shook his head. 'No, he doesn't drive as far as I know and has no car. He travels on foot or by bicycle, I believe.'

Jane finished her drink. She couldn't help a sneaky feeling of relief that this was one thing at least that counted in Father Dermott's favour. Arthur had helped her build quite a convincing case against him the previous day. Even so the brigadier's often repeated mantra kept sounding in her head: *Trust no one.*

'I expect Chief Inspector Thorne will send a constable

around the village to make enquiries and to examine all the motor vehicles for any sign of damage.' Arthur sounded thoughtful.

'True. It was a shame that Bendigo didn't see what happened. He may have recognised the car,' Jane said.

Arthur looked at her. 'It is probably as well for him that he didn't. He may have found himself next on the list.'

'Yes, I suppose you're right. We need to think this all through after dinner. I feel, at the moment, as if this fog has seeped into my brain and I can't think straight.' Jane uncurled herself from the armchair. She wanted to go and check on Marmaduke and escape from the chaotic ideas running around her mind.

Arthur agreed. 'I think so. We need some sort of plan going forward if we are to solve this.'

He looked weary and Jane guessed Georgette's death had shaken him more than she had realised perhaps.

'Very well then, after dinner,' she said.

CHAPTER TWENTY-ONE

Dinner was a quiet affair. The layer of gloom permeating the dining room was only lifted slightly by the appearance of a nice pair of pork chops with kidneys for their main course. Arthur's mind was too busy working through everything they had learned to make light conversation. Not that making good dinner conversation had ever been one of his skills.

Jane too was preoccupied, focusing all her attention on her food. That was one of Miss Treen's good points, he realised. Jane never prattled in the way some women did just to fill a gap. She could be a very sympathetic companion when she wasn't fighting her corner somewhere.

Mrs Mullins brought their after-dinner coffee into the drawing room.

'Mr Benson has gone to do his fire watch duties, sir. So, if there is anything else this evening it will be myself as you'll need to call,' she informed him as she set down the tray.

'Of course, Mrs Mullins, thank you.' Arthur had forgotten that his manservant had volunteered to be part of the fire watch for the village. He and Bendigo Mullins would be on the church roof armed with binoculars and access to a stirrup pump should any incendiaries fall on their village.

He often wished his own health would permit him to assist but he knew he would be more of a hindrance than a help in such matters. On a night such as this, with the cold and the sleet, he didn't envy them. His own part of the war effort would have to be cerebral rather than physical, no matter how frustrating that might be at times.

Mrs Mullins left them to enjoy their coffee. Jane immediately pulled out her cigarettes and used her lighter.

'Right, where are we with all of this, then?' she asked, before taking a pull on her cigarette.

The scent of tobacco smoke drifting towards him irritated Arthur's nose and he wafted his hand in front of his face in an attempt to ward it off. He pulled a notebook and pencil towards him on his side table and opened up the book. He usually found he worked much more effectively if he could jot his thoughts down on paper.

'I suggest we liaise with Chief Inspector Thorne tomorrow to establish if he has identified the vehicle that hit Georgette.' Arthur scribbled a note in his book. 'Or if he has located any more witnesses to the accident.'

Jane blew a thin stream of smoke into the air, thankfully directing it away from his face.

'Agreed. That would seem to be sensible,' she said. 'What else?'

'Perhaps we should talk to Andrew and Diana Fenwick again. Diana was friendly with Georgette. You said you saw them talking at the station in Exeter. Perhaps she may know about Polly and Georgette having this quarrel that the woman in the library referred to.' Arthur looked at Jane.

'Yes, you're right. Although Georgette was at pains to assure me this morning that she and Diana were not particular friends.' Jane extinguished her cigarette and poured them both a cup of coffee from the tall chrome pot.

Arthur added a note to his book. 'Georgette seemed to have quarrelled with a few people before she died. Polly, Diana, and maybe more? We can also find out if Diana or her brother ever posted mail for Georgette or ran other errands for her. You know, to help her out.'

Jane's neatly pencilled eyebrows rose slightly. 'Hmm, we can try but I'm not certain they would tell us.'

Arthur set down his pencil to accept a cup of coffee from Jane. He could see what she meant but it had to be worth a try. Sometimes people slipped up during seemingly innocent conversations.

Jane settled back in her chair and stirred her coffee. The door to the sitting room eased open and Arthur found himself being stared at by Jane's beastly one-eyed cat. The wretched animal looked smugly at him as it strolled past, tail in the air, to be greeted with cries of delight from Jane.

Arthur watched in horror as Jane scooped her beloved pet into her arms, crooning exclamations of pleasure and endearments into its ragged ears. Stray ginger cat hairs floated down onto the Turkish carpet.

'Jane, I really must insist the cat goes back to the kitchen.' He could almost feel his eyes starting to water.

Miss Treen regarded him with the same baleful glare as her pet before standing up with a huff. 'Very well. Come on, Marmaduke. Don't worry, Uncle Arthur doesn't mean to sound so grumpy,' she said as she started to walk out of the room.

'I am not grumpy,' Arthur said grumpily. He sneezed loudly. *Uncle Arthur?* How had it come to this?

He caught the faint tinkle of Jane's laughter from the hall.

'And I will not be uncle to a cat!' he called.

This time, in response, all he heard was the soft thump of the baize-covered door to the servants' area closing behind her as Jane presumably deposited the ginger feline menace back in the kitchen area.

With Jane temporarily out of the room he used his handkerchief to dispose of the stray cat hairs in the fire before she returned. She was smiling as she re-entered the room and he glowered at her from his seat.

'If we could return to our conversation now?' he said once Jane was back in her seat, her feet tucked under her once more.

'Of course. I was about to say that there is something that's troubling me about all of this. From the very first murders.' She looked at him. The merriment that had been present in her gaze was disappearing and a more troubled expression replacing it. 'Those messages, the Bible quotes, the ones found with the first murders.'

'Who left them? Or the purpose behind leaving them?' Arthur asked.

'Both, I suppose. I thought initially, as did you, that there was something personal behind those messages. Something that linked to the people involved in Operation Exodus. After all, why else simply target those people? And draw attention to it in such a way?' Jane asked.

Arthur knew what she meant. He too had agreed with Jane that the messages had seemed personal. Now, however, like her, he too was having doubts. 'You think that there is another reason behind those messages?'

Jane's frown deepened. 'Well, everything we have discovered so far indicates that there is a problem which extends beyond Operation Exodus. It even appears that there is a group of people, fifth columnists if you will, that are seeking to undermine the sovereignty of this country and are attempting to cost us the war.' She paused to look at him.

He nodded. 'Go on.'

'Those messages may have been left to serve more than one purpose. They could have been personal, implying that the rest of those agents were in danger. That someone was out to avenge another death that had happened during the operation. But they've also served another purpose, haven't they? It seems clear that whoever killed them knew of the existence of the diary so, perhaps, the only way they could get to the other agents involved and eliminate them was by highlighting that they were in danger. They knew the department would act to try and protect them, but that in turn would reveal where they were, having quite the opposite effect. After all, if the agents were abroad and seconded onto new tasks, they wouldn't know who had the diary.' Jane halted.

'I think I follow you. You believe that the existence of the diary became known to whoever is masterminding all of this. That person didn't know which agent had it in their possession or what was in it and so began to flush them into the open, then killed them?' Arthur began to see what Jane was driving at. 'They thought the diary had the information that could lead to this network of traitors being uncovered. Then, when the blue-prints vanished, they would know it had to be Polly or Anna who had taken them. They invited Polly back to Pennycombe probably with some kind of promise of revealing who the traitors were. Polly returned and was murdered. By then Anna had been posted abroad, but they knew Georgie Porgie had visited and been to Cornwall.'

'Yes, and they obviously knew Anna regularly saw Father Dermott so they pieced it all together in the way we did, except we found the parcel first. I wish we knew where Maura Roberts is. I think she has to be the key to all of this.' Jane peered disconsolately at her empty coffee cup and took out her cigarettes.

'I think you're right and she is a key figure, but I'm not certain that she is the top dog, so to speak. It's like looking at a jigsaw and we have completed the borders but there are pieces missing.' Arthur resisted the urge to cough as some of Jane's cigarette smoke wafted his way.

'Do you think there is someone else co-ordinating all of this? Someone above Maura?' Jane asked.

'I think it very likely.' Arthur wished he could say that it wasn't the case and that once they managed to get hold of Maura, they would have all the answers. However, he had a feeling this wasn't the case. It was a disturbing thought that someone higher up at Whitehall might be a traitor.

'That is the other thing I feel we are missing. If Maura is the department mole, then how is she linked to here? And to who – someone in the village?' Jane asked.

Arthur had no answer to that question. Except he could only believe that was why the diary had been so sought after. Whoever it was had been afraid the diary would name them. He only wished it had.

Chief Inspector Thorne called at the house shortly after breakfast.

'Good morning, I thought you might both like to know that we have identified the car that hit Miss Darnley.' The policeman had been shown into the sitting room by Mrs Mullins and was seated on the sofa.

'Oh? Who does it belong to?' Jane asked, leaning forward in her seat. She was eager to know who it might be and if they were connected in any way with the other deaths.

'It was the doctor's car. He reported damage to the front fender first thing this morning. He says he didn't take the car out yesterday.' The chief inspector scratched his forehead.

'And do you believe him?' Jane asked. 'I take it he is not the kind of man who would lie?'

She blushed a little as she spoke, hoping the chief inspector wouldn't think her question rude. It was important though that they discovered not only whose car had been involved in the accident, but who may have been behind the wheel. Until now the doctor's name hadn't really come up in the investigation.

Chief Inspector Thorne gave her a sharp look. 'Yes, Miss Treen, I believe him. The doctor normally keeps his car keys hanging on a hook in the kitchen near the back door. Now, the accident occurred while the doctor was in his surgery seeing a patient. The back door of his house, in common with many in the village, was unlocked. His wife was out arranging flowers at the church. And it was certainly his car: the damage matches what was done to the bicycle. The paint from the bicycle matches that left on the car.'

'So, anyone could have spied their chance at an empty house and helped themselves to his keys. Then they returned the car after the accident and replaced the key on the hook.' Arthur looked most unhappy at this news.

'It certainly seems that way, sir, yes,' the chief inspector said.

'Then Georgette's death was murder. Someone took that car with the sole intent of killing her.' Jane shivered as she spoke. The cold-blooded motive behind Georgette's death was frightening.

'I believe so, Miss Treen. I thought you and Mr Cilento would like the update. Obviously, we are checking for any clues as to who may have taken it, but no one seems to have witnessed anything. The weather was so bad yesterday there weren't many people out and about.' The chief inspector stood and collected his hat from the table. 'If anything else does arise, I'll keep you both informed.'

Jane rose to see the policeman out. Arthur appeared rooted to his chair, clearly deep in thought.

'Thank you for calling.' Jane opened the front door for him. Benson had the day off since he had been up on watch all night.

'I wish I had better news for you, Miss Treen.' Chief

Inspector Thorne placed his hat on his head and strode away down the drive towards his car.

After the murky weather of the previous day, a watery sun had ventured out from behind the clouds and the air felt a little milder. Jane closed the door and returned to the sitting room.

'Well, it seems another promising lead has petered out,' she remarked as she opened the drawing room door. It seemed, however, that she was talking to herself since Arthur had vanished.

She turned around in the doorway as she heard the telephone ring in the study across the hall.

A moment later, the door of the study opened, and Arthur appeared. 'Jane, it's for you.'

She hurried across the tiled floor. It had to be the brigadier, or knowing her recent run of misfortune, it would be Stephen.

'Jane, my dear, there you are.' The brigadier's voice boomed in her ear, and she moved the receiver away from her head a touch.

'Yes, sir, I was about to call you. I'm afraid there has been another murder.'

'Who?' The brigadier's question was sharp and succinct.

'A young woman, Georgette Darnley, she worked for Major Hawes. She was knocked off her bicycle late yesterday afternoon and killed.' Jane perched herself on the corner of the desk, ignoring Arthur's disapproving frown.

'Hawes, Hawes, hmm, yes, I know the name. The blueprints you found were the ones sent to him. I take it the police are involved with this one too?' The brigadier sounded thoughtful.

'Yes, sir, the chief inspector just called to let us know the latest information on Miss Darnley's death,' Jane replied in a cautious tone. You never knew who might be listening in on these smaller village lines.

'This is not good, Jane. Whoever is doing this is highly dangerous. Are you and Arthur any closer to solving this thing?'

'We have a few lines of enquiry to follow.' Jane looked at Arthur, who looked slightly alarmed at this.

'Well, be careful. I called to tell you to come to London tomorrow. Your man Georgie Porgie is due back in the country, and I want you and Arthur to meet him from his train to escort him to Whitehall.' He gave her the details of the station and time of the train.

She jotted them down on the back of an envelope on Arthur's desk. 'Very good, sir. Let's hope this gets us somewhere.' She replaced the receiver.

'We are to go to London tomorrow to meet Richard Trent from his train and to escort him to Whitehall.' Jane looked at Arthur.

'Trent? I take it they have retrieved him from his mission?' Arthur stroked his chin thoughtfully.

Jane stood and straightened her skirt. 'It would seem so. He is landing back, being debriefed, then put on a train and we are to meet him and escort him to the brigadier.'

'So we are to go to London? On a train again?' Arthur looked disgruntled.

'Yes,' Jane replied firmly. 'Finally, we might discover something useful. In the meantime, where is that list we made last night? We still have work to do here.'

'You mean talking to Andrew and Diana Fenwick?'

Jane raised her eyebrows at him, and he reluctantly stood up. 'Very well, we shall go and pay them a call.'

CHAPTER TWENTY-TWO

Arthur left instructions with Mrs Mullins to tell Benson they would be going to London early the next day. Once that was done and Jane had ensured that her beloved Marmaduke was safe and content in the kitchen, she and Arthur set off for the vicarage.

Jane was forced to slow her usual brisk walking pace once more to accommodate Arthur. Even though the weather was much improved from the day before he was still wrapped in layers of wool and walking at the speed of a tortoise.

Eventually, they arrived at the vicarage and Arthur rang the bell. Jane looked around while they waited for someone to come to the door and noticed Diana's bicycle was propped up against the privet hedge. Clearly, she hadn't yet set off for Exeter.

The front door opened, and Diana appeared. She was dressed for her shift at the station tea room.

'Arthur, Miss Treen, what a lovely surprise. Do come in. I was just getting ready to set off for work. Andrew is in the study finishing his sermon for Sunday.' Diana led the way inside the house and into the large, untidy drawing room.

'We thought we should call in case you hadn't heard the

news about Georgette,' Arthur said as he unravelled himself from his woolly layers.

'And do please call me Jane,' Miss Treen added.

Diana took his coat and hat along with Jane's things and carried them out into the hall. 'Gosh, yes. We heard last night. Then the chief inspector called before breakfast. He wanted to look at the car.' Her voice floated back into the drawing room. 'It's simply ghastly. The police were asking all kinds of questions, but we haven't used the car now for at least two weeks. Andrew is very upset; he doesn't want me to cycle to the station today.'

Diana shuddered as she came back into the room and went to poke at the lacklustre fire glowing in the hearth.

'The terrible thing is that it seems now that poor Georgette's death was not an accident after all.' Arthur took a seat close to the fireplace.

Jane watched keenly to see the girl's reaction. Diana appeared to pause for a second as if gathering herself before turning to face them, poker in hand. 'Not an accident? I don't follow.'

'The chief inspector called on us too this morning. The doctor's car was taken and used to run her down on the road. It was murder,' Jane said.

'The doctor's car? I don't understand.' Diana sank down on the other fireside chair opposite Arthur, her lovely eyes wide with disbelief. 'That's impossible. I mean, who would do such a thing? And why Georgette of all people?'

'I should imagine those will be the very questions that the police will be asking too,' Jane said.

Diana replaced the poker in the rack with an unsteady hand. 'I can't believe it.'

The drawing room door opened, and Diana's brother entered the room. 'Hello, I thought I heard voices. Diana, my dear, are you all right?' He paused to give his sister a concerned look.

'Oh, Andrew, it's poor Georgette. Arthur and Jane said it wasn't an accident after all. Someone stole the doctor's car and deliberately ran her off the road.' Diana looked up at her brother.

The vicar sat down heavily on the opposite end of the sofa to Jane.

'Oh dear. That's dreadful. Poor Georgette. It was bad enough thinking it was an accident, but murder? And so soon after your cousin.' He looked at Jane.

'I mean, it was definitely murder?' Diana asked. 'The doctor didn't, I don't know, take his car out yesterday and well...' Her voice tailed off.

'No. He didn't use his car yesterday and he keeps the key on a hook near his unlocked back door.' Jane's tone was crisp. 'His wife was out at the church arranging the flowers, so the house was empty.'

It occurred to Jane that both Diana and her brother would have been well placed to know when the doctor's wife usually went to the church to sort out the flowers for the week.

Diana shivered. 'First your cousin and the burglary, and now Georgette. What is happening?'

'When did you last see Georgette? You were friends, weren't you?' Arthur's question to Diana was much gentler than Jane's.

'Yes, well, not very close friends but we knew each other well. It's what comes of living in a village,' Diana said. 'I think it must have been yesterday morning. I was going to the post office to drop some things in for Andrew.'

'You weren't at work, yesterday?' Arthur asked.

'No, it was my day off. I had quite a few errands to run and I met Georgette outside the library.' Diana frowned as if trying to recall the meeting.

'That must have been when she was on her way to us.'
Arthur looked at Jane.

'She did say she was very busy,' Diana agreed.

'How did she seem in herself?' Arthur asked.

Diana blinked. 'Distracted, but Georgette was often like
that. Her mind was always full of a million things. Just her
usual self, I suppose.'

'She seemed distracted when she called at the manor.' Jane
agreed with Diana's assessment.

'Do you know if she had quarrelled with anyone recently?
Or if there was anyone who disliked her?' Arthur asked.

Diana shook her head slowly. 'No, well certainly not
enough to wish to kill her if that's what you mean.'

'The librarian thought she had a boyfriend,' Jane said. The
woman had hinted she thought Polly and Georgette's falling out
was over a man. It struck her that if that was true then Diana
might know something about it.

Diana gave a sad laugh. 'Georgette? No, she was one of life's
spinsters. I always thought she was destined for a life alone
accompanied by her knitting and a cat.'

Jane refrained from commenting on this.

'Georgette was a very sweet girl. She wouldn't have harmed
a fly. She was one of those people who was always helping
others. I often thought people would take advantage of her,'
Andrew Fenwick said.

'She always seemed very pleasant. I know she ran a lot of
errands for Major Hawes,' Arthur agreed blandly.

'Gosh yes, his right-hand woman in many ways. Her and
Sarah, of course. I don't know how he'll manage without her.'
Andrew Fenwick sounded thoughtful.

'He certainly kept her busy.' Diana rose from her seat. Some
colour seemed to have returned to her cheeks.

'Well, I must be off I'm afraid, if I am to get to the station in
time for my train.'

'Of course, my dear. Do be careful though.' Andrew looked worried as his sister said farewell to Jane and Arthur and headed out to collect her bicycle.

'I hope she'll be all right.' He turned to Arthur and Jane. 'As if the blackout and travelling alone in the dark wasn't enough to worry about. Now it seems there is a murderer on the loose.'

'It is quite unnerving,' Jane agreed. 'I hope Georgette's death hasn't upset Diana too much?' She did her best to sound sympathetic.

'I know what you mean. Diana is a very sensitive girl really, but she does her best not to show it. Stiff upper lip and all that, so one is never quite sure.' He looked worried.

'I'm sure she would come to you if there was anything seriously troubling her,' Arthur attempted to reassure him.

'And I expect a girl as vivacious as Diana must have lots of friends,' Jane added.

Andrew ran his hands through his hair in a distracted fashion. 'I'm not sure, to be honest. Oh, she talks about some of the women she works with, and she goes to tennis parties and such in the summer. Still, she lost someone dear to her I think about eight or nine months ago. She never said much about him, but I know they were corresponding, then the letters from abroad stopped. Since then, well, she's sort of closed in on herself. Grief, I suppose.'

'That's so sad. This war feels never-ending sometimes.' Jane spoke with feeling. She too had borne losses, although she never spoke of them to anyone. Except Marmaduke, and he was good at keeping secrets.

She thought she caught a slightly surprised look in Arthur's eyes at the trace of emotion in her voice.

'Yes, it does rather. I expect you knew Georgette well too? Despite spending a lot of time here and living with my uncle I didn't have the same connections since I was away a lot,' Arthur said.

'What? Oh yes, well, Georgette came here quite often to see Diana. She would accompany Major Hawes when we had a bridge evening, that sort of thing. Yes indeed. The library will miss her, the whole business is very upsetting.' Andrew looked troubled.

'We should get back,' Arthur said, rising from his seat.

'Yes, thank you for seeing us. I'm sorry we were bearing such horrid news.' Jane joined Arthur.

The vicar appeared lost in his own world for a moment and Jane wondered what he was thinking.

'Ah, yes, coats. I'll see you out.' He appeared to recollect himself and led the way back out into the draughty hallway. Jane and Arthur put on their outdoor things ready for the walk back to the house.

'I expect I shall see you both again soon. If you require some help with the funeral for your cousin, Jane, you must let me know.' Andrew opened the front door.

'Yes, I will. The police have yet to say when it can take place,' Jane said as she stepped outside. Arthur followed her.

'I do worry so about Diana, you know.' Jane wasn't sure if he was trying to assure them of his concerns or if he was talking to himself.

'Absolutely,' Arthur responded, shaking his hand in farewell. 'Only natural.'

He fell into step beside her as they crunched their way from the house across the gravel drive.

'What did you make of that?' Jane asked, once the vicarage door had closed and they had rounded the corner of the privet hedge onto the footpath.

'Interesting. He's very concerned about Diana, isn't he? And I don't think it's just over the business of Georgette or her safety cycling to the station and back,' Arthur said, adjusting his scarf as he spoke so she could hear him more clearly.

'Have the Fenwicks always lived here?' Jane asked.

'They came about four years ago, I think. The same time as Father Dermott. I remember my uncle writing to me about how strange it was that both churches changed incumbents at the same time,' Arthur said.

'Oh look, isn't that Sarah?' Jane caught hold of his arm, forcing him to halt.

The young housemaid was coming towards them from the direction of the butcher's shop. A large wicker basket over her arm.

'Morning, sir, miss, I was just seeing if there was anything nice as I could get to cook the major for his dinner. I wanted to try and cheer him up a bit, you know.' She shifted the weight of the basket and peered up shyly at them.

'That's a kind thought. You must have been terribly upset yourself. The major said you and Georgette had been at school together,' Jane remarked.

'She was a few years ahead of me, but I've known her all my life. The police came this morning and told the major it was murder. Why? Who would do such a thing, and so soon after your poor cousin, miss.' The girl looked at Jane with a troubled gaze.

'You don't know anyone she'd fallen out with? No young man or anything like that?' Jane asked. Despite Diana's scorn and Georgette's obvious interest in Arthur, she may have had a boyfriend. It had to be worth pursuing just in case her death was down to a spurned lover and not connected with Polly's murder after all.

'Miss Georgette wasn't courting, so far as I know.' Sarah bit her lip and Jane sensed the girl had more to say.

'And anyone she had quarrelled with?' Jane pressed.

Sarah's cheeks flushed. 'I'm sure as it's nothing but well, just lately, since Christmas really, she wasn't herself. Like as if something was on her mind. Then, when your cousin was killed she was really, well jittery. That's the only way as I can describe it.'

Arthur exchanged a glance with Jane.

'We know she had argued with Jane's cousin just before she left the village,' Arthur said.

Sarah's colour deepened. 'I don't know about that, but I know she had words with Miss Fenwick the other day. The day you and Mr Cilento went to Cornwall. She had run into her at the station, and she came to the house later on in the afternoon. She seemed like her feathers were ruffled so I asked her if she was all right. She said as she had had words with Diana Fenwick.' She looked at Jane.

'They were friends, weren't they? Diana and Georgette?' Jane asked.

Sarah shrugged and shifted her basket on her arm as if eager to be off. 'I don't know as friends were exactly the word. Miss Fenwick always seemed to be bossing Miss Georgette about. Still, they did spend a fair bit of time in one another's company.'

'Let us hope the police catch whoever did this soon,' Jane replied in a kindly tone.

The girl responded with a wan smile of agreement, and they continued on their way.

Jane could tell that Arthur was pondering everything they had learned during the course of the morning so far. Her stomach growled, reminding her it had been quite a while since breakfast and once again no refreshments had been forthcoming at the vicarage.

When they arrived back at the manor, Benson opened the door to them.

'I'm pleased you have returned, sir, miss. There is a visitor waiting for you. I have shown him into the drawing room.' The manservant helped them with their coats.

'Who is it? Have they been waiting long?' Jane asked, alive with curiosity over who it might be.

'Only about five minutes, miss. It's Father Dermott. It seems he has heard the news about Miss Darnley,' Benson said.

Arthur's eyebrows rose slightly at this. 'Perhaps a tray of tea, Benson, if you might be so good,' he directed.

Jane followed Arthur into the drawing room wondering why the priest had called. The discussion of suspects that she and Arthur had recently was at the forefront of her mind and she hated having to feel so suspicious of everyone.

Father Dermott was seated on the end of the sofa as they entered the room. He jumped to his feet and greeted Jane with a smile and Arthur with a handshake, introducing himself to Arthur as he did so.

'I do hope you've not been waiting long, Father. Benson is bringing some tea.' Jane took her seat opposite Arthur in the fireside chair.

'Not at all, my dear Jane. I wasn't going to wait but Mr Benson thought you would be returning shortly.' Father Dermott's brow was creased with worry lines and his ready smile faded.

'I assume you have heard the sad news about Georgette Darnley?' Jane asked.

The priest nodded. 'I did. I also heard that your house had been burgled.' He looked at Arthur.

'Yes, on the day we returned from our journey to Cornwall. Jane also had her bag stolen in Exeter. It has all been very eventful just lately,' Arthur said.

Benson entered the room bearing a tray of tea which he set down on the low table in front of the sofa, before discreetly withdrawing again. Jane set the cups out on the saucers as Father Dermott cleared his throat.

'Now, how can we assist you, Father?' Arthur asked as Jane busied herself pouring tea.

Father Dermott dug his hand deep into the pocket of his black cassock and produced a card which he handed to Arthur. 'I received this.'

Jane's gaze jerked upwards to the card, and she spilled a

drop of tea onto the saucer. Recollecting herself, she set down the teapot and studied Arthur's face as he looked at the card.

'Well?' she asked when Arthur didn't say anything.

He passed the card across to her. It was a plain, blank white postcard, with just Father Dermott's address on the one side. The postmark was obscured by the amount of black ink that had been used on the stamp, and the card had clearly been wet at some point, smudging it even further.

The writing on the other side of the card was also smudged and a little hard to decipher. Arthur took over, adding milk to the teacups while she read.

Jane frowned. 'It's so hard to read. It looks like, *Exodus, tell Miss Treen. A.*'

'I believe Anna has sent it in the belief that you will understand what she means.' Father Dermott accepted a cup and saucer from Arthur.

'I see.' Jane was perplexed. Anna was abroad so far as she knew, she certainly wouldn't be aware of anything going on in England. At least she shouldn't be aware, let alone be able to send mysterious postcards. The card also bore an English stamp.

'When did you receive this, Father?' Arthur asked.

'This morning, first post. I didn't know what to make of it. Coming on top of the news about Georgette, I was worried. I thought you might be in danger so that's why I came straight here.' The priest's face appeared to betray his concern and he sounded genuinely distressed.

'Thank you, that's kind of you. It is most perplexing.' Jane wasn't sure what to make of it.

'We have just been calling on Reverend Fenwick. We were concerned that Diana might be distressed about Georgette. They were friends, I believe,' Arthur said, before taking a sip of his tea.

'Hmm, Georgette was not one of my flock, but I know she

and Miss Fenwick certainly appeared friendly.' Father Dermott rubbed his chin thoughtfully. 'Although, since the New Year I've not seen them together as much. In fact, now I think of it, Georgette seemed to be avoiding Diana.' He gave a small shrug. 'I expect there had been a tiff of some kind.'

'Oh, what makes you think they had quarrelled?' Jane asked.

'Well, I was in the grocer's and Miss Darnley flew in through the door and busied herself looking at the tinned goods at the back of the shop. It seemed so unusual for her, she never said hello or anything like she would normally do. She kept peeking out as if she were nervous and then I saw Miss Fenwick wheeling her bicycle past the shop. As soon as she had gone by, Georgette came out and spoke to me, apologised and seemed flustered. She looked through the shop window, saw Diana had gone, and scurried away,' Father Dermott said. He drained his tea and set the cup back in its saucer. 'I hope those girls had made up before Georgette's death. It's not a nice thing for Miss Fenwick to have on her mind otherwise.'

'No, indeed,' Jane agreed.

'I had better be off, I have a parishioner who is very ill with pneumonia. I'll leave the card with you. Please take care, Miss Treen.' Father Dermott rose and extended his hand to them both before leaving.

Benson met him in the hall and showed him out.

Jane leaned back in her chair, staring at the postcard lying on the table. 'What an interesting morning.'

CHAPTER TWENTY-THREE

Benson had organised train tickets for the early train the next day. Arthur calculated they should arrive at the station some thirty minutes before Richard Trent's train was due to arrive. This would allow for any delays to their train.

Jane had fretted all the previous afternoon about the postcard and if they should have acquired tickets for that day instead of waiting for the morning train. Her flat was free, and they could have stayed there overnight if necessary.

'With the bombing that is taking place in London at the moment it would be foolish to leave a day early,' Arthur had assured her.

Jane had been forced to agree. She knew it made more sense to remain at Pennycombe where there was less likelihood of being bombed. Even so she would have preferred to be in London earlier waiting around on the platform. She had slept badly, images of bicycles and Polly floating in the river had haunted her dreams.

The postcard Father Dermott had received bothered her too. It was almost as if they were being taunted. Someone had wished to remind her that this was all connected to Operation

Exodus. As she sat beside Arthur in the chilly, crowded carriage of their train, she wondered what had become of Maura.

The brigadier hadn't mentioned her when he had telephoned and, so far as they knew, there had been no more sightings of the girl. She sighed and shifted her position on the seat once again.

'Jane, I am starting to think you have a flea,' Arthur muttered as she nudged him once more.

She glared angrily at him. 'I can't help it. I am a little squashed,' she muttered back.

The generously proportioned gentleman sitting on the other side of her sniffed indignantly and moved his briefcase, so it dug into Jane's arm. By the time they arrived at Paddington, Jane was certain she had a large bruise forming.

Arthur and Benson helped her down from the carriage, and she tried to get her bearings as people scurried past her on the busy platform at Paddington. There were fewer uniformed personnel on the platform here than at Exeter. Instead, there was more of the usual hustle and bustle of city life, men in bowler hats and smartly dressed shop girls and typists.

Benson consulted the large silver fob watch that hung from a chain on his pinstriped waistcoat. 'Our train was a little late due to the signals. I think Mr Trent's train is due in the next fifteen minutes.' He looked at Jane and Arthur.

'I suggest we move a little out of the crowd. It seems that there are a great many people waiting to board it when it comes in.' Arthur took Jane's arm and led her away from the edge of the platform to the relative quiet further back.

'Shall I station myself at the other end of the platform, sir? We may stand a better chance of seeing him if we are standing in different sites,' Benson suggested.

'Yes, good thinking. You remember his features from Jane's photograph?' Arthur asked.

They had all studied the files that Jane had left in Arthur's safe the previous afternoon.

'Yes, sir.' Benson disappeared into a crowd of schoolchildren and black-suited businessmen on the platform.

Jane peered over the hat of the woman in front of her to look at the large, white-faced station clock hanging above the platform. 'The train is late.'

'Probably held at the same signals our train was stopped at. I think I hear it coming now.' Arthur nudged her.

Sure enough she could hear the whoosh of the brakes and the release of steam as the train clanked and rolled to a stop at the platform edge. The waiting crowd moved forward slightly, jostling for position as the passengers on board the train began to disembark.

'I assume he will not be in uniform?' Arthur asked as they peered at the faces of the men coming away from the train.

'I wouldn't have thought so.' Jane wished she could see their target.

Almost everyone had disembarked from the train now as far as she could tell, and the waiting passengers were being allowed to board. The engine driver and his mate were talking to the railway guard near the engine while new supplies were being organised.

There was still no sign of Richard Trent.

'Did he board the train?' Jane asked in bewilderment, looking at Arthur.

The words were no sooner out of her mouth than a commotion started on board the train in one of the carriages further down.

'I rather fear that he did.' Arthur's mouth was set in a grim line as they, along with the railway guard, hurried towards the scene of the kerfuffle.

Benson too moved as swiftly as possible to the affected carriage. A uniformed soldier jumped down onto the platform assisting a middle-aged woman in grey. The woman's complexion was the same colour as her coat. More soldiers spilled from the carriage all talking at once.

''Ere, what's all this about, then?' The railway guard pushed his way through the crowd. Benson slipped unobtrusively behind him.

'Murder! That's what. There's a bloke dead in the carriage,' the soldier supporting the woman said.

The woman's knees buckled as he spoke, and she almost fell as a couple more men stepped in to support her.

'Blood, there was blood.' The woman looked as if she might be sick.

The railway guard pushed through and entered the carriage. Benson followed on his heels to take a quick peek before stepping smartly back down into the crowd.

Jane and Arthur looked to the manservant to see if what he had seen was the body of the man they had come to meet. Benson gave a slight incline of his head as the railway guard re-emerged, his face pale.

'This train ain't going nowhere. Where's the police?' he asked.

The hubbub around him grew louder and people started to look out from the windows of the nearby carriages. Jane spotted the navy serge uniform of a policeman approaching.

'We should slip away,' Arthur suggested.

Jane nodded. 'Yes.' They moved discreetly away to meet up with Benson as the scene around the carriage grew busier as more of the passengers were evacuated from the train.

'I take it the body was definitely that of Georgie Porgie or, as he called himself now, Richard Trent?' Arthur asked once they were away from the melee.

'I'm afraid so, sir. It seems he was stabbed, with the wound being concealed beneath a newspaper. I would surmise that as the lady boarded, she noticed that blood had started to seep through the layers and was now visible.' Benson's expression was grave.

'Was it a closed carriage or was there a corridor?' Jane asked.

'Closed. Whoever killed him was a fellow occupant of that carriage, miss,' Benson said.

The train had been so busy, and the carriage must have been so crowded with people standing as well as sitting that it was doubtful anyone would have seen anything. That was even if they could trace any possible witnesses. The passengers having long dispersed now from the station.

'Someone knew he was on that train,' Arthur said.

A cold chill ran along Jane's spine. 'How though? Did someone find out from the brigadier's end? Or was it during his transfer back across the Channel? Or was it from someone at our end, in the village?'

'It seems there is little we can do here.' Arthur eyed the large, disgruntled stream of rail passengers all leaving the station.

More policemen arrived as he spoke, all heading towards the train.

'I expect they will clear the station while they uncouple the carriage and shunt it into a siding,' Benson said.

A uniformed railway employee started to approach them.

'We should leave,' Jane said. 'We will need to inform the brigadier and let his department handle things. There is nothing more we can do here for now.' They turned and started walking towards the station exit.

It didn't sit easily with Jane that they had no other choice. She and Arthur were civilians and any attempt to involve themselves in the investigation would certainly be viewed as interference rather than help. It was also clear that they could be of no assistance now to Richard Trent.

Benson cleared his throat as they emerged onto the street

outside the station. 'If I may suggest we adjourn for refreshment, while a course of action is considered?'

Arthur looked at Jane.

'Oh, very well. I suppose it would help to have a plan in mind when we head to Whitehall,' she agreed somewhat grumpily. Another of her agents was dead and right under her nose.

Benson led the way just off the main street to a small café which was probably used mainly by employees of the railway and cab drivers. Jane was squeezed onto a rickety chair next to Arthur, while Benson collected battered white enamel mugs of a steaming dark brew from the miniscule counter.

He placed the mugs down on the battle-scarred polished wooden table and took his place on the vacant seat.

'I know you only got a quick look, but did you see anything useful to us when you looked inside that train carriage?' Arthur asked.

'The gentleman we were expecting was seated in the far corner of the carriage. He was dressed in civilian clothing, a dark-grey suit. A newspaper was open across his chest and to the casual observer it would have looked as if he had fallen asleep. However, he had obviously been stabbed and the resulting blood loss had since seeped out and made itself visible through the paper. This presumably drew the lady's attention, and she raised the alarm.' Benson gave a short factual summary.

'Was the weapon used visible?' Jane asked, scowling at her tea, and wishing it was coffee.

'I believe I saw what seemed to be the short bone handle of what was probably a narrow-bladed knife,' Benson said, before taking a sip of his tea.

'The like of which is probably to be found in kitchens all over the country,' Arthur replied disconsolately.

'You're right. I doubt that will be of any use unless the police are able to recover any fingerprints from the handle.' Jane pulled her cigarettes from her bag, ignoring Arthur's disapproving look.

She lit her cigarette and considered their situation. 'With Trent dead, our chances of finding whoever is behind all of this have been somewhat reduced.'

'More like considerably reduced, I'd say,' Arthur said. Jane frowned at him. She suspected he was about to calculate the exact odds of their chances of success in solving the murders. Right now, she guessed they would be pretty poor.

They had been counting on Trent to fill in some of the gaps for them. He might have given them some names that he, Anna and Polly had suspected.

'Where do we go from here?' Jane looked at her companions.

'After you've briefed the brigadier and delivered the bad news?' Arthur asked.

'Obviously, after *we've* seen the brigadier,' she emphasised the word *we*. She was not going down for this failure alone. She had said to Arthur that she thought they should have arrived earlier. Not that it would have made any difference, she supposed, but even so.

'I fear it may be difficult to get a train home for quite a while. Mr Trent's murder is likely to cause considerable delays on the railway,' Benson said.

Delays and disruptions were commonplace these days. Labour shortages, materials shortages and damage from bombs or delays due to warnings of bombs all played a part.

'You can both stay at my flat, if necessary,' Jane offered. She had a miniscule spare bedroom and Arthur would probably fit on her couch since he was shorter than Benson. The manservant had brought Arthur's medical supplies with him so that wouldn't be a problem.

She was somewhat annoyed to see that neither of her companions appeared impressed by her offer.

'Um, thank you, Jane, that's most kind,' Arthur mumbled.

'If only we could track down Maura.' Jane stubbed the remains of her cigarette out in the chipped white china ashtray.

'Ahem, if I may make a suggestion, Miss Treen,' Benson said in a slightly apologetic manner.

'Of course,' Jane agreed.

'It strikes me that we are some distance from Whitehall and the buses are disrupted so it may take us considerable time to get to see the brigadier in person. I wondered if perhaps we should telephone instead and make our plans from there on,' Benson suggested.

Arthur looked hopefully at her. 'He makes a good point and there is a telephone box right outside.'

Jane looked through the steamed-up window of the café to see the blurred red outline of a telephone box in the weak wintry sunshine.

'Very well, give me any change you have. Since my purse was taken, I mainly have notes.' Jane accepted the suggestion and the pile of coins and reluctantly left the warmth of the café to make her call.

'Jane, an unexpected pleasure, where are you?' Stephen picked up the call.

'I'm in a telephone booth near Paddington station. I haven't much change and I need to speak to the brigadier urgently.' Jane's tone was crisp as she tried to stifle her irritation at hearing her colleague's smug, laid-back voice in her ear.

'No can do, dear girl, I'm afraid. He's been called to an urgent briefing. Has something gone wrong with the pick-up?' Stephen asked.

'Our man was dead on arrival. Someone got to him on the train,' Jane said.

'I see. That is very troubling.' Stephen's voice had lost its usual nonchalance.

'Listen, the pips will go in a second. I'm on my last tuppence. Do you have any news on Maura?' Jane hastily fed the last of her change into the slot and hoped she wouldn't be cut off before he could answer her question.

'Last reports were that she was still in London. Some sightings around the train stations and a rumour that she had been seen near where her house used to be. You know the address?' he asked.

'Yes. Tell the brigadier we are going to try to locate her. I'll report back later.'

'Jane, be careful. She is likely to be danger—' Stephen's voice was cut off by the chirping of the pips signalling the call was at an end.

Jane replaced the receiver and went back inside the café to brief the others on her plan.

'You want to try and hunt down Maura? How?' Arthur asked incredulously when she had finished telling them the outcome of her call.

'We know her last address and there have been sightings of her locally around there as well as at the railway stations,' Jane said.

'It will be very difficult. You said when you first arrived at Half Moon Manor that the area had been badly damaged during the bombing raids.' Arthur looked most unhappy. 'Do you know that part of London?'

'I have been to that area before. We have to try something. No one else has the time or the resources to try and find her. We should at least give it a go whilst we're here. As Benson has pointed out, getting back to Half Moon Manor may prove difficult until the trains are running properly again.' Jane tried to sound firm while she wracked her brains for memories of the area where Maura had lived.

'It sounds more like a wild goose chase to me,' Arthur said.

'Do you have a better suggestion? Another of my agents has just been killed. Whoever is behind all of this has to be stopped. It's our patriotic duty to do all we can, even if you think it may be foolish.' Jane's voice wobbled slightly. Trent's death had upset her greatly.

'I'm sorry, Jane. You're right, of course.' Arthur placed his hand on hers and gave it a gentle, reassuring squeeze.

'Then this map I brought with us may be useful,' Benson said, pulling a folded-up document from the inside pocket of his coat.

Jane watched as he unfolded it on the table, moving their mugs aside. She wondered how much it would take to persuade the manservant to work directly for the brigadier rather than for Arthur.

Arthur wondered what else Benson might have concealed about his person.

CHAPTER TWENTY-FOUR

Arthur produced a pencil from his pocket so that they could mark out the areas near the East End they intended to search.

'Should we split up, do you think? To cover more ground?' Jane suggested, frowning at the streets Arthur had marked.

'I think we can do that when we are in that area. It may be safer, however, if we stick fairly close together. This woman may well be very dangerous, assuming we find her,' Arthur said. 'Also, until we arrive in that part of London, we won't know just how extensive the damage might be. It's been targeted since September because of the route the planes take to try and hit the docks.'

'With respect, I suggest we go and assess the area where Maura Roberts was last known to reside. If there are any buildings still standing and occupied then we can ask around,' Benson suggested.

'Very well,' Jane agreed.

'I believe if we walk a little way along this street, there is a bus that should take us in that direction.' Benson started to fold the map ready to return it to his pocket. Before leaving the café, he persuaded the man behind the counter to break a pound note down into coins so they would be able to pay the conductress for their bus tickets. Something Jane hadn't thought about.

Jane slowed her pace again to accommodate Arthur as they made their way to the bus stop. The sun had come out more strongly now and the puddles on the pavements were drying at last.

There was a lengthy wait for the bus and Jane's stomach rumbled, reminding her that it had been a long time since they had eaten breakfast. She rather wished now that they had ordered toast or sandwiches to accompany their tea whilst they had been at the café.

The bus, when it finally arrived, was like the train, overcrowded and rather sweaty. Benson and Arthur were forced to stand, hanging on to the leather straps and metal poles for support. Jane was perched on the edge of a seat next to a garrulous elderly woman who appeared to mistakenly believe that Jane would be interested in the state of her bunions.

As the bus rumbled its way through the streets, they were able to see for themselves the extent of some of the damage from the bombs. Large craters pockmarked the rows of buildings. Walls stood exposing the interiors of what must have once been people's homes or places of work, with scraps of different coloured wallpapers on display to the world. Jane shivered and hoped her own flat a mile or so away was still intact.

At least Marmaduke was safe at Half Moon Manor for now. She had found him as a small, angry kitten amongst the ruins of just such a building. He had been injured and starving, mewling furiously and spitting at her when she had rescued him. She had nursed him back to health despite his objections and now he was the best of companions. No matter what Uncle Arthur thought.

Eventually they reached the area of the East End which Benson and Arthur had marked on the map. Arthur offered his hand to assist her down from the bus and they stood for a moment on the corner of the street to get their bearings. The devastation was much heavier here, as the enemy planes had tried to bomb the docks. The weapons had fallen short and hit the terraced streets of the densely populated area.

* * *

Arthur suppressed a sigh as he took in the enormity of the task before them. Finding any trace of Maura Roberts in the midst of so much destruction seemed to him to be the human equivalent of searching for a needle in a haystack.

Even the midday sunshine seemed to be mocking them as they looked around for any landmarks they could use to work out which direction to try first. Broken glass, fragments of wood and broken pieces of red brick were scattered all over the pavements. As they walked along the road, in the distance ahead of them they could see where some places had been barriered off with makeshift blockades. Those parts having been deemed too dangerous to enter just yet.

Benson looked around as he walked, the manservant's immaculate appearance at odds with the disarray of his surroundings.

'I believe we need to turn this way.' Benson paused at what had once been a street corner. The sign still hung precariously on the remains of a soot-stained brick wall.

There were more signs of life as they ventured into the street. More buildings were intact and obviously still occupied. The glass in the windows taped up lattice fashion to prevent injury should they be shattered. Steps had been swept and scrubbed. A few small children were playing in the street outside the houses. The boys with a few marbles and two little girls holding home-made rag dolls.

They attracted a few curious stares as they walked along the street looking for house numbers or names.

'Here.' Arthur halted in front of a pile of rubble. 'This is where Maura's family's house stood.'

All that remained of the building was a heap of bricks mixed with tattered pieces of fabric that might once have been curtains.

Jane looked around. 'The houses opposite are gone too.'

A woman was approaching them, wheeling a pram along the street.

'Excuse me, we were looking for the Roberts family. They used to live here?' Jane stepped forward to speak to the woman.

'All killed love, except the girl.' The woman's voice was as weary as her eyes.

'Maura?' Jane asked.

'Actually, it was Maura we were hoping to find,' Arthur said quickly.

'What you want with Maura?' The woman peered suspiciously at them, clearly noticing they did not have local accents.

'I work with Maura and—'

Arthur interrupted Jane, '—and we are with the insurance company that hold a policy that may be to her benefit,' he said smoothly.

'Oh.' The woman appeared to consider this as she looked at them. 'Maura was 'ere yesterday seeing as if there was anything else as she could salvage.'

'Is she living locally?' Arthur asked. He could hardly dare hope that they might actually be lucky for once.

'I don't know as I should say,' the woman prevaricated.

Since the wheels of the pram had stopped rolling the baby grew restless and started to cry. The woman rocked the pram back and forth attempting to soothe it as the wails grew louder.

'We would be glad to reimburse you for your trouble,' Arthur said, sensing the woman wished to get moving again so she could soothe her child.

He took out his wallet and produced a crisp pound note.

The woman's eyes brightened and widened. She glanced around swiftly as if to make sure the transaction was unobserved before accepting the money, tucking it inside a worn red-leather purse. Arthur suspected that like many people who had lost most of their possessions, some extra money to buy a few things was to be treasured.

'You'll find her at her aunt's house, near the green.' She gave them the address. 'Don't say as how you found her though. She keeps herself to herself, that one. Don't like people talking about her.' The woman seemed quite warm and talkative now.

'Thank you.' Benson stepped aside, and the woman continued on her way.

'Very good, well done, Arthur. At least we have an address.' Jane seemed to perk up now there was new information.

Once the woman had turned the corner and vanished from view, they used the battered remains of a wooden gatepost to spread the map out once again. Arthur quickly picked up their route.

'We need to continue along this road until this point then follow the street if we can, and I think we should be in the right place. The woman said it was near the green,' he said, using his finger to trace the road.

'Very good, sir.' Benson refolded his map.

'Let's go.' Jane was clearly eager to be off.

Arthur hoped there would not be too much more walking. Despite the sunshine, the air was still cold and there was a distinct tang of smoke in the air. All of which left him feeling somewhat breathless.

They seemed to be walking for quite some time. The landscape was not dissimilar to the one they had already passed through. It was clear, however, that the closer they drew to Maura's aunt's house the area was slightly more affluent. The terraced houses gave way to villas with pocket-handkerchief-sized front gardens surrounded by clipped privet hedges or low walls which once had iron railings.

The damage here was less too. Although it had been hit, the desolation was not so extensive.

'That must be the green the woman told us about,' Jane said as they approached a wedge of scrubby grass interspersed with laurel bushes and holly opposite a row of houses which bore names like 'Rosemont' and 'Claredon'.

'We should think how we are to approach this.' Arthur halted next to a large shrub. 'If she sees you, Jane, she may take fright and refuse to open the door, or make a break for it.'

'I agree, Miss Treen. Perhaps you should remain here for now and myself and Mr Cilento will try the insurance agent approach once more,' Benson said.

Arthur could see that Jane perceived the wisdom in their suggestion, but clearly disliked not being in the thick of the action.

'Very well, but be careful,' she said.

Jane remained where she was, just out of sight amongst the laurel bushes, while Arthur and Benson approached the address the woman with the pram had provided.

The house was one of the slightly scruffier ones in the row. The step had dried mud and leaves on it and the brass knocker on the door needed a polish. Benson took hold of the knocker and rapped loudly on the door. The sound seemed to reverberate in the quiet street.

Arthur's heart thumped as loudly in his chest as the knocker on the door. He disliked confrontation of any kind and was thankful that Benson was beside him. At first, he thought that the house was empty, and they were not going to get a reply.

After a few minutes, just as Benson was about to knock again, the front door was flung open. A woman dressed in a large floral pinny with a turban on her head and a child on her hip stood glaring at them.

'Whatever you're selling, we don't want none,' she said, preparing to slam the door shut again in their faces.

'No, madam, forgive us for intruding on you but we are not salesmen.' Benson discreetly inserted the toe of one of his highly polished brogues in the doorway.

'Who am you then?' The woman adjusted the weight of the child on her hip. 'The rent is paid up till Tuesday.'

'We are from the London and Provinces Insurance Company and are looking for a Miss Maura Roberts.' Arthur thought Benson sounded very convincing.

'Maura? Don't know nobody of that name,' the panicky expression in the woman's eyes as she spoke convinced Arthur that she was lying.

'Oh dear, we have this address on our files as that of Miss Roberts's aunt. It's in regard to a policy taken out some years ago by Miss Roberts's mother,' Benson said, sounding slightly regretful.

'An insurance policy? You mean as there might be some money?' The woman shifted the child's weight once more. She suddenly sounded more amenable.

'It would be in Miss Roberts's interest to see us, yes. Still, if you say we have an error in our paperwork, we shall have to resume our search for her elsewhere.' Arthur half-turned on the step as if about to leave.

''Ere, hold on a sec, don't be hasty. I might know Maura.' The woman licked her lips and looked hopefully at them.

Arthur turned back to face her. 'Do you know Miss Roberts or not? We have it on file that this house belongs to her aunt. Are you a relative of hers?' He injected a sterner note into his voice.

The woman's face took on a sulky expression. 'Maura is my niece. Her mother was my sister, Rosalind.'

'And where can we find Miss Roberts now? We understand that she has not been back to her workplace since the unfortunate events that destroyed her home.' Benson's tone was smooth with a hint of sympathy.

'She's been busy. Funerals to sort out and trying to find somewhere to live. She can't stay 'ere much longer. I got seven kiddies, house is full as it is.' The woman sounded defensive.

'We do understand the difficulties at this time. Will she be returning later today?' Arthur asked.

'Reckon as she'll be 'ere about four. She usually gives me an 'and with getting the supper on before me 'usband comes back from work,' the woman said.

'Thank you, may we call again then? It would be to her advantage to speak to us about the policy,' Arthur said.

'I suppose it won't do no 'arm,' the woman grudgingly agreed.

Benson made a show of patting down his pockets as if searching for something. 'Oh dear, do forgive me, I seem to have left my cards in the office.'

Arthur picked up on his manservant's cue. 'I gave my last one to Mrs Frost at our previous call.'

'Not to worry, we will return later with the papers for Miss Roberts to make her claim.' He lifted his hat politely to the woman.

Arthur turned away once more and he and Benson strolled leisurely away, certain that they were being watched from the front bay window of the house. Once they were sure they were out of sight they doubled back and met up with Jane.

'Well? Was she there? What happened?' Jane demanded as soon as they reached her.

Arthur gave her a quick précis of the conversation with Maura's aunt.

'So, we need to come back? Or hang around here in case she returns early?' Jane asked.

Benson consulted his fob watch. 'It is only two o'clock. If my memory serves me well, the map indicated there were some shops further along this street. We might be able to obtain something to eat and return here well before Miss Roberts is expected back.'

'I think that sounds like a sensible suggestion,' Arthur agreed. His feet hurt, his chest ached, and he was hungry.

There was a reason he didn't do this kind of physical work. His role was a cerebral one, none of this hiding out in bushes business.

'Very well, but we need to be quick. We can't afford to miss her,' Jane warned.

CHAPTER TWENTY-FIVE

Jane had to admit that a sit down in a nice warm café with a bowl of vegetable soup and a bread roll was very welcome after being out in the cold for so long. The café was at one end of a small row of shops only a minute's walk from Maura's aunt's house.

It was taking something of a risk not to stay watching the property, but Arthur had started to look quite unwell and, in turn, that appeared to make Benson anxious. She had been starving ever since they had left Paddington station so a few minutes' respite to warm up and eat was very welcome.

She mopped up the last of the soup from the thick, white china bowl with the remains of her roll. 'That's better,' she said, after finishing off her meal.

Arthur looked much improved too for the break. The grey tinge had receded from his cheeks.

'How are we going to approach this?' Jane asked.

'Obviously, you need to remain out of the picture for now, at least until we have established what Maura's role in this thing actually is,' Arthur said.

Much as it irked Jane, she knew he was right. They had to at least get Maura to start talking before Jane made her appearance. 'How do you intend to play it? Go with the insurance angle?' That seemed sensible to her.

Neither Arthur nor Benson would be known to Maura so she wouldn't recognise them. It troubled her that Maura's aunt had said her husband might be home. He would be an unknown quantity and could turn nasty if he didn't like what Arthur or Benson had to say to his niece.

'I think that should be our opening gambit. I think we need to draw her from the house. I expect at that time of day the household will be somewhat chaotic, so she may be willing to step outside for a moment.' Arthur scratched his chin thoughtfully.

'We have no powers to detain or arrest her. She could simply refuse to see you or answer any questions you ask.' Jane frowned. 'She could just take off.'

'True, but we might learn something, and even if we just manage to lull her into a sense of feeling safe at that address for a while longer, we can request the brigadier to alert the police with any evidence we have,' Arthur said.

'If she thinks you are insurance men, you mean? Do we have evidence though? It's all circumstantial really, even though the pieces fit together. I'm not certain she is at the top of the tree. What I really want to know is who's she working for? That's the key and we all think whoever that person is has to be connected to your village.' Jane leaned back on her wooden chair.

'We can try some names and see if she reacts,' Arthur suggested.

'Let's get back there. I noticed a bench behind the trees in the park. Luckily at this time of year the branches are pretty bare so we should be able to keep watch.' Jane gathered her bag and gas mask.

Arthur followed her lead and got somewhat reluctantly to

his feet. Together with Benson they made their way back to the small park area near Maura's aunt's house. The bench Jane had noticed offered a good view of the front door, but protected them from being seen thanks to a clump of scrubby bushes.

They settled themselves on the bench and prepared to wait.

'I hope Maura is prompt, it's frightfully cold. The blackout will probably be just after four thirty and then we will struggle to get her away from the house,' Arthur said as they watched a hopeful pigeon strut past their feet.

'This is our best shot at discovering something useful. I wonder if the brigadier or Stephen has learned anything more about Trent's murder today.' Jane huddled further into her coat. The sun was lower in the sky now and the temperature was dropping rapidly. She wished she could have saved Georgie Porgie; it hurt her that she had lost another of her agents to the murderer.

Arthur was already rearranging his multiple layers of wool to cover his mouth and nose. The street was quiet. The only people appearing were children, clearly finished with school for the day and arriving home to the various houses. No one walked through the park except an elderly man with a fat stumpy-legged dog on a lead.

'Over there, is that her?' Arthur placed his hand on Jane's arm.

Jane squinted through the gap in the bare tree branches at a small, slim figure in a dark-blue coat hurrying towards the front door of the house they were watching. As the girl reached the door, she looked back over her shoulder as if to check no one was watching her, before unlocking the door and going inside.

'Yes, that's Maura, go quickly. We don't want the aunt telling her too much about your visit before you get hold of her.' Jane's pulse raced as Arthur and Benson set off back to the house.

She got up from the bench and crept slightly closer to stand in her previous hiding place amidst the laurels. She doubted she would be able to hear or see much more than she could from the bench. At least, though, she felt as if she were doing something.

The light was already fading, and she shivered as she watched Benson knock on the door of the house. After a moment, the door opened, and she could see them speaking to whoever had opened it.

The figure in the doorway came closer to the step and someone switched on the hall light. Jane bit her lip, longing to know what was being said. Maura came out of the house a little way as if she was about to step onto the path when there was a sharp crack.

Maura fell to the floor in a crumpled heap and Arthur and Benson dived down onto the ground. Jane looked around her trying to ascertain where the sound had come from. Surely, that had been a gunshot.

Maura had been shot, but by who?

As she searched for any sign of the murderer, Jane caught a glimpse of a tall figure in a dark coat hurrying away in the direction of the parade of shops where they had eaten their lunch. Without stopping to think, she set off in pursuit.

Behind her she could hear the sound of a woman screaming.

'Jane, wait!' Arthur came puffing and panting up behind her. 'Benson has stayed with Maura's family. They have sent a lad to fetch the police.' He wheezed the information out.

'Is she dead?' Jane asked, her gaze still fixed on her quarry who had slowed to mingle with a crowd of munitions workers who had just come out of the factory gates.

'I think so. I didn't wait to find out. Did you see who shot her?' Arthur was struggling for breath as he tried to keep pace with her.

'Yes, stick with me. I don't want to lose them; they've gone into the crowd.' It was getting harder to keep tabs on her quarry, who seemed to know that Jane was on their tail. The light levels had dropped considerably now, and a low mist had started to swirl around them.

They emerged on the other side of the crowd and for a split-second Jane thought she had lost sight of the murderer. 'Down there, come on.' She pulled on Arthur's coat sleeve to speed him along.

'Jane, this is madness. They still have a gun,' Arthur wheezed.

The alley led between the houses and back into the badly bomb-damaged streets they had walked along earlier that day.

'I know, but we have to catch them. If they get away now there will be no proof. They'll deny everything.' Jane's pulse pounded in her ears.

'For heaven's sake, Jane.' As Arthur spoke the familiar wail of the sirens went off. 'We have to take cover! Find a shelter!'

'There isn't anywhere here. There are no signs.' Jane could already hear the drone of the aircraft approaching in the distance, barely audible at first with the wailing sirens. 'Come on, you have to hurry.' She pulled Arthur along, ignoring his splutters of protest.

They had to find somewhere they could shelter and keep track of Maura's murderer who also appeared to be seeking shelter. The planes were getting louder, and Jane's body thrummed with the vibrations of the sound and the wailing of the sirens. There was no sign of an ARP warden or of a public shelter.

It was almost completely dark now and they were tripping over the rubble and debris from the previous raids. Up ahead, Jane could just see the figure she was pursuing also stumbling over the potholes trying to get out of the open.

'Jane, there, a public shelter.' She could hardly hear Arthur's voice as he pointed to the black-and-white painted sign ahead of them.

The aeroplanes were almost overhead now, and Jane

guessed they must be heading towards the docks again. The sound of rapid gunfire split the air. Flashes of light were visible in the sky and Arthur pulled her into the shelter of a nearby wall.

'Stay low!' A loud explosion rent the air and Jane was knocked to the floor by Arthur pushing her down to shield her with his body. Fragments of dirt and brick rained down on them and Jane screamed in shock.

'That one was close.' Jane could hardly make out what Arthur was saying to her. Her ears were still ringing from the noise of the explosion, and everything was muffled. The planes were still droning overhead, and she thought she could hear gunfire and distant explosions. It was all just noise though and she couldn't be certain of what was happening.

She lifted her head and peered around, trying to recover her breath. Disappointment filled her when she realised she could no longer see the woman she had been chasing. It had definitely been a woman. Then in the gloom, further down the street, she caught a glimpse of colour on the floor.

The same explosion that had almost caught them had also knocked her quarry off her feet as well.

'Come on, Arthur!' She extended her hand to pull her companion to his feet.

Arthur too seemed dazed and shaken by the blast. She doubted he had heard her; she couldn't really hear herself. She put her arm around his waist to steady him as he staggered to his feet. In the faint glow of the searchlights which were trying to pick out the airplanes, and what seemed to be a building that was on fire nearby, she could see her target lying on the ground.

Arthur wheezed loudly in her ear as he accepted her assistance to move forward. She hoped he wasn't about to collapse. Benson had some emergency medication in the leather bag he always carried with him, but right now they were stranded in the middle of an air raid with a murderer in their sights.

The air had grown thicker, and the acrid scent of smoke had mixed with the mist from earlier sending Arthur into a paroxysm of coughing. A surge of adrenaline carried her forwards. The planes seemed to have rained incendiary bombs all around them and the sky had turned an ominous shade of orange. He fumbled with his scarves to cover more of his mouth and nose.

They were closer now to the prone figure. Jane wondered if their quarry was unconscious or dead. They were forced to pause to allow Arthur to recover. The noise in her ears had started to recede and the sirens stopped. If the killer was alive, they needed to retrieve the gun they had used to shoot Maura before it could be turned on them.

Another loud explosion somewhere to the side of them seemed to shake the ground beneath their feet and Jane clung on tight to Arthur for support. Fires seemed to be starting all around and there was a crash as another of the already unstable brick walls of the damaged houses collapsed.

The smoke was enveloping them now and everything was tinged with an eerie glow from the flames of the many fires. Jane's ears were still deaf from the cacophony of noise surrounding them. Everything sounded muffled as if they were underwater.

They finally reached the figure lying sprawled on the floor. Her dark-green hat had been knocked from her head and lay to one side revealing a wound to her head which was oozing blood, stark and sticky, onto her blonde hair.

Jane let go of Arthur in preparation to try and see if the woman was still alive and to find the gun. Before she could even bend forward the figure on the ground rolled over to look up at them.

'Diana,' Arthur half-wheezed, half-coughed as he recognised their quarry.

Jane raised her hands as the gun the other girl held in her hands was trained right at her. Her heart raced at the full realisation of Diana's treachery.

'I wouldn't use that if I were you.' Arthur's voice was suddenly stronger and louder. Jane risked a quick sideways peek to see that he too now held a gun, and it was aimed at Diana. His hands wobbled slightly, but he tightened his grip on the handle.

'You know I can kill her now and I wouldn't care if I died too. Who do you think is fastest on the trigger, Arthur?' Diana shouted to make herself heard as she slowly manoeuvred herself into a sitting position.

'Why, Diana? Why all of this? Maura, Georgette, Kate, Richard and I suppose the others too. At least the ones in England,' Jane asked, her own voice equally loud.

Diana's lip curled in a cruel semblance of a smile. 'Have you ever been in love, Miss Treen? I mean really in love with someone who was the other half of you? Then had them cruelly taken away, killed, leaving you alone, a half person in a world of complete people?'

'I imagine there are many people who feel that way at this point in time.' Jane kept her voice calm and steady even though her heart pounded as she tried to think of a way out of the impasse they found themselves in.

Diana gave a tiny shake of her head. 'No, you don't know, do you? The man I loved was killed overseas by you.'

'Me?' Jane frowned. 'Was he an agent involved in Operation Exodus?'

Diana laughed, the sound barely audible amidst the crashing of falling bricks and crackling of flames. 'No, you still don't see it, do you?'

'This man, the one you lost. He was on the other side. One

of the enemy,' Arthur said. His breath sounding slightly better now they were no longer running.

'He was involved in the last operation, as a double agent. You thought he was important and needed to be sent back to England. Maura knew about him. She had been receiving information for months and feeding it back to me to pass on to my contacts. As well as doing her part to derail the operations she was involved with abroad. All things she discovered from Rose and your office,' Diana gloated.

Jane felt sick at the extent of corruption and betrayal Diana was revealing. Her hearing was clearing now and she could hear Diana's voice more distinctly.

'This is the man you were receiving letters from?' Arthur asked.

'Poor Andrew, he thought they were from a serviceman. He was right in a way, I suppose. Henrik was more than my lover, he was my life and you and your operation killed him. That wasn't supposed to happen. We met years ago along with Maura at a youth church camp abroad. We all shared the same ideals, we were going to be together in a brave new world.' Diana moved as if she were about to stand, her eyes gleaming in the light from the fires surrounding them.

'I think you should stay still. I take it your brother didn't know anything about all of this?' Arthur's tone was surprisingly firm given his difficulty breathing.

'Andrew hasn't a clue. Even when I used him to find those quotes to leave with the bodies. He thought I was finally taking an interest in his work.' Diana stilled her movement but focused her gaze on Arthur.

'Why did you leave those quotes?' Jane asked.

Diana gave a small shrug. 'A calling card, like the postcard to Father Dermott. To let you know why they had to die.' Her eyes narrowed. 'I must admit though, I didn't know that Arthur knew you, Jane. Something Maura failed to mention. The house had been let through a solicitor so after Polly died, I didn't expect you to arrive and stick around, poking your nose into everything.'

'How did you say you knew Maura?' Jane shouted her question once more as the surrounding noise suddenly increased again. She couldn't believe that Maura had been as committed as Diana to their cause.

'This was Andrew's old parish when I was a child. I've known her for years. She shared my beliefs for a better Britain. We went to the church youth camp together. She would write to me after I moved to Pennycombe. We wanted to cut this war short, save the waste of life and all this destruction. Germany will win, you know,' Diana sneered.

'And Polly's murder served a dual purpose I suppose? Revenge and you wanted to ensure she couldn't convey her suspicions about you, after she found you had stolen those blueprints with the amendments from Major Hawes?' Jane said.

'It was like taking candy from a baby offering to post things for poor, beleaguered Georgette. Then Polly saw the envelope in my bag, and right after that it went missing. I knew she had taken them from me. I arranged to meet her after she had left the village, as I wanted them back to send to my contacts. They could have been useful to Germany. I told her I had information for her. I didn't realise then that Anna had already worked with Richard to conceal the blueprints along with some kind of diary.' Diana glared at Jane. 'Maura had found out about the diary from Lucy Locket. I started to panic about it, I had to try and recover it in case my name was in there.'

'And Anna was long gone, back on another mission. Polly was thought to be safe, about to leave to go abroad herself but then she agreed to meet you. You got Maura to impersonate me, thinking Anna might have given them to Father Dermott for safe keeping.' Jane nodded, satisfied they were getting to the truth.

'Then I found out that Richard Trent had taken the papers and the book and hidden them. I knew you and Arthur were trying to find them, so it was easy to keep track of you both. I had plenty of help. Georgette had said Polly had borrowed library books on Trelisk and I discovered that was where he had gone on the train.' Diana sneered.

'You orchestrated the burglary and taking my bag at the station?' Jane asked.

'Of course.' Diana raised an eyebrow as if Jane had said something stupid. 'I have a lot of helpers. Like the ones who locked you in that chapel and searched your rooms at Trelisk.'

'Why kill Georgette? She was your friend,' Arthur said.

'She had guessed that I must have taken the blueprints. She confronted me and I denied it, but I could see she was unhappy. I knew she would blab,' Diana explained. 'Now, I think we've delayed this for long enough.' She steadied the gun at Jane once more.

CHAPTER TWENTY-SIX

Arthur sent up a silent prayer and braced himself, preparing to shoot should Diana fire first. But an almighty bang louder than a clap of thunder sounded close by, and the world went black.

Arthur opened his eyes, his ears and head were ringing. He wasn't sure how long he had been unconscious. Even with his scarf covering his mouth and nose he could taste dirt on his tongue. He seemed to be covered with a fine layer of dirt and stones. His gun was still in his hand covered by some fragments of wood and broken glass.

He lifted his head cautiously from the floor and blinked, shaking his head to dislodge the soil from his hair. His hat had disappeared. One of the already damaged houses close to where he was lying was fully ablaze, the flames licking hungrily at the night sky. The heat from the fire reached him as he looked around for Jane and Diana.

Someone to the side of him moved and groaned, dislodging more dirt and debris.

'Jane?' He tried to shout so she would hear him.

'I'm all right, I think. Are you hurt?' Her voice was muffled.

'I think I'm uninjured.' He scrambled to his knees as Jane did the same.

'Where is Diana?' Jane asked once she was on her feet. She clung to him for support, her long brown hair loose around her shoulders and streaks of dirt on her cheeks.

Arthur looked at the spot where Diana had been. All that was there now was a small pile of broken brick and pieces of what looked like window frames.

'She's managed to get away.' Jane looked around at the burning buildings and the fresh craters and huge potholes revealed by the glow of the flames.

'No, she's over there.' Arthur spotted Diana's silhouette, black against the red of the fires. He tugged at Jane to point her in the right direction knowing her hearing was probably as muffled as his own. Diana seemed to be trying to pick her way through the ruins to try to escape out onto the main road where the bus had dropped them off several hours before.

'What is she doing?' Jane asked as Diana appeared to stumble and fall before getting to her feet once more.

There was another small explosion and the last remaining wall of a house next to where Diana had been standing crashed down showering dust and ash high into the air. Jane turned her head and buried it against Arthur's shoulder. He could feel her shaking as he held her.

He couldn't see how anyone could have survived that amount of masonry falling on them. The fire was also raging now over the place where they had last seen her. He slipped his gun away back into the special inside pocket of his overcoat.

The warning wail of the air raid siren had stopped, to be replaced by those of the fire engines. People were starting to emerge despite the all clear not having sounded. An ARP warden emerged out of the dusk, shouting something indistinguishable and waving his arms to get Jane and Arthur to evacuate.

'We need to go back and find Benson,' Arthur spoke close to her ear.

'And my other shoe.' Jane's own voice was shaky. He looked down and realised that one of her brown lace-up brogues had been blown off in the last blast.

He looked around until he saw it, half buried under a pile of wood. He shook off the dust and pieces of broken glass and she replaced it on her foot. Thankfully the bombing seemed to have halted, and they made their way slowly back towards where they had left Benson with Maura's body on the doorstep of the villa.

The following day saw Jane, Arthur and Benson seated in the brigadier's office. They had spent the remainder of the night in Jane's flat after a gruelling journey through the blackout across London. Arthur had narrowly avoided being admitted to hospital thanks to Benson's administration of his medication.

Jane had been relieved to see that Arthur, although still somewhat short of breath, had largely recovered from their ordeal. Benson had used the medication that he always carried and had also affected to repair the damage done to Arthur's attire using sponges, clothes brushes and an iron.

Jane would have liked to have arrived at the office early, before Stephen had taken his place at his desk. Arthur, however, had needed to rest and take more of his inhalers before they had secured a taxi, so it was closer to lunchtime when they finally made it to the offices.

The brigadier listened attentively to her report without interruption. All the time she was speaking his gaze surveyed them all keenly as if weighing up all the points she made. When she had finished, he nodded his head.

'Operation Exodus was a vital operation. We managed to save some of our best people who had been working secretly right at the heart of power in Berlin. Losing it was a terrible blow. Maura's actions, orchestrated by this Diana Fenwick, cost us dearly. We could have retrieved so many more of our people.'

'Yes, sir. I feel I should perhaps have noticed sooner that something was amiss,' Jane said. She couldn't help feeling guilty that the operation had failed and so much death had followed afterwards. She had been responsible for overseeing Maura, amongst others, so she couldn't help but worry that she had missed some clue that Maura was a traitor.

'Nonsense, Jane. You have acted very promptly and efficiently, as always. You will, of course, write all of this up in a report for me. Do not send it to the typing pool, give it directly to Stephen to process.' The brigadier gave her a stern glance.

'Yes, sir.' Jane felt an overwhelming sense of weariness now it was over. It all seemed such a waste of life: Polly, Richard, Lucy, Jack, Peter, Georgette, even Maura and Diana herself. She felt as if she had let her agents down after they had tried to do their best for their country. Unlike Diana and Maura who had been led astray by enemy propaganda.

She knew from their conversation at her flat earlier, before leaving for the office, that Benson and Arthur also felt guilty. Benson had been troubled by his failure to recognise Diana as a 'wrong 'un', and Arthur, because he had been too willing to trust people he had known before the war. All of them had vowed to be much more cautious in future. They would all need to remember the brigadier's mantra: *Trust no one.*

'I am sure you all realise the implications of this affair?' The brigadier frowned, his eyebrows coming together like two bushy, silver caterpillars.

'The network Diana alluded to? It sounded worryingly extensive and well organised,' Arthur said. He coughed as he spoke, and Benson gave him a concerned glance.

'Yes, that's worrying, very worrying. Clearly, they were co-ordinated enough to follow your movements, even into Cornwall, and then they discovered Trent's recall back to London and stabbed him.' The brigadier pushed himself up from his seat and strode about his office. 'There is a lot of work to be done there, finding the leaks and plugging them.'

Jane knew this was something he always did when he was thinking.

'Hmm, Mr Cilento, you specialise in examining mathematical data and patterns for the ministry. This has proved very useful I feel in this case. A logical approach to assessing complex matters is always an asset. Mr Benson, I can see clearly, is of great assistance to you in this.' The brigadier nodded benignly at Arthur's manservant who had been seated quietly at Arthur's side.

'Thank you, sir.' Benson acknowledged the brigadier's praise for his support of his master.

The brigadier paused for a moment and looked at Jane.

'I had hoped when I asked you both to work together that you would make a good team. Jane has strong leadership qualities and experience. She also has leaps of inspiration and a keen mind.' He now appeared to be addressing Arthur.

Jane's cheeks pinked under the unexpected praise from her superior. She sensed though that the brigadier was building up to something. She also sensed that she might not like what else he was going to say.

'This affair has highlighted a grave risk to this country, and it is clear that even here in this building there are issues. That is something I shall need to attack. From what this Diana told you, it sounds as if, beyond her own personal connection to this Henrik fellow, she had bought into the ideology that Hitler and his government are purveying. Double agents are not a new thing, but we were clearly blindsided by Maura covering his tracks. I can't believe their connections did not come to light during our security checks. This is deeply troubling as they had known each other for such a long time. Operation Exodus was vital as a way of assisting personnel safely out of Germany. Its end was a bitter blow. Jane, my dear, your work within the department is invaluable but I should like to ask you, all three of you, to continue to work together as a unit.' The brigadier stopped his pacing and looked at them as if assessing what they might say.

'I don't quite follow you, sir,' Arthur said.

'I want you all to form a new department, led by Jane, of course. You will answer only to me, and the other departments will remain unaware of your existence. I suggest you continue as usual with your normal workloads. However, when something arises which I feel needs a combination of your specialist skills, then I shall call on you to work as a team to resolve the case,' the brigadier explained.

Arthur exchanged a glance with Jane. 'Right, yes, I understand.' He gave another cough and rubbed the centre of his chest. Benson nodded his agreement, his expression carefully blank.

They emerged from the building a few minutes later into the weak late morning sunshine. 'I feel as if we have just been played,' Arthur remarked to Jane as Benson went to try and find a taxi to take them to the station.

'I think you're right. A secret detective agency, you might say. Hmm.' Jane wasn't sure how she felt about being part of a specialist secret field unit. She liked her office and her job. She liked her small flat and the security of returning home each day to Marmaduke. This new idea sounded as if they could be sent anywhere at any time. It also meant she would have to continue working closely with Arthur.

She decided not to examine how she felt about that too closely at this point in time either. After much difficulty Benson procured a taxi and they set off for the station to return to

Pennycombe. On arrival at the station, Benson went to obtain tickets, while Jane and Arthur studied the timetable.

'Janey, my darling honey pie, cooee!' a loud American female voice sang out above the hum of the crowd and Jane shrank down inside the collar of her coat. Maybe she could just ignore it.

It was no use.

'Janey, my treasure! What a heavenly surprise!'

Jane turned around and fixed a smile on her face. She hoped Benson wouldn't take too long returning with their tickets. It seemed half the station was now watching them. Which, after all, would be exactly the effect the attractive older woman wished to achieve.

'Have you just arrived, honey? Or are you leaving?' the woman asked as she adjusted the fur collar on her coat.

'We're leaving. Work, you know how it is,' Jane said.

'Oh, what a shame. Stephen told me your department was busy. When will you be back? We can meet for afternoon tea, my treat, and we can catch up.'

Jane was aware that Arthur was eyeing both her and the woman with a curious expression on his face.

'Of course, I'll telephone you when I get back.' Jane wished she would leave.

The woman glanced at Arthur but thankfully refrained from asking who he was. A train pulled up to the platform and people started to move forward.

'I think we have to go.' Jane didn't know if it was their train or not, but she wanted to get away.

'Oh.' The woman pouted in disappointment before embracing her in a hug and kissing her cheeks. She departed in a waft of perfume leaving Jane feeling shaken and with red lipstick smudges on her cheeks.

Benson was approaching them with their tickets. 'Excuse

me, Miss Treen, but was that lady...?' he asked, staring at the glamorous, departing fur-clad figure.

'Elsa Macintyre, the actress, yes,' Jane said tersely. 'My mother.'

Benson's eyebrows rose fractionally, and he looked at Arthur. 'I have secured tickets home, sir. Our train is due after this one.'

Jane knew her companions had questions on the tips of their tongues about her mother and Jane's own relationship with her. None of which she wished to answer.

'Then we had better find a place to wait.' Jane led the way to the busy café.

Meeting her mother unexpectedly had disturbed her. It always disturbed her. Perhaps a cup of coffee and a cigarette would restore her equilibrium. Arthur found them a seat and Benson once more went to obtain refreshments.

'Do you want to talk about your mother?' Arthur asked quietly.

Jane shook her head. 'I'd rather not. It's complicated. I just want to get back and see my cat.' She looked at him, hoping he understood.

He placed his hand on hers. 'Of course. You are welcome to stay for longer at Half Moon Manor if you can be spared. You... and the cat.'

She managed a weak smile. 'Thank you. I rather think though I should collect Marmaduke and get back to work. There is a war to win after all.'

Benson deposited three mugs of indeterminate lukewarm fluid in front of them.

'Then, until our next case.' Arthur raised a mug to chink it against Benson's and Jane's cups.

She wondered what they would be required to tackle next.

'To victory,' Benson said.

'To the secret detective agency,' Jane murmured. She caught Arthur's eye and they both smiled.

A LETTER FROM HELENA DIXON

Dear reader,

I want to say a huge thank you for choosing to read *The Secret Detective Agency*. There are lots more adventures ahead for Arthur, Jane and Benson. Not to mention Marmaduke, of course! If you enjoyed it and would like to keep up to date with all my latest releases, just sign up at the following link. Your email address will never be shared, and you can unsubscribe at any time. There is also a free story – *The Mysterious Guest*, starring Kitty Underhay's friend, Alice, who features in my other 1930s-set series.

www.bookouture.com/helena-dixon

The Second World War was a difficult time and I have endeavoured to stay true to events that happened during this period. Many things are still secret even after all this time. Crime and criminals were still present, despite the conflict and despite keeping calm and carrying on, people were still people. I do hope you loved *The Secret Detective Agency* and, if you did, I would be very grateful if you could write a review. I'd love to hear what you think, and it makes such a difference helping new readers to discover one of my books for the first time. You can get in touch on social media or through my website.

Thanks, Helena

KEEP IN TOUCH WITH HELENA

www.nelldixon.com

 facebook.com/nelldixonauthor
 x.com/NellDixon

ACKNOWLEDGEMENTS

My grateful thanks go to my fabulous agent, Kate Nash, who read the start of what was fondly known as my 'Friday Night Project' and fell in love with it. Also to Maisie, my editor, who also loved Jane and Arthur. The Bookouture team, who have been so brilliant with team Kitty and are now also team Jane. My fabulous niece, Sophia Pritchard, who has diligently researched and fact-checked all my historical references to make sure that this book is as accurate as we can possibly make it. Her knowledge of World War II and the home front is unsurpassed. My thanks also go to the Coffee Crew and the Tuesday zoomers, my brilliantly supportive writing friends. Thanks also to the Friday night Roller girls. Finally, much love and thanks go to my museum contacts and local historians who are so generous with their knowledge and time. Thank you!

PUBLISHING TEAM

Turning a manuscript into a book requires the efforts of many people. The publishing team at Bookouture would like to acknowledge everyone who contributed to this publication.

Audio
Alba Proko
Sinead O'Connor
Melissa Tran

Commercial
Lauren Morrissette
Hannah Richmond
Imogen Allport

Cover design
Debbie Clement

Data and analysis
Mark Alder
Mohamed Bussuri

Editorial
Maisie Lawrence
Sinead O'Connor

Copyeditor
Jane Eastgate

Proofreader
Shirley Khan

Marketing
Alex Crow
Melanie Price
Occy Carr
Cíara Rosney
Martyna Młynarska

Operations and distribution
Marina Valles
Stephanie Straub
Joe Morris

Production
Hannah Snetsinger
Mandy Kullar
Jen Shannon
Ria Clare

Publicity
Kim Nash
Noelle Holten
Jess Readett
Sarah Hardy

Rights and contracts
Pcta Nightingale
Richard King
Saidah Graham

www.ingramcontent.com/pod-product-compliance
Lightning Source LLC
LaVergne TN
LVHW042129270325
807131LV00031B/626